A
Harlequin
Romance

OTHER

Harlequin Romances
by ESSIE SUMMERS

957—NO LEGACY FOR LINDSAY
982—NO ORCHIDS BY REQUEST
1015—SWEET ARE THE WAYS
1055—HEIR TO WINDRUSH HILL
1093—HIS SERENE MISS SMITH
1119—POSTSCRIPT TO YESTERDAY
1156—A PLACE CALLED PARADISE
1283—ROSALIND COMES HOME
1326—MEET ON MY GROUND
1348—REVOLT—AND VIRGINIA
1375—THE KINDLED FIRE
1416—SUMMER IN DECEMBER
1445—THE BAY OF THE NIGHTINGALES
1502—RETURN TO DRAGONSHILL
1535—THE HOUSE ON GREGOR'S BRAE
1564—SOUTH ISLAND STOWAWAY
1702—A TOUCH OF MAGIC
1731—THE FORBIDDEN VALLEY
1854—THROUGH ALL THE YEARS
1884—THE GOLD OF NOON
1917—ANNA OF STRATHALLAN

Many of these titles are available at your local bookseller,
or through the Harlequin Reader Service.

For a free catalogue listing all available Harlequin Romances,
send your name and address to:

HARLEQUIN READER SERVICE,
M.P.O. Box 707, Niagara Falls, Y.Y. 14302
Canadian address: Stratford, Ontario, Canada   N5A 6W4

or use order coupon at back of books.

NOT BY
APPOINTMENT

by

ESSIE SUMMERS

Harlequin Books

TORONTO • LONDON • NEW YORK • AMSTERDAM • SYDNEY • WINNIPEG

Original hardcover edition published in 1976
by Mills & Boon Limited

SBN 373-02000-7

Harlequin edition published August 1976

Copyright © 1976 by Essie Summers

Except for use in any review, the reproduction or utilization of this work in
whole or in part in any form by any electronic, mechanical or other means,
now known or hereafter invented, including xerography, photocopying and
recording, or in any information storage or retrieval system, is forbidden
without the permission of the publisher. All the characters in this book have
no existence outside the imagination of the author and have no relation
whatsoever to anyone bearing the same name or names. They are not even
distantly inspired by any individual known or unknown to the author, and all
the incidents are pure invention.

The Harlequin trademark, consisting of the word HARLEQUIN and the
portrayal of a Harlequin, is registered in the United States Patent Office
and in the Canada Trade Marks Office.

Printed in U.S.A.

CHAPTER ONE

Jocelyn had never before seen her father take the manse phone off the hook. He must always be available to his parishioners, he'd said.

He answered the question in her startled eyes. "I feel that for once I must be ready to listen to you as I've always been for parishioners' daughters and sons when something has disrupted and disturbed *their* lives."

So much for Jocelyn's hopes of being able to treat it lightly, to hide from her parents the extent to which she had suffered. However, she made one more attempt to diminish it.

"Oh, Dad, it's not as serious as all that. It's only giving up a job, after all."

The Reverend Niall Alexander looked searchingly at his daughter. "Jos, we've known you twenty-seven years. Don't you think we're bound to recognize immediately that something is very wrong?"

She didn't answer immediately. He grinned, boyishly. "I expect you thought your mother would guess because of this womanly intuition we hear so much about, but not me. That's about as solely the right of women as logic is supposed to be of men. This is far more than just deciding you'd rather live in the South to be nearer us. We both know how devoted to your job with Leigh you were, how much he relied on you. What happened? The very fact you rang to say you were coming for a holiday and now, ten minutes after your arrival, you've announced you've left Auckland, means something is behind it."

Jocelyn pushed back a strand of smooth, acorn-colored hair from her forehead, shifted her gaze from her feet and looked

5

squarely at her parents. Love and trust were reflected in each face. She smiled, her look no longer evasive. "Let's sit down. I might have known I couldn't keep it from you. And it'll be a relief to tell someone. I know you'll have no doubts, that you know Leigh well enough to know that he—" She paused.

Her father filled it in. "That Leigh never for a moment ever overstepped the barriers of friendship with you."

Jocelyn's hazel eyes widened. "Dad . . . you guessed? How could you?" Her eyes went to her mother's, saw the same knowledge there.

Ingrid Alexander said, "Jocelyn, we knew Leigh's wife so well. We knew there was a danger, that anyone living with a woman so neurotic, so temperamental, would some day compare the two of you, compare his nurse with his wife. We didn't warn you—we felt it might make you self-conscious. We rather hoped someone else might come along to interest you. When we left Auckland for Dunedin we prayed no sudden temptation might ever rise up to confront either of you. But we've known it could happen."

Niall's eyes were fixed on his daughter's face. "And what did?"

"Simply a set of unfortunate circumstances. Horrible timing. Leigh and I had just finished surgery hours and were having a cup of coffee. The phone rang. You may remember that child of seven I mentioned in my letters? With that dreadful hip trouble. I won't be too technical about it, but little Marguerite, a spunky kid if ever there was one, had operation after operation, but none was successful. Her parents had taken her back to their farm in the Bay of Plenty. She was being built up for yet more surgery.

"She was lying on their verandah when she saw her brother thrown from his horse. She screamed for her mother who was too far away to hear her, and she got off the couch and was halfway along the passage yelling her head off when her mother heard. The boy was only knocked out. It was a miracle. They called the local doctor, of course. The next day, when Marguerite walked again, he rang Leigh." Her eyes were ashine at the memory, just as they'd been when it happened.

6

"Leigh turned from the phone and, looking as if someone had handed him the world on a golden platter, said, 'Jocelyn, Marguerite is walking!' and he caught hold of me and hugged me. It could have happened in front of anyone, but we were alone. The next moment Eloise pushed the door open and stood there. It was hideous—for her and for us. We realized in a split second how it looked and I suppose we looked guilty because we did. Leigh rushed into speech—told her about the phone call, tried to make light of it, but it was no go. I felt that if only a report of it, newly opened, had lain on his desk, it could have been convincing.

"I'd guessed, of course, that she was given to tantrums, was highly strung; but honestly, I've never heard anything like it. Words just poured from her like pus from an abscess. Oh, sorry, that's horrible; but we get used to such terms. I've never seen anyone go so white and tense as Leigh did. Finally I said to Leigh, through the vituperation, 'Leigh, we've got to get her calmed down so she can listen to reason. Can you give her anything?'

"A dreadful look crossed his face, a sort of recollecting look. He said, 'It's not quite as easy as that. It can go on for hours. Will you go home, Jocelyn, and leave me here? Lock the door behind you. Ring home for me and tell Mrs. Simkins that Eloise has had one of her turns and I won't bring her home till she's out of it. She can tell the children I've taken their mother out to dinner.' All this time Eloise was ranting on. I felt so sick leaving him there to cope.

"Later he rang me to say she was now heavily sedated and Mrs. Simkins was with her. He came across to my flat. We talked it over and I said I was sure I could convince Eloise, when she recovered, that there had been nothing in it except exuberance of spirits at the thought of this child walking.

"Leigh said, very slowly, 'You can try, Jocelyn, and because you have the same integrity your parents have, it *may* convince Eloise. But, you see, her underlying trouble springs from a deep-rooted and abominable selfishness. She'll never understand the joy we felt for Marguerite's sake. Her world revolves round herself.' The hopelessness of his tone just tore at me.

I realized he must have tried time and again. I let him talk on—the first time he'd ever done so, to anyone. They just keep her on an even keel with tranquillizers and that's all." Jocelyn sighed. "And if he did go off the rails with anyone, he'd be rated as the guilty party, not her! I made him some toast and tea—he'd not eaten anything since it had happened, and I had some with him. We both felt battered."

She paused. Then, "I think I'll tell you the lot. I know how safe things said within these walls are. When he was going, I told him how much I admired him for keeping it to himself all these years. That I'd guessed his wife was temperamental, but hadn't known it was like this, and, unfortunately, I added: 'Maybe you should have talked it out with me long ago, Leigh. I can understand your loyalty, but sometimes, as Dad is so fond of quoting from Macbeth, we have to give sorrow words.'

"He had his hand on the doorknob, but he turned at that and said, 'I hadn't dared, Jocelyn. Not to *you*. Haven't you guessed? You've not only been my right-hand man, my second pair of hands, my memory when I might have forgotten things necessary for my patients' welfare . . . did you never realize how much you've come to mean to me? You gave me back my faith in women. Only—' he paused, and I filled it in for him, 'Only there's nothing we can do about it.'

"He nodded. I never admired him more. I want you to know that we didn't exchange as much as a kiss. He said, in a flat tone, 'Eloise needs me. Even when she's storming at me, she needs me.' He made an attempt at a smile and added, 'And you have a life of your own, Jocelyn, which must never be tangled up with anything sordid.' And he went out.

"Three days later I went across to see her, on my own, without Leigh knowing. I was terrified I might be doing the wrong thing, but I felt I must. I'm sure God helped me, gave me the words to say." Jocelyn laughed. "It's a bit of a nerve to say that, because what I did was practice a bit of deception. I pretended I was furious anyone should have thought I'd even look at a married man and that also I was simply terrified that it might come to the ears of someone I'd met on my visit to your new parish—someone I'd fallen head over heels in love with. That he came from a very strait-laced family, and in any case I'd been on the point of giving notice to Leigh and going to Dunedin if I obtained a good post there. It worked. The change in her was immediate and terrific. She's like the little girl in the nursery rhyme—when she's good, she's very, very good. Though it's a lifelong habit to view things only as they affect herself.

"I managed to contact Leigh by phone, at his rooms, and told him what I'd said. I wanted no tête-à-tête in my flat, or even at the surgery, to be remarked upon or misunderstood. Providentially, he managed to get a nice middle-aged nurse, well and truly married, and I left feeling much happier about Leigh and Eloise. That's all, my dears."

They all stood up. Niall said gently, "No, it's not all. We can only guess at what you've left unsaid, but we'll leave it at that. We'll just say we know it cost you something too, to leave. Now . . ." he replaced the phone on the hook, "let 'em all come . . . callers, telephone rings, both important and petty. We've put our own house in order. Let's go and scramble ourselves some eggs."

Later, Ingrid Alexander said shrewdly, "I've an idea you won't want to go back to hospital life."

"No, I've been away from it too long. Before I make any final decision, I'd like to go exploring Fiordland and Central Otago, then come back here and get a job before Christmas. I've a yen to do private nursing."

Her father pursed his lips. "Private cases can be difficult. People get demanding, possessive, resent you having any sort of life of your own. You might have no company for relaxation."

His daughter said, "I want something pretty stiff, something of a challenge. I need it as much as a case would need me."

Niall's smile broke up the deceptive severity of his face. "The panacea of work. The old, old story. And like most trite things, true and effective. Right; go to it, lass. But I'm glad you're going to see a bit of beauty first, and beauty you'll surely find abounding in Fiordland. Ingrid, she could stay for a few days with the Ronaldsons at Te Anau. We've been up to see their new place and it's just glorious, Jos. They said that on your next holiday you must spend at least a week with them. They're so enraptured with the loveliness of their retirement setting they spend half their days showing people round. They're on a gloriously solitary road, you can't see another dwelling. You go to your window in the morning, and down below you is nothing but trees and mountains and lake. It's just beyond Te Anau Downs. The main road curves past there, but theirs runs parallel to the eastern shore."

"That sounds marvellous. They don't know Leigh, so they won't ask awkward questions. We could ring to ask if it's convenient."

"Yes, and you must call at the Seven Forks Manse. Brian Newbury has gone there, and he and Sybil are still feeling a little lost and strange. The more old friends who call in, the less isolated they'll feel."

From then on, they didn't mention Leigh. That is, till Jocelyn was getting ready to travel some days later. Even then her mother referred to it only obliquely.

Jocelyn had donned white trews with a loose brown jacket that had revers and cuffs spotted in white, and had tied her hair back with a gauzy lime-green bow. She'd slipped brown bare feet into white thonged sandals and her eyes looked more brown than green today. Her mother said, "Oh, Jocelyn, you look exactly like a beechwood."

Jocelyn laughed. "Then I'm heading in the right direction since Fiordland is full of native beech forests. Oh, thanks for the picnic basket."

Then Ingrid met her daughter's eyes, mirrored, as Jocelyn leaned forward to inspect her eyebrows. Jocelyn's gaze was arrested immediately. Ingrid's eyes were burningly blue, a heritage from Scandinavian ancestors. She didn't dither. She said forthrightly, "This is the start of a new life for you, Jos. You may feel, as I did once, that your entire sum of happiness for a lifetime is behind you. I thought mine was all in my past. But it wasn't, it lay ahead with your father . . . I'd not even met him by then. Now I can't imagine a time when I

10

didn't know him. Sometimes I think I must have been stupid not to know that somewhere a man like that existed for me."

Jocelyn was startled. She'd always looked on her father and mother as an ideal pair. Not that they were angels, not that it could be said they never quarrelled, but fundamentally you knew the bond was strong, enduring.

Ingrid answered that look with a rueful grin. "Jocelyn, when I was a couple of years younger than you are now, I walked the floor night after night with the pain of knowing I loved someone I couldn't have. I told myself passionately I'd never, never marry anyone else, that I'd met my soulmate, that circumstances had decreed we were to be forever parted. Oh, it was highly dramatic and I thought romantic—one of the loves of the ages—that is, when it wasn't so painful as to be almost unbearable. You know how sweet your grandparents are. They suffered with me, told me there was a lot of life ahead of me, during which time I'd look back and wonder why I'd agonized so much and spoiled some of the best years of my life. And all the time, Niall was waiting for me. My father said, 'Lassie, God will have many dear surprises ahead of you. Some day you'll turn a corner and find love waiting.' I didn't believe him. You never do, not till you've proved it for yourself. But just last night I felt history repeated itself.

"I was reading my magazine. You know those snippets they have from the editor's scrapbook? I came across this. It's by Gerald Massey. I've no idea who he is, but this, I feel, was meant to be read by me, last night. It may not mean much now, but I've a feeling it will, later." She unfolded her hand and there, tucked into her palm, was a tiny clipping. She read it aloud:

> "Not by appointment do we meet delight
> Or joy; they heed not our expectancy;
> But round some corner of the streets of life
> They of a sudden greet us with a smile."

There was a small silence. Jocelyn turned, caught her mother in her arms, hugged her. "Thanks, Mother. Don't worry about me too much. I'm trying not to look back to

11

those years with Leigh. And . . . thank you for telling me about . . . about that other man in your life. I'd thought there was no one, ever, but Dad. It's good to know these things. There have been times when I've envied you—thought how wonderful to know such contentment, such bliss. One doesn't realize it mightn't always have been like that. Can I take that clipping with me? I might be able to build myself a whole new future on that."

SHE HEADED SOUTH. Beauty of surroundings helped to ease the ache. How Leigh would have loved a road like this! His waiting-room tables overflowed with books on trees and birds and shells. Watch it, Jos; Leigh belongs to yesterday.

The road skirted the lower slopes of Saddle Hill, dipped down into miniature green valleys, wound over rivers with names that sounded themselves like running water, the Taieri and the Waipori.

Lake Waihola filled up a vast hollow in the circle of the westward hills, and every emerald curve was reflected in its glass-still waters this day.

To Gore, and turning west, with every mile a delight, and with new vistas opening before her, mountains becoming higher, sculpted and carved out by the Ice Age into fascinating shapes and bluffs, some shorn off, some gently planed. She lunched by a willow-bordered stream, the afternoon wore on, the miles went into three figures.

Seven Forks was some miles off the main road, in such delightful country she wished she could stay longer than an hour or two with the Newburys. It would be better not to stay for the evening meal, though, because even with this long southern twilight, she would only just reach Kamahi Point before darkness fell.

The road turned a corner, dipped down a hill, across a stream, and there was the church, with the white-painted wooden manse beside it. Jocelyn sounded a gay tattoo on her horn. The front door flew open and out rushed Sybil, as welcoming as ever, Jocelyn thought affectionately. But it wasn't a welcome. It was a rueful warning.

12

"Jocelyn, above all things, both children have gone down with German measles! It came on so suddenly. We've not heard of any in the parish. They woke up in the night and seemed a bit feverish, but about ten this morning I discovered the rash. I rang, but you'd already left. I thought you'd have been bound to have had them, anyway, but your mother said it was the one infectious thing you'd never had. I oughtn't to invite you in for even a cup of tea. How maddening, and I was so thrilled you were coming."

"Oh, not to worry. I'm very sorry about the measles—for the children's sakes, and yours, but I'm glad you're sensible. I'm hoping to take a private case if I can track one down, and I'd be anything but popular if I arrived covered in spots. I'll just go on to the Ronaldsons'."

Sybil said unhappily, "And that's another thing—the Ronaldsons. They rang just an hour ago. Their son who's in Indonesia has had a sudden trip to New Zealand—a conference in Wellington. He was asked to substitute for someone else at a moment's notice, so got here and rang them from Wellington Airport. They're flying up to have three days with him. They knew you'd already have left, so they rang here. They only had time to get to Invercargill and then fly from there.

"When I told her about the measles, she said you might like to use their place just the same, and to stay on till they get back, of course. But if you didn't fancy staying alone in so isolated a spot, that there are some very good motels in Te Anau. If you leave a message for them at the Fiordland Travel to say which one, they'll call on their way back Friday. But she told me where she put the key if you'd rather stay at Kamahi Point."

Jocelyn made a lightning decision. "I can't think of anything nicer than having a whole house to myself for three days. Imagine doing nothing but read and sunbathe, with no need to be polite and make conversation! Sounds like the bonus of the year to little Jos. I'm all for it. Where's that key?"

"Well, seemingly they gave you instructions how to get to the Point. She'd no time to repeat, she just had to gabble at high speed. Evidently the house faces away from the road, so

13

you go in by the back porch. It's more like a conservatory and——"

"If I know Emmie Ronaldson it certainly will be," said Jocelyn. "She loves pot-plants."

"So there's a row of cactus, then a big jar of *toe-toe* fronds. It's quite dry, so the key is dropped down in there. You'll find stacks of food in the fridge and deep-freeze, but you can take bread in if you like."

They chatted for a few moments, then Jocelyn was on her way. Sybil told her she needn't go back to the main road, she could go on past the village store, over the hill, and when she came to the quarry take the road to the right.

"Oh, good. I love a road I haven't been on before. Bye-bye for now, Sybil, and here's hoping the children recover quickly."

She called at the store, got bread and fruit, and carried on. What an enchanting township, tucked into the folds of the hills, and thick with trees that must be a glory in autumn— oaks, sycamores, maples, poplars. Jocelyn loved to sketch poplars. Well, she didn't need to hurry now. She'd sketch that old barn with the three Lombardies right now. It leaned right over to one side . . . she could title the picture "Anno Domini."

Then driving on, she came to the quarry. Goodness, that road to the right was little more than a rutted track! Besides, the main road lay off to the left. Trust Sybil. Brian always said she'd no sense of direction whatever! Jocelyn took the road to the left.

It was a bonny road, it meandered, dipped, climbed, and got her nowhere, fast. Finally, miles on, she went into a farm that was at least half a mile back from the road, found no one at home, retraced her way to a farm she'd seen earlier, and was told she ought to have taken the road to the right. It curved back towards the main road two miles farther on. By this time she decided she'd be better to stick to the road she'd come in by; it was longer, but safer.

Now the kilometres seemed longer, because after a couple of hours or so she was getting a little anxious. It wasn't like driving up to a lighted house; Dad had said it was set in bush,

14

which of course meant it was forested, and once the sun went behind the westward mountains, the twilight would purple to darkness very quickly. There was a wild, untamed loneliness about the deep South that was quite different from the more densely populated rural areas round Auckland.

At last she came to Te Anau, the little township lying symmetrically on the flat reach of land by the eastern shore. The lake was pewter-pale, giving a hint of the great depths, presided over in brooding withdrawal by enormous dark mountains lit with silver peaks where the snows of July and August had covered them to the bush-line. Hard to realize that the purple slopes that looked like stippled oilpaint dabbled too thickly on a canvas, were formed of giant forest trees of jungle density. Or that what looked like deep shadows were indented fiords reaching back into almost unexplored territory, some of it forbidden to hikers because deep in its hidden fastnesses were, it was hoped, some fifty or so pairs of *takahe*, nesting—a bird once thought to be extinct.

It was just light enough to distinguish *kowhai* trees drooping goldenly over the water, and immense gums, aromatic and stately. The streets were still astir with overseas people from the big buses drawn up outside modern tourist hotels. A little float-plane rocked gently at its moorings, and rhododendrons and azaleas glowed in the duskiness.

Jocelyn knew she'd finish up at Kamahi Point in the dark now, and remote country roads never carried any lights, but never mind—the Datsun had powerful headlights and she had a good flashlight. Nevertheless, she'd check her directions.

Ah, a drugstore was open. Quite a number of shops stayed open in tourist areas. She'd buy some insect repellent anyway. Mother had warned her about the sandflies.

The druggist knew the Ronaldsons well. "Yes, it's on a little-used side-road, but it's well signposted. Te Anau Downs Homestead is eighteen to twenty miles up-lake—I can't think in kilometres yet—continue past there, then you'll come to a signpost with a lot of arms. The one you want is marked: 'Kamahi Point, No Exit,' and you don't need to know about the others, it would only confuse you. After all, you can't

15

miss Ronaldsons' place—it's the only house on that road."

When she was heading out on the lake road, Jocelyn grinned. Her father had said once, "I always hate it when someone says: 'You can't miss it.' It's a hoodoo on my peace of mind. I invariably end up lost." What a stupid thing to think now. The road led at first through rather scrubby-looking *manuka* country, rolling, with very few sheep on it, some cattle. There was still an afterglow, but suddenly she could no longer distinguish the white-tops. They looked a little blurred now, those darkening mountains. She'd heard they were often misty—in fact Mother had said, "One moment they're shrouded so thickly the world is featureless, the next everything is standing out in angular relief. One moment it's like the Scottish Highlands, the next a truly Kiwi scene with bold escarpments and towering heights."

She rounded a corner that turned left towards the lake, and next moment her car was engulfed in swirling mist, a condensation from the expanse of water after the unseasonable heat of the day. It was terrifying as all visibility was cut off, leaving her isolated in the small, rectangular world of the car.

She switched from dim lights to full right away, but it only put the evil of this writhing menace a little further away. It just enabled her to make out the edge of the road and though it dipped where the tarseal met the shingle and vegetation, there was no deep ditch there, no drop. She edged cautiously along, away from the bend behind her, and saw thankfully that the shoulder widened a little here as if it was a place for cars to stop for lake-viewing. She crawled on to it and stopped. She hoped all cars would take utmost caution. Even here, it would only take some driver, disorientated by the fog, to veer to the left and crash into her. She got the flashlight, shone it in front of her on the passenger side, opened that door, and stepped gingerly out, relieved to find firm turf beneath her feet.

She knew she dared not go far from the car or she would lose all sense of direction, but she wanted to find out how long this wider stretch was. It was a fair length, and solid. She got back in the car and moved it along, repeating the

16

maneuver several times till she could be reasonably sure she wouldn't cause an accident.

She dared not drive on with visibility just one degree above nil, especially on a strange road. It might curve back toward the lake. How easy on such a night to find oneself going over the edge.

She was there two hours. They seemed an eternity, and the fact there was nothing to do made her skin crawl with apprehension at times. She thought she couldn't stand the blanketing silence one moment longer when suddenly a beast bawled nearby and Jocelyn came out of her seat a couple of inches and flopped back. She'd thought it was a car-horn. She hoped the calf wouldn't bump into the car. Thereafter she was thankful for the silence.

All of a sudden there was a faint whispering sound . . . leaves stirred by a breeze? Oh yes, yes, please! It was a minor miracle. One moment white dense mist pressing against the windscreen, the next a thinning, then a parting, a widening clear passage, and suddenly one star shining out over the lake. In ten minutes it was all gone and even if she couldn't see it, there must be a moon somewhere, its light illuminating a silvered peak across the waters. She could see their glimmer now. She was nowhere near it, thank goodness. There were paddocks of *manuka,* gorse, pig-fern between the road and the shore.

She looked at her watch, pulled a face. No wonder she was feeling deathly tired but hadn't dared drop off to sleep. Now what would she do? She looked at the mileage gauge she'd checked before leaving Te Anau and decided she was much nearer Kamahi Point. The shorter distance was preferable if that mist came down again. Besides, it was disappearing with a curious funnelling effect, towards Te Anau. It was clearer ahead.

Jocelyn saw the signpost for Te Anau Downs, climbed a hill, dipped down, sped on, found herself going through a tunnel of tall native beeches that would be a fairyland in daytime, but at night was intimidating, crowding in on one. How awful if one's car broke down here in almost solid blackness! The darkness ahead lightened a little . . . tussocky flats spread each side as the trees stopped. How much farther, for goodness' sake? But then an unknown road always seemed longer . . . ah, what a beautiful sight, on the left, a yellow signpost, with finger-arms pointing in several directions. Now be careful, Jos, make sure you get the right one!

She drove the car till the beams were pointing directly on it. Well, no mistake about that . . . she turned at the one that said: "Kamahi Point. No exit."

What a surface! Well, roads that served only one homestead were likely to be rough stony ones in New Zealand. The cost was enormous as it was. No open land here. A darling tree-bordered road, dappled now by moonlight whenever there was a gap in the density. Not that Jocelyn was in a mood to appreciate its beauty. All she wanted was a hot drink . . . that mist had cooled the temperature . . . and bed.

She caught a silver glimmer of water to her left and a cleared space to her right. Then new gateposts, the name Ronaldson dimly glimpsed, and she rattled in over cattle-stops.

The glances she got as she swung up the drive, in the headlights, were enchanting. The lights picked up the gold of daffodils, the white blurs of narcissi, and the purple of lilacs all growing wild in long green grass. She saw a few outbuildings, what looked like an old-time stable and an ancient barn—how odd, she thought, the Ronaldsons had bought just two or three acres from a farmer and built a new house on it. But perhaps this was on the site of an older dwelling, long since crumbled to dust.

She swept round to the back of the house just as she'd been told. What a lovely sight! Shelter, safety. Now to find the key. She'd just take her overnight bag and picnic basket in for now. She grabbed the flashlight, went up the steps.

The porch-cum-conservatory was more of a patio with a closed-in end with a fine array of hot-plants. Oh yes, there was the row of cacti, now for the vase of *toe-toe*. She waved the light up and down. Nothing like any sort of pampas could be seen. She turned to the other side. All kinds of ferns and

18

mosses. Too wet to hide keys in. A faint feeling of panic seized Jocelyn. Then she took hold of herself. At least she was here and not stranded in fog. She could sleep in the car, couldn't she?

But it was funny, because Emmie was a very practical person, not dreamy like Cosmo. But of course they'd been in a frantic rush. What if she's said to Cosmo to put the key in the *toe-toe* and he'd put it in something else? He always vowed he didn't know one pot-plant from the other. But then *toe-toe* wasn't a plant in a pot! Perhaps Emmie had forgotten she'd thrown the *toe-toe* out and Cosmo had put it in the next best thing . . . in a cactus pot.

She moved seven before she heard a faint tinkle. Ah, here it was. Good deduction, Jos. In two minutes she had the lights on and was inside. She went through a small passage into the kitchen.

Why, this was charming. Some brand-new houses lacked charm, but this was patterned on the style of an older one, and had the best of both. A long kitchen with east and west windows, lined with cupboards sufficient to delight any woman's heart, had a row of copper-bottomed pans, a dresser with blue-and-white Cornish-ware basins on it, all modern appliances, and an enormous map of Scotland framed on one wall.

Jocelyn knew she must eat and drink before she dropped. She opened the fridge. It certainly was well stocked. Dear Emmie, even in her great rush, had left some grapefruit ready segmented for breakfast! But why two? Oh, don't be stupid, Jocelyn, if you have two halves you almost always sugar both. Any note? No . . . probably thought her phone conversation to Sybil was sufficient. Well, everything was at hand. She switched on the electric kettle.

She wouldn't bother hunting through Emmie's tins tonight. Just something from the picnic basket would do. Jocelyn had a ginger biscuit with her tea, ate a queen cake, had a second cup, then, feeling her eyelids drooping, decided she must seek her bed without delay and explore the house in the morning.

19

The second door on the left upstairs was her room, according to the message Sybil had relayed. She opened the door, then blinked. This wasn't a bedroom. It was carpeted and had draperies, and an enormous desk stood in the window, and another had piles of stationery on it; but apart from that it was a junk-room—packing-cases, straw, a few books unpacked. What on earth . . . ? The Ronaldsons had been here for months! Then a thought struck her. Ian Ronaldson must be coming back to New Zealand. He was an anthropologist. Maybe these books had been in store during his term in Indonesia. His parents must be sorting them for him.

She backed out, grinning. Sybil had been right about which road to take, but wrong about this. It must be the second door on the *right*. So it proved. It was obviously a guest-room, twin-bedded. Ah, yes, and one bed was made up. She found bathroom and toilet, came back to undress and get into bed. What a wonderful moment!

There was a good lamp over the bed and a book and magazines on the bedside table. Not particularly women's reading—travel magazines.

She picked one up, and her attention was caught by a picture . . . enormous cliffs, barren, sheer as if sliced down by a knife. And on a reef of rocks a tall stack, as symmetrical, almost, as a chimney. Why, that was the famous landmark of the Orkneys, "The Old Man of Hoy." Mother and Dad had a slide of it. All these magazines were of Orkney. How sweet of the Ronaldsons. They'd remembered that her mother and grandparents were Orcadians and had sorted out things to interest her.

She was too sleepy to finish even one article, enthralling though it was. She yawned, snapped off the light, and sank into billowy sleep.

SHE COULDN'T BELIEVE how strongly light it was when she woke. Perhaps this room faced east and of course in this remote spot in an upstairs room she hadn't bothered to draw the curtains. She brought her arm out and blinked at her watch. Heavens, it couldn't be! But it was, nine-thirty! Oh, well, what odds? She wasn't very likely to have callers.

She went across to the windows and was caught spellbound. She hadn't realized the Ronaldsons had a private inlet of the lake all to themselves . . . it was almost a half-circle, beautifully wooded at the edge, with a path winding in and out of the trees . . . a path that would entice anyone's feet. Three launches floated on silver waters that were so still, each boat had a twin image beneath it.

On the right arm that curved round the bay, alien willows made a fringe of lighter green against the dark slopes of native trees that rose above them. On the left was a white strip of shoreline, a bathing-beach, surely, and two jetties jutting into the water, one old, one new.

It was so endearingly small, an intimate, family bay. The headlands almost met, which was probably an illusion. Beyond, across an immense stretch of water, reared the mysterious mountains-of-the-mist, living up to their name, for their lower slopes were barred by mist, and their tops floated like disembodied peaks.

Jocelyn dropped her eyes to the garden below, a wild, rambling one that must have been lovingly planned years ago. So the Ronaldsons *had* built on the site of an old homestead. The rhododendrons in their rich purples and pinks, crimsons and pearly whites sheltered cinerarias in the same colors beneath them and pale primroses, like embroidered flowers, carpeted the ground.

But she was starving. Breakfast first, then a shower. She picked up a glamorous housecoat her mother had given her last Christmas, a delicate thing in eggshell blue, patterned with lilac and rose, tied its drawstring round her slim waist, slipped her feet into feathery satin mules, gave her hair a few flicks with a styling-brush she'd had in her sponge-bag, and ran downstairs. Breakfast, wash up, shower, make her bed, explore the bay. That delectable bay. That was her order of the day. What bliss! What serenity! This was the life!

It didn't take long. The grapefruit, toast and marmalade, a pot of tea. She propped one of the magazines about Orkney against the cosy and read as she ate.

Then it happened. She heard a sound from outside. But what? A car door slammed? Steps, heavy ones, on the back patio. Oh, well, Emmie and Cosmo had probably told some neighbour—if you could call anyone neighbours in this solitude—to look out for her. But she wished she wasn't in this flimsy garment. It would look a bit dissipated at ten in the morning to some farmer who'd been up since five!

There was no pause, no knock. She heard the back door flung open so violently it banged against the passage wall . . . Jocelyn felt her heart lurch . . . what on earth could be—the footsteps thundered along the passage, the kitchen door was wrenched open and the largest man she'd ever seen . . . and the angriest . . . erupted into the room.

Jocelyn stood up, opened her mouth to protest, but was silenced as he barked: "What the hell d'ye think you're doing here?"

She gaped, then pulled herself together and to hide her fright said with spirit, "And who the hell are *you*?"

It was his turn to gape. He recovered, said furiously, "Well, of all the cool cheek! You——"

"And," interrupted Jocelyn, her cheeks flaming, "how dare you rush in here without knocking!"

His words shot out so fast he almost choked. "Without knocking? Can you give me one good reason . . . one faintest glimmer of a reason, even, why a man should knock on his own back door?"

CHAPTER TWO

The irate stranger got no further, though this time Jocelyn's voice was faint, not angry. "What did you say? *Your own house?* But how is it? I mean. . . ."

Her voice tailed off as the enormity of what she must have done took her in the midriff. She simply hadn't enough breath left.

His rage restored her. "*What* do you mean?" he barked.

Jocelyn drew in a deep breath, steadied herself by the edge of the table, said, "Er—isn't this the Ronaldsons' house?"

He boggled, then managed, "Are you some kind of nut or something? You aren't going to tell me you thought this was Ronaldsons'? That's on a completely different road, and anyway, if you're a guest of theirs, why wouldn't they have been here? I mean who'd let you in?"

It was like trying to fit a jigsaw together, but nothing fitted in this, and this man's hostility and disbelief was getting at her and making anything she might attempt to say sound really feeble.

Which question to answer? The last, perhaps. She said, trying to sound reasonable, "I let myself in, with the key."

He set his jaw. "How ridiculous! There are only two keys. One is in my pocket and my manager's wife has the other. You broke in, *didn't* you? But why?"

A sort of calm superseded Jocelyn's panic. She drew herself up, said coldly, "I think you'd better start believing me. If you'd let your blood sugar subside, it would be a good beginning! Most things that happen can be explained. Mine is fairly simple. For a start, I'm a qualified nursing Sister, not a stranded hitch-hiker who broke into an empty house!"

His tone was impatient, but slightly less furious. "I'm not likely to think that. You've got a brand-new Datsun outside. But how——"

"If you'd keep quiet for long enough, you'd *know how*! If you keep interrupting me every two seconds, I'll *never* be able to offer you my explanation."

His blue eyes seemed rapier-bright. He was going to try to discredit everything she'd say. But when he'd heard it all, he'd have to eat a large slice of humble pie. Somebody had interfered with that signpost, so clearly the mistake was understandable.

She said, "In the first place, I'm not a nut, or a scatty teenager. I'm the daughter of a very respectable Presbyterian minister in Dunedin. The Ronaldsons were in my father's parish when we lived in Wanganui. I was asked to spend a week with them. I was on my way when they got word that their son Ian—you may know he's in Indonesia—was to be in Wellington for three days, so they flew off to see him—they only just had time to get to Invercargill.

"They knew I was going to call in at the Newburys at Seven Forks Manse, so they left a message there to say I could stay in their house, alone, if I wanted to, or go to a motel at Te Anau till they returned."

She paused, and saw disbelief in his eyes.

His lips curled as he said, "And you expect me to believe that the Newburys would let you come on to stay in an empty house? It doesn't sound like manse hospitality to me!"

She said, stung, "You seem to be the most extraordinarily suspicious person I've ever had the misfortune to meet! Normally I'd certainly have stayed there, but their two children had just gone down with German measles, so I didn't as much as go into the house."

He said scornfully, "And I'm supposed to believe that a fully-qualified nursing Sister hasn't come into contact with German measles before, and would be nervous of them in addition?"

She actually gritted her teeth at him. "My dear man, it's

24

the only infectious complaint I've not had, and though, normally, I'd just love to have them, I certainly wouldn't want them just now—I'm hoping to take up private nursing somewhere in this wonderland, and it would scarcely be a good start to arrive covered with spots, or to carry them to a patient!"

He heaved an insulting sigh. "Now I know you *are* nuts! You say normally you'd *love* to have the measles. Of all the daft statements I've ever heard, that's the daftest! I'm sure *I'd* never *want* measles!"

She glared madly back. "Of course you wouldn't. It's not within the bounds of possibility that *you* could ever become pregnant!"

In the succeeding moment she thought she was going to burst into hysterical laughter at the look on his face.

He gazed at her with great concern. "I say, perhaps you've already got measles! You must be running a temperature . . . that's it. You're positively scarlet. You sound a little—a little——"

Jocelyn said, *"Nutty* is probably the word you want."

He said helplessly, waving his hands in frustration, "No, it isn't. I meant perhaps you're a little delirious—you don't know what you're saying. I mean . . . about becoming pregnant . . . me . . . how . . . I mean how in——"

"If you say 'how' once again I'll scream, just to relieve my feelings. It's your fault I'm talking about pregnancy because you will keep asking irrelevant questions. You asked why I'd welcome measles—except on holiday—it's because it's best for every girl, before marriage, to have rubella—German measles—so that if in early pregnancy she comes in contact with them, they'll do her unborn child no harm! I've seen something of the resultant damage."

He put up a hand and brushed his forehead. Then he said feebly, "Oh, I see. Well, that's a relief. I thought you were really bonkers. Well now, how on earth did you get here? We're the only house on this road, and it's well enough signposted.

Nettled, Jocelyn said, "I was *told* it was well signposted. In fact the Te Anau chemist said I couldn't possibly miss it. The only trouble was the signpost pointed the wrong way."

He made an impatient gesture. "That's absolutely absurd. You must have mistaken it or you wouldn't be here. Why not just admit it? Plenty of folk have no sense of direction and can get mixed up no matter how clearly roads are marked—and there are so many right there."

Her lips set in a mulish line. "I know I didn't make a mistake . . . I went straight along the way the arrow pointed."

He made an exasperated sound. "Leave that. But how on earth didn't you discover your mistake when you got here? And what's this about a key? Had they left a key with the Newburys? And did it happen to fit by some unlucky coincidence?"

"They had no time to make it to Seven Forks. I was told the key would be in a glassed-in porch inside a vase of dry *toe-toe* just past a row of cacti in pots. I couldn't find any *toe-toe*, so I lifted the pots in turn and found the key." She added, at his puzzled look, "Truly it was. Look, it's in the inside of the lock now. I wondered myself, then reasoned that after Emmie had told Mrs. Newbury where they'd put it, she probably let Cosmo lock up, and told him where to put it. That perhaps she'd forgotten she'd thrown the *toe-toe* out, and he'd be in such a rush, he'd do the next best thing and put it under a dry cactus." Then she thought of something else. "But I *know* I saw the name Ronaldson on the mailbox at the gate!" She looked completely bewildered.

He said, but more patiently, "There isn't a mailbox. Ours is at the crossroads by the signpost. They don't come right down here for one house. You weren't very observant—which proves my point about the signpost—it's a name-plate and it says 'Ronaldsay Downs.' "

Jocelyn retorted: "I was only too thankful to see it after all I'd been through. The headlights just flickered over it. I'd spent two terrifying hours on an unfamiliar road in dense fog, and having been told there was only one house at Kamahi Point, and having no reason to think I was on the wrong road, I was only too thankful to see what I thought was confirmation."

His expression altered a little, "Oh, it was after dark . . . and you'd been caught in the fog? Well, that explains the mistake with the road, doesn't it? Anyone can go adrift in fog."

She set her teeth again. "The fog had completely gone when I got to the crossroads. And I put my headlights full on the sign."

He said hurriedly, "All right, all right. Though I'd have thought anyone coming into a friend's house would have realized this wasn't it. Didn't you find my gear unrecognizable? And——"

"I was dead beat. I did think it odd when the second room on the left upstairs was full of unpacked books. Though I thought they might have been storing them for Ian. I'd been told that was the guest-room, but you know how people mix up relayed messages—so when I found a bed made up in the second room on the right, I thought that must be it." She looked at him challengingly. "I even saw books on Orkney beside the bed. I thought how sweet of Emmie to take the trouble. My mother and grandparents come from Orkney."

"Well, so did my forebears and I'm just back from there myself. That's why they called this place Ronaldsay Downs. And it was my bed—Meg had it ready for me. But enough of this. I've got to get you out of here faster than sound. I'll be in a hell of a mess if you're here when Ina comes."

"Ina? Your wife? But surely if *you* can believe me, *she* can! She'd just better!" Indignation sharpened her tones.

An extremely grim expression crossed his face. "Ina is my sister-in-law and wouldn't *want* to believe you. Get yourself dressed and out of here as fast as you can."

"I certainly will," she flung at him, "but not so much from a desire to spare this Ina her suspicions, but because the sooner I'm out of your company, the better I'll like it. I could understand a wife thinking it odd finding her husband here with a strange girl at breakfast-time, even if it isn't exactly the crack of dawn, but a sister-in-law . . . really! Is

27

she very prim and proper? And why wouldn't she want to believe my story?"

A strange look passed over his face, distaste and anger and something else . . . but what? It almost looked like woe.

He said grimly, "I'm taking my recently orphaned niece and nephew away from her. She's their aunt on their mother's side. Their late father was my twin brother. She's all out to prove I'm not a fit and proper person to have charge of them. This would indeed be grist to her mill!"

Jocelyn looked horrified, then rallied, "But surely no legal situation could develop from a stupid mistake like this?"

Again the expression crossed his face. "I already have a bad reputation. Though it's far enough in the past not to weigh in too heavily at the present, unless something stirs it up. Like you sleeping in my house, for instance, and only one bed slept in at that."

Jocelyn felt sick. It had been no more than an unorthodox and stupid adventure till now. She said swiftly, "I can't tell you how sorry I am. But I'll gather up every trace of my presence. I brought only an overnight bag inside. When will your sister-in-law arrive? This morning? Because I'll need to be well clear of the crossroads."

"She won't be here till lunch-time. The wife of my manager is coming over to cook that lunch. I want Ina to realize the children will be well cared for."

"You're not married?"

A grim look again. She seemed as if she could do nothing but touch the tender spots.

"No; scandal put paid to my engagement a few years ago."

"Then how are you going to look after the children?"

"Till yesterday I thought I had that under control. I'd engaged someone. She was ideal, not too young, not too old, and had had nursing experience. That was desirable because, as I don't want Ina hinting at irregular relationships under my roof, I'd asked my Aunt Clarissa to live with us. She needs some attention, mostly massage. She's arthritic, and is in a wheelchair most of the time. But no better chaperone could be imagined, and Ina knows that.

28

"This woman asked us to pick her up at Lumsden, but when we got there her friend told us that Miss Belgarde's mother in Christchurch had been rushed to hospital and she'd had to go to her, naturally. But it put me in one hell of a hole. The friend put her phone at our use and I rang everywhere I could think of . . . nursing services and friends, but very few people can come at such short notice, and don't want to come to a spot as remote as this. Besides, I need time to make sure I get someone really suitable. Not just to look after the children's physical welfare, but to make them happy. Someone not crotchety, yet a disciplinarian. They're bewildered, mixed-up little things at the moment.

"By the time I'd exhausted all avenues, we decided to come on here and make the best of it. Meg will help for a day or two. At Te Anau we heard there was fog on the road, so we went to a motel."

Jocelyn shivered reminiscently, "I wish I'd met someone who'd known. I didn't know the road, and in that density I could have gone into the lake! Do you wonder I was in no state to take much notice of my surroundings? Well, I'll be out of here in a quarter of an hour. Where is this Ina coming from?"

"From Lake Wanaka. She was spending the night there. She and her husband live in South Canterbury. She was coming through the Lindis Pass, so she's got to cross the Crown Range before even getting to Lake Wakatipu, then right down to here. Nevertheless, I want you away and all traces of your occupancy removed, in double-quick time. I don't even want Meg Watson to know you've been here. I can't risk any hint of it getting out. Make sure you remove every single vestige, no tights left about, no toilet articles, not as much as a hairpin!"

"I won't," said Jocelyn coldly, beginning to have some sympathy with the children's Aunt Ina. This was going to be a hopeless set-up for children recently bereaved. What if they'd rather be with their aunt? Still, it was nothing to do with her and she must vamoose as soon as possible. She said crisply, "Would you wash up while I get dressed and gather

29

up my things, even if it's hardly likely they'd even get here by twelve?"

At that moment the telephone rang. He strode to it, picked it up. His bellowed, *"What?"* stopped Jocelyn right in her tracks. There was complete consternation in it. She turned back from the doorway, eyes wide.

His voice was unbelieving. "She's at the farm? Oh, no! Colin, you've got to delay her for a few moments—I haven't time to explain. Keep her as long as you can without arousing her suspicions. Say you want to show the kids something—kittens, puppies, anything. I'm not ready for her. Go to it, man."

He banged the receiver down. "Hell and damnation—she spent the night at Queenstown and left early. She's coming through the track from the farm. What can we do with you? We'll never get you away—you can't travel in that ridiculous garment . . . you haven't time to dress and pack. You'll have to hide. Look, I'll get you into one of the sheds. I'll put your car in one of the garages and lock it. Don't stop to change, grab your clothes, your bag, and dress in the shed. I'll try to get rid of her as soon as possible, but no matter how long she's here, you aren't to emerge. You aren't to as much as peep out. She can think this breakfast is mine. *Don't just stand there, scram!"*

Jocelyn said quickly, desperately, "If he can't delay her, there won't be time to get me into a shed and it would look a thousand times worse if you get caught trying to hide me. Look, can't you pretend *I'm* the nurse you engaged? After all, I am one!"

He looked a little hopeful, then groaned, said scornfully, "I'm afraid not. You're too young and glamorous. Look at you!"

She said, "I'm not when I'm out of this ridiculous garment." She grabbed her car keys off the dresser, flung them on the table in front of him. "Unlock the boot of the car, bring in my blue case—I've got my uniforms in it. I can look a hundred per cent less glam in two minutes flat. Don't just stand there, get going. The *blue* case, and I'll be in that bedroom I slept in, getting out of this. Just open the door and throw the case in."

As she saw him obey, vanishing out of the door, she ran upstairs and by the time he'd thrust the case in, she was into her underwear and was madly plaiting her hair after parting it with more speed than she'd ever achieved in her whole life. She twisted a couple of rubber bands round the ends, rummaged frantically in her sponge-bag, drew out some hairpins, coiled her plaits round her ears in the fashion of the early twenties, and skewered the pins almost into her scalp.

She unzipped the case, drew out a uniform, shook out its starchy folds, donned it, pinned her veil well back on the center parting so the plainness of the style was emphasized, grabbed at some white no-nonsense shoes, pushed the offending negligée into the case, and shoved it under the bed. She ran down to find him piling her dishes into the sink. He turned round, saw this Miss Prunes-and-Prisms in the doorway and said, "Good grief! How'd you manage it?"

"Easy. I was got up like this in a play not so long since. For heaven's sake fill me in before this Ina gets here. What's her surname? What's your name? And don't you forget my father is a minister. That ought to weigh in on the side of respectability. You've got to explain Aunt Clarissa's absence. So you'd better say she wasn't too good last night, so I came on here in my car to get things ready for her, while you stopped on in Te Anau with her. But your name? I'm Jocelyn Alexander."

"Isbister. Magnus Isbister."

"Oh, splendid! It's a name familiar to me. I've a cousin married to an Isbister from Orkney—up in North Canterbury. You'd better call me Sister Alexander. That will add tone and credibility."

"You're an Alexander? You . . . you aren't a cousin of Grant Alexander of Challowsford? He married——"

"Yes, he's my cousin. Married Sarah Isbister. Grant is my

mother's cousin really, but so much younger he was named after my father. You mean you know them?"

"*Know* them? Sarah's *my* cousin. Also not a first cousin, but near enough. What a coincidence!" Despite the urgency of the moment they gazed at each other in thunderstruck silence, then Magnus Isbister said, "That's it, then, a godsend. We'll say we're cousins—we won't say cousins-by-marriage— and that when this woman I'd engaged as a nurse had to go to her mother, my cousin stepped into the breach. You see, I'd mentioned the name of this nurse to Ina on the phone. Oh, splendid!"

"You'd better call me Jos. But won't Ina think it odd your brother and her sister have never as much as mentioned me? And won't the children give it away? Or are they just toddlers?"

"No, they're nine and eleven, but they couldn't. I had more to do with Sarah and Grant than Eric had. Someone from Orkney wrote to ask my mother if someone could represent Sarah's family at the wedding, so she and I went up for it. I stayed with them two or three times after that, whenever I was travelling up there, but Eric never even met them. He had a bit of trouble with his marriage at first, and never seemed to get——"

Jocelyn's voice held surprise. "You were at the wedding? So was I. In fact I was a very junior bridesmaid. To keep Sarah's young sister Pauline company."

He stared. "I recall Pauline very well. Oh, were you the spindly one?"

She had to laugh. "I was. How providential! I'm beginning to think I was meant to come here. Do you think this Ina will stay long?"

Again the grim look. There was no doubt but that this man detested his brother's sister-in-law. "No fear! I want no prolonged farewells to upset the children."

Jocelyn looked apprehensive. "You mean they won't want to leave her? That they'll be hostile to you? To the idea of living here?"

"Good lord, no. This is their home—at least the farm is. They were a pitifully homesick pair when I got back and went to South Canterbury."

"Got home? Were you away when——"

"When their parents were killed on an accident. Yes, I was in a remote part of Orkney, marooned by hideous gales on a temporary inaccessible island. You've got to know all this so you drop no clangers. Eric's wife, Jan, was Ina's younger sister. Ina was terribly possessive. She made mischief between them, but long enough ago. Jan finally saw through it and put first things first. She can't have a family of her own—Ina, I mean—and thinks if she adopts these two, it will hold her own marriage together. Her husband wants children. There's no reason why they shouldn't adopt—except that she's house-proud and bone selfish, and thinks older children would be less bother. Now——"

The phone rang again. He answered it briefly, turned round, said, "They're on their way. Less than five minutes to D-Day. For God's sake watch what you say, take a lead from me. The children are Ninian and Una. What are your parents' names? I'll have to speak of them as Aunt and Uncle."

"Niall and Ingrid. My brothers are David and Robert. All Flett family names—Mother was a Flett from Orkney. And Dad has St. Cuthbert's parish in Dunedin, was in Auckland before that, and earlier Wanganui, where we knew the Ronaldsons. You might be expected to know that. Maybe Ina knows them. That would add a touch of authenticity. I came down to be with them. I was receptionist to an ortho-pedic specialist in Auckland till last month. It was providential you knew this—you called in at the manse on your way, perhaps? Then when this woman's mother took ill—don't say just when—you asked me to take it on. And where is Aunt Clarissa to sleep? I might be expected to know which is her room."

He hustled her through to a room which opened on to a wide patio and had views of both garden and lake. The manager's wife must have fixed it like this. It had everything

33

for an invalid's comfort. A room for the nurse led off it.

They heard a car. Jocelyn said hurriedly, "I'll emerge from here with a vase in my hand as if I was just about to put flowers in it. Off you go, they're swinging round to the back."

She'd glimpsed an expensive car, well-handled, she thought, come close to the house-corner and disappear. She felt her heart thump quickly and painfully. What a situation! She only hoped she was doing the right thing. What if these children really wanted to stay with their aunt and uncle? It would be a more normal family situation. She wanted nothing to do with anything that savored of family disruption and discord. Oh, well, she must play it along for the time being at least, and work out the rights and wrongs of it later. Having complicated this matter by her unfortunate mistake, she must try to retrieve it.

She picked up a vase, walked out quickly and, she hoped, with what looked like confidence, to the kitchen. She'd missed the greeting between the children and their uncle, so had no means of gauging whether they were glad to be with him or not.

Her large, fiery-headed host turned as she opened the door, said easily, "Ah, there you are, Jos. I've just been telling Ina how fortunate I was that you were coming into this area to look for some private nursing."

Jos said primly, "Fortunate for me too, of course. Much nicer to feel one is helping out in the family as well as earning one's own living. This will be Eric's sister-in-law. How do you do, Mrs. Chester . . . or may I call you Ina, seeing we're connections? And these are Ninian and Una. Hullo, children. Now what about us all having a cup of tea? It's too early by far for lunch. Magnus, you can put out some cakes and things. I'm not sure where yours are yet, but that tin in my picnic basket has some of Mother's queen cakes in it."

Magnus said pleasantly, "How marvellous. I always feel no one makes queen cakes like Aunt Ingrid. I saw David eat four at one sitting once. I'll switch the kettle on."

Jocelyn had imagined a tall, hard-faced woman, one of

34

the matriarchal type, who were so often possessive. She saw instead an appealingly fragile youngish woman, exquisitely dressed, with a gentle manner. It almost threw Jos. She had an idea she'd have relished helping Magnus Isbister thwart a battleaxe, but this was the sort of woman who'd have been a very maternal little girl, fussing over dolls even as Jocelyn had done herself. A pang of pity shot through Jocelyn's heart for her.

But the children must be put at ease first, poor scraps. They were the ones who were going to be left with a strange nurse, and Jocelyn realized that in this hair-do and uniform, she looked more than a little forbidding.

She smiled at them and said, "As soon as you've had something to eat you'll want to take your things up to your rooms, I suppose. You'll know which ones, of course."

Magnus said, very hastily, "Not really—they've not been here since Ronaldsay was rebuilt, and before the fire when they used to stay with Nan and Grandpa, they occupied the same room. But when I was here last week, kids, I brought your old treasures over from the other house. I've not sorted them yet, I only had time to get them across. Anyway, that'll be a job for you. And Cobby and Punch will be brought over to the paddocks here this afternoon and you can have a ride. What do you want . . . Coke or lemonade?"

He set out the cakes, buttered some crackers while Jocelyn made the tea. As she poured out he said, "Are you staying at Queenstown again tonight, Ina?"

The incredibly long lashes swept up from the deep blue eyes. "That depends on you, Magnus. If you'd rather I stayed on a few days to get the children settled in, I'm quite willing. Harold can manage on his own quite well. He was so concerned about them, having another upheaval, and adjusting to still another situation, so soon after their . . . their cruel loss—he doesn't mind how long I stay."

Magnus Isbister's tone was crisp, entirely lacking in sentiment, "Oh, it won't take much adjustment. After all, it's a coming home. Their mates are here. It's the school they've attended all their lives, and it's the farm Ninian will manage when he's old enough."

Ina said, "I'm so afraid their noise will be too much for Aunt Clarissa. People with arthritis can get so crotchety. They can't help it, of course, poor darlings. It's the pain. I'd thought the children could have a much more normal life with us, a perfectly secure home, with a mother and father." She glanced up at him appealingly. "I'm only thinking of the children. Of what is best for them."

Magnus Isbister sounded hatefully dry and mocking. "Are you now? That's interesting. I believe you even deceive yourself. But in any case, none of it matters. Eric *and* Jan left their children in my care, I'm their guardian as well as uncle. It's as simple as that. And they grow up, as their parents wished it, in my home, on their father's farm. Their name is Isbister, they grow up on the Isbister estate."

Jocelyn wished herself a thousand miles away. She saw a glimmer of tears in Ina's eyes. Ina said gently, "Of course they aren't all Isbister. They're half Sheldon. But I know the legal position, Magnus. That's why I obeyed you and brought them here. I was hoping, though, to appeal to your better judgment, even at this late hour. Thought you might look at it, at last, from the standpoint of what is best for the children."

"I am."

"I feel it's so unfair to them. It will be so unsettling for the poor darlings if you tire in well-doing, as so often happens. In the first flush of enthusiasm people take things on, then tire of them."

Magnus Isbister looked all stern Norseman then. His face was nothing but planes and angles, his chin jutting. "We aren't talking of *things*. We're talking of my brother's children. My *twin* brother's children, who've been like my very own."

Jocelyn felt as if something in her stilled every movement. She knew she ought to do something to make this less painful for the children who were as silent as herself, only their eyes, watchful and moving from one speaker to the other. But she couldn't. She was the stranger here, even if Ina didn't know it.

36

Ina said, "And you really think that because Eric was your twin, whereas Jan was my younger sister, they're closer to you, more to you, than to me?"

Surprisingly, Magnus's voice gentled. "I think you must accept that, Ina. It needn't have been so, but the mischief you made—the mischief you *tried* to make between Eric and Jan separated you somewhat from your sister. You might as well admit it. Perhaps you're trying to make up for that now, by offering them a home, but it so happens I'm their guardian. It's what Jan and Eric wanted, their children to grow up here if ever anything happened to them. It seemed just a remote contingency then, but these things ought to be provided for, and thank God they were. You'll be able to see them from time to time. You and Harold can have a lakeside holiday in the old cottage any time that's also convenient to me. But this is their home—Ronaldsay Downs."

Tears welled up, spilled over. Ninian glanced at his sister, and Jocelyn thought he put out a hand to hers under cover of the table, as if protecting her from being upset over their aunt's tears. His gesture moved her to action.

She said crisply, "Magnus, would you like me to take the children upstairs while you and their aunt finish this discussion?"

Ina stopped the handkerchief operation to concur. "A very good idea. Magnus, your cousin can see exactly how painful this is for the children, trying to decide their future."

His voice rasped. "Oh, come, there's no decision. The children are home and home to stay. And when Eric and I were kids we suffered far more if we were banished when family discussions were on. Eric once said when they were talking over the choice of boarding-school or correspondence lessons for our high school education that he'd much rather hear all that was said."

Ina seized on that. "That's another thing. If they lived with us, they wouldn't have to go to boarding-school for their higher education. An excellent high school is just a quarter-hour's walk away. It's a big point."

For the first time Ninian spoke. He was a smaller edition of Magnus, copper-headed, and had a Norse profile to match. His voice was surprisingly mature. "My name has been down at John McGlashan College in Dunedin for years. My father saw to that. He wanted me to go to his own school. And Una's is at Columba, nearby. So that doesn't come into it."

Magnus actually chuckled. "And if you change your mind between now and then, Ninian and Una, a very good Form One to Six co-ed high school is going up in Te Anau township. I wonder you didn't see it coming through, Ina."

There was a silence, then Ina said, "It's a big job taking on a ready-made family, for a bachelor. Let me take Una back with me?"

Jocelyn saw the color recede behind the little tanned cheeks, the lips tighten. Again she was sure Ninian's hand reached out to Una's.

Magnus stood up. "The discussion is closed, Ina. Thank you for bringing them down. As I told you over the phone, I would have come up for them, though when you insisted you'd bring them yourself, it did make it easier for me to get Aunt Clarissa here. As I said, she's in Te Anau. I'll go in for her after lunch now my cousin's got things ready for her."

Ina said quickly, "Why not go now, Magnus? I could help your cousin unpack the children's clothes, and fill her in on their likes and dislikes and so on. Their funny little ways."

His look was bland. "She'll never know they have any if you don't point them out, Ina. They're perfectly normal kids, and Jos grew up in a family and has done children's nursing as well as every other kind. I never dreamed when you were a bridesmaid for Sarah and Grant, Jos, that some day you'd be Aunt Clarissa's nurse at Ronaldsay Downs. What funny quirks fate takes!"

Ina looked from one to the other. She was obviously assessing Jocelyn's age, thinking that if she had been a bridesmaid then, she must be well up in her thirties! She'd never guess, with this old-fashioned hairdo, that she'd been a child attendant. Jocelyn was rapidly changing her mind about Ina. There

38

had been a few moments at first when she'd actually felt sorry for her, losing her sister's children to an overbearing man like Magnus Isbister.

Ina said, turning to her, "However are you going to manage with a helpless invalid and a huge house, to say nothing of two energetic children and a man who——"

Una burst out laughing. "Oh, Aunt Ina! Aunt Clarissa's not a helpless invalid, she's fun. She only uses that chair to get places more quickly. And she knows things, about birds and trees."

Once more Ina turned to Jocelyn. "I don't suppose you've realized how little your cousin will be able to help you, how long his hours are. I——"

Jocelyn interrupted. "I'm not completely a city girl. My father had a country parish on the outskirts of Wanganui. I know it's very often a case of the woman helping outside when seasonal work is on. I——"

Magnus's voice cut her off, "Oh, cut it out, Jos. My manager won't expect any help from you. In fact his wife has offered to help you with the house. I don't even expect any help in the garden from you. After all, most authors like to garden for exercise when their day's stint of typing is done. So that'll be my responsibility. I ought to have told you that."

Jos felt a little sick. She'd almost given the show away. She hadn't thought of him as anything else but a farmer. That was one thing a cousin, a true cousin, would be bound to know. Magnus Isbister? She'd never heard of an author by that name.

She grinned and said, "You might find it hard to keep me out of the garden at that. I searched Auckland for a flat with a garden big enough to satisfy me when Mother and Dad moved South."

"Oh, good show. Not to worry, Ina. I'll cut down study hours so I can give enough time to the kids to make them still feel part of the family. I might even send some work off to be typed, though as a rule I can't bear anyone else to touch my manuscripts."

Jocelyn said decidedly, "Oh, you mustn't do that, Magnus. You must go on polishing up your phrases to the very last. It would affect the quality of your work otherwise. Anyway, with a little help from Meg, we'll manage fine. In fact we might be able to do without her altogether when I get into the running. And this house is so new and well planned, it won't be hard to manage. And Mother said she'd come up any time we need her."

"Oh, great. It would be a change from manse life for her, and she and your father could spend all January here. He'd enjoy the fishing. And Aunt Ingrid and Aunt Clarissa get on so well together."

"Ingrid?" asked Ina. "That's not a common name."

"Not in New Zealand perhaps, but of course, like Magnus's family, we have a lot of Scandinavian names, all Orcadians do."

"But your own isn't," said Ina perceptively.

Jocelyn shook her head. "I was named after Dad's mother. But I bear the middle name of Christane. That's a Flett name."

Ina said suddenly, pettishly, "I don't think I'll stay for lunch. No point, seeing I'm not needed. I'll go home by way of Gore. I've an old school friend living there. I'd just like to say, Magnus, that when you find the children too much, they'll always be sure of a home with me."

"Thank you," he said smoothly, but inflexibly. As if that ended it on a polite note, but was beyond the bounds of possibility. He flicked a glance in the children's direction. They rose with alacrity. Una said, "Thank you very much, Aunt Ina, for looking after us when Uncle Magnus was in Orkney. We're sorry we can't stay on with you as you want, but this is our home. Please give our best wishes to Uncle Harold too."

Ina gave a tinkling laugh. "Goodness, poppet, you sound all formal! You don't have to be that way with me." Jocelyn saw Una compress her lips into a tight, unchildlike line.

Ninian added, "Give him my best wishes too, and thank you, Aunt Ina, and goodbye."

40

Jocelyn looked away as large tears rolled down Ina's cheeks. Magnus merely looked long-suffering. He swept the children out to the door with a movement of his long arm, said to Jocelyn, "Come on outside too, you've hardly had time to admire our views, you've worked so hard."

As Ina reached the car she said to Una accusingly, "Why, you'd left Belinda-Ann in the car." She reached over and got it, put it into Una's unenthusiastic arms. "It would never do to leave that with me."

She flung her arms round each stoical child in turn, still crying, then said, from the driving seat of the Jaguar, "Goodbye, Jocelyn, and don't forget, when you have problems, I'm at the end of a phone. Don't upset Magnus with expensive toll-calls, though. Reverse the charges. Harold, my husband, is not a penny-pincher!"

Not a word was said by the group till she went over the first cattle-stops, then Ninian said violently, to relieve his feelings, "Harold is a *nit!* He's a *clown!*"

Una said passionately, "He teases all the time. He thinks children *like* teasing. He never takes us seriously. He just acts dumb all the time with us."

Jocelyn said, "I used to hate people like that. We had one in our Wanganui parish. Dad was there for years, so I was very small. I used to call him the Teasy Man. When you live in a manse you're supposed to be so darned polite to everyone, supposed to treat them all alike. But you can't help loving some people more than others. Mother told us once that if it was too much of a strain, to just make sure we were polite to everyone, but not to worry too much about the loving. That's what I liked about what you did just now—you thanked your aunt and sent best wishes to—" she paused because she'd completely forgotten his name.

Ninian's blue eyes gleamed with mirth, "To the Nit," he suggested.

"To the Nit," agreed Jocelyn.

Una looked up. She was completely unlike either brother or uncle. She had brown hair, in a page-boy bob, brown eyes, a brown skin against which her teeth looked dazzlingly white. She said, "Isn't it funny? Your voice sounds younger than you look."

For the first time Jocelyn saw Magnus Isbister look other than stern or furious or coldly forbidding. His face crumpled up and he began to laugh. The children stared at him "That was just to impress your Aunt Ina, to look older and more responsible. She doesn't always wear her hair like earphones. It just flows out."

Jocelyn said hastily, "Oh, not really. I find it too hot. I tie it back, or pile it up. But I hadn't even brushed it this morning."

She remembered she mustn't refer to their early and dramatic encounter in front of the children and said, "Now please . . . let me take my fill of the views. Between fog last night and sleeping in, I've not had a chance. But from my window I saw that darling tiny bay. May we go round to see it? What do you call it?"

Ninian laughed. "Guess. Its name matches your description."

She considered it. "Dwarf Bay? No? Let me see. Um . . . Midget Bay? Little Bay? Oh, does it have a Maori name? What's small in Maori? I know . . . *iti*. Iti Bay? Or is that word tacked on to something else? Wai-iti . . . little water? No? Oh dear, I'm not doing very well. What's bay? Whanga. Whanga-ete?"

They shouted with laughter. "It's not the Maori," Una said. "Let's give her a clue. The burn that runs into it is called the Swift Burn. Know why?"

She thought Magnus looked at her gratefully. This was taking the children's minds off their too-long separation from home. Now they were on their native heath, showing a stranger round.

"How does that make it a clue? I expect it's because it runs swiftly, but——"

"It doesn't. In summer it's only a trickle. Uncle Magnus says it ought to be called the Sluggard Burn."

Magnus said, "I'll help you, cousin dear. There's a waterfall away through there. It's called the Jonathan Falls." She looked at him uncomprehendingly for a moment then said, "Jonathan? Jonathan Swift. Author of *Gulliver's Travels*. Um . . . oh, I know, it'll be Lilliput Bay. Is it? Oh, what a perfect name! Let's go round the front."

They wandered through the tangled old garden, badly in need of attention, yet with a wild charm of its own. October was probably its most colorful month, because under the giant beeches and oaks and poplars on its perimeter, the rhododendrons and azaleas were massed, in glowing jewel-colors like rose quartz, rubies, amethysts, garnets, lighting up the darkest, leafiest corners.

A narrow white ribbon of path, beaten by the feet of many years, ran under sycamores and maples and great aspens, aquiver in the sun, to a broad sweep of lawn terraced to keep it level for mowing, then the garden lost itself in a downward slope of rockeries and little pebbled paths that followed down to the daffodil-dotted green sward that fringed the bay.

"Lilliput Bay," repeated Jocelyn softly. "Do you mean you own this bay, cousin Magnus? That it belongs solely to your family?"

She wished the words unsaid because there wasn't much family left, seemingly. But he took it easily. "Yes, in actual fact; but my dad, and my grandparents before him, always allowed access for fishermen and bathing parties. Up to that little curve of willows that shuts off the far beach. And you'll often see a boat load of tourists coming in from the lake, through the Gates of Lilliput—those headlands."

"Are the islands yours too?"

The children answered, vying with each other for the telling. "Yes, but you'd never guess those names. One is St. Olaf's Isle, and one is St. Ringan's Isle."

Jocelyn turned to Ninian. "That last one is named for you? Or an earlier Ninian?"

The boy gave a delighted laugh. "An earlier Ninian, the first to arrive from Orkney. How'd you know? Not many folk know Ninian can be Ringan too."

His uncle said, "Of course she knew. She's family, and as Orcadian as you are. Children, I hear the ponies coming." They were off like streaks of lightning.

Jocelyn and Magnus were left alone.

CHAPTER THREE

Jocelyn was most relieved not to have to keep up the pretence any longer. She said, "This is a golden opportunity to tell me all those things I must know. Will the manager and his wife be with the ponies, and how much are you aiming to tell them? About me, I mean?"

"Very little more than we told the detestable Ina. They must think you are really my cousin. If I say we weren't tidy enough to receive Ina and impress her they'll accept that. She's house-proud. I'll say you came on ahead and slept in, and didn't even have the breakfast-table cleared. The Watsons are fine people, but Meg just might tell it as a joke, to somebody, and you know how news like that spreads. If Ina had the slightest hint that things weren't what they seem, she'd try her darnedest to prove I wasn't at all a right and proper person to have her sister's children under my care." He looked grim. "And there's an awful lot of ancient mud that could be stirred up, believe me."

Jocelyn knew a nasty taste in her mouth. She said, "It seems as if I'll have to go along with this for a bit. I didn't like Ina. She's smarmy. But I'm warning you, Mr. Isbister, that any hint of anything I can't approve of might make me inclined to think living with their mother's sister might be the better choice of two evils. I realize that since my unorthodox adventure of last night put you in an awkward position, I must play this your way for a while, but if I feel they're coming into contact with anything undesirable, I could throw my weight in with the other side."

She expected him to fire up. He had the color for a ready

temper, and she'd seen him hot to the point of fury earlier, but he took it. "I can promise you, my dear cousin, that irregular relationships with the opposite sex simply can't flourish side by side with my Aunt Clarissa. There'll be none in this household while the children make their home with me. I'm glad you've realized you owe me something and will stay on. Otherwise I'd have had to insist on it."

"Well, don't push your luck too far. I'm choosing to stay till you can get someone more suitable—but for the children's sakes, not yours. Anyway, no amount of pressure could make me act against my own inclinations."

"Couldn't it? Isn't that just what is making you do it? The pressure of your own conscience . . . trying to redeem the consequences of your own stupidity in not being able to read a simple signpost right?"

She felt a wave of sheer temper sweep over her. Just as well that at that moment Colin Watson came round the corner. Magnus made her known as his nursing-cousin-who'd-stepped-into-the-breach. Colin took it as a bit of good luck and said Meg was at the house now with the lunch she'd prepared, but the children had said their aunt hadn't stayed for it.

Jocelyn liked Meg immediately. She was quite candid at being glad she didn't have to entertain Ina. "I never liked her from the first moment we met. Though Jan had her here as seldom as possible. Oh, it's good to see those children back here. Why that woman couldn't have left them here till you got home, Magnus, is beyond me. I said why uproot them when you'd be back as soon as you got the news when they got you off that island? I'll never forget the gloating anticipation in her eyes when she said, "How are we to know he'll ever get back? I believe that island is difficult of access any time, and with freak storms, anything could happen. I felt sick. I'll never forget the look on those children's faces when they went off with her . . . the way they looked back till the car was out of sight. They had that frozen, resigned look children get when they can do nothing for themselves. I didn't sleep all night. And . . . and when Ninian secretly posted back Una's battered old teddy-bear that Ina had thrown into the dustbin, with a note in it to say keep it for his sister, my thoughts were violent towards her. I had it dry-cleaned and it's on her bed right now."

She chuckled. "I was so determined she'd have nothing to cavil at in the lunch, I've overdone it. But you can put the balance in the deep-freeze."

"Better still, stay and have it with us, Meg. Jos hardly knows where things are yet. Then if you wash up, we'll away in for Aunt Clarissa. And cousin dear, you can take your veil off and the pins out of that ridiculous hairdo. It's served its turn." Magnus turned to the Watsons. "This was her idea of impressing dear Ina with an illusion of age and respectability. It put ten years on her." He leaned forward and neatly snicked out the bobby-pins that held her veil in place, and managed to loosen one coil. Then he grabbed her protesting hand, had the other down, and pulled the rubber bands off. Her hair uncoiled from the plaits—so she ran her fingers through it, spreading the strands, shook it free, walked to the dresser where she'd noticed a darning-basket, rummaged, came up with a pair of bootlaces and tied her hair back with one. She was slating him for doing it as she did so.

"Wouldn't believe the difference, would you?" asked Magnus, twinkling at the other two. He sounded very cousinly. "I hardly recognized her myself when she appeared like that. The children will like you better now—Una has already said your voice is younger than your looks, Jos."

Jocelyn had an idea this man could be fascinating, given half a chance. He had a sort of audacious confidence that would be hard to resist.

The four children—because the Watson offspring had arrived too—came tumbling in, madly excited by the reunion. It was a beautiful lunch—Cornish pasties piping hot, a tossed salad, lettuce, sweet corn, pineapple, juicy raisins, with sliced tamarillos and watermelon to give color. Some delicious bread, still faintly warm with a crisp crust, and boysenberry jam rich and dark, whipped cream, shortbread, and fresh scones.

47

Meg saw Jocelyn look apprehensively at the wholemeal bread. "Oh, don't worry. We're not so isolated that that's a regular chore. It was in Magnus's grandparents' day, I believe. We get bread every time we go to Te Anau, and keep it in the deep-freeze till needed, but I was foolish enough to try one of those packets of hot breadmix lately, and they've got too fond of it. Best bread I've ever tasted. But I tell them it's only when I've time."

It was good the children didn't want to accompany them to Te Anau. Magnus told her a bit about Aunt Clarissa Archer as he drove. "The difference in her since I went overseas has to be seen to be believed—some new drug that not only lessens the pain but attacks the stiffness. It used to hurt me to see how slow she was with her patchwork, her stamp collection, her letter-writing. But her fingers are quite nimble now. She's using her wheelchair less and less all the time, her daughter said. We'll tell her the lot."

Their private road was a gem, even as Jocelyn had guessed, in the darkness last night. They swung round the last bend and there before them was a lovely sight . . . the best sight of all as far as Jocelyn was concerned . . . workmen doing something to that signpost!

Just as Magnus drew up beside them, they began to swivel it round. Jocelyn sat there smirking. He leaned out. "What goes on?"

"Vandalism. Not smashing things this time. Not taking pot shots at the A.A. signs . . . just turning the signpost round—irresponsible sort of joke, that. Fortunately, the bus for Milford Sound spotted the switch and rang us from Cascade Creek. Otherwise the Ronaldsons might have had private tourists turning up asking where the Homer Tunnel and the Tasman Sea had got to, and the road to the Sound would have been dubbed 'No Exit.' As it is, no harm's been done."

"No," agreed Magnus, "no harm at all. Perhaps we need electric fencing round our signposts." He drove on.

The next moment their eyes met and they burst out laughing.

"All right," said Magnus, subsiding. "You don't have to go on wearing that smug expression. I grovel. Everything conspired against you—the fog, the vandalism, the key under the cactus. And *am* I glad! It's purely selfish, and you may not want to stay, but for the time being it saved the situation. As far as Ina's concerned, I've only to put one foot wrong, and she'll try to get the children away from me."

"You said she wanted the children to try to save her marriage. Why?"

"Harold would like a son to carry on his business. It's quite a good one. In fact I was surprised when Ina asked for Una. I've a shrewd suspicion she thought they'd fret apart, and in time I'd let Ninian go too. It's a stupid thing—even if they had a son of their own, it's not to say he'd want to follow in his father's footsteps. Many sons do, but they should never be forced into it.

"Take us," he went on. "If ever anyone had an excuse to want just that, Dad did. We weren't born till our parents had been married fifteen years. I never wanted to be anything but a writer. That came from Mother's side. Eric wanted to be a surveyor, pushing on into barely explored country like Fiordland. Dad hid his disappointment well, built a manager's house and sent us both off to Otago University. He said we weren't just Isbisters, we had other ancestors, and if their traits cropped out in us it made family life more interesting."

Jocelyn nodded. "Yes, Oliver Wendell Holmes said that man is an omnibus in which all his ancestors ride."

Magnus's voice quickened with interest. "Oh, marvellous! Look, there's a ballpoint and notebook in the pocket in front of you—write that down for me, will you? It'll do splendidly for a quote for my current thriller. I've a hero despised by his father because he's got a fine contempt for the money he'd make if he followed on in the family fortunes. After a couple of hundred pages of conflict and adventure, the son becomes such a hero the father sees his name a household word over the entire communication network. Ah, thanks, that's a good girl. Cardinal rule for writers, never fail to jot.

Otherwise other things happen and overlay the very thing you thought impossible to forget. And it leaves your mind receptive for the next bit of inspiration."

Jocelyn nodded. "My father finds this too—for sermons. Mr. Isbister, what——"

He stopped her. "It's got to be Magnus. You're my cousin, remember. Ina's got friends not too far away, and coincidence has already played a big part in our—er—first confrontation. The fewer who know the better. I know Ina, she'll appear unexpectedly some day—taking some friend to Milford Sound. She's devious. You'll have to call Clarissa 'Aunt' too. Put her wise to all your relations—who will be presumed to be hers too. It would be so easy to put a foot wrong, like today when you thought I was farming. I knew a moment of panic, but the next moment you were handling it most expertly. It seems as if Grant Alexander has never told you his wife's cousin is an author?"

"I've not seen them for five years. It's been just a case of cards at Christmas lately. I've got to confess, Magnus, that I've never heard of you, much less read one of your books."

He grinned. "Well, thousands—millions—of people haven't. I don't go round expecting all and sundry to palpitate at the name of Magnus Isbister. And my type of book mightn't be yours. You may not read thrillers."

"I do. But I've just not caught up with yours. Dad and my brothers read a lot of them. I must ask them if they've had yours."

"Better not. They may feel they must, then, and nothing kills enjoyment of reading more than being told you ought to read a book."

She chuckled. "That's so. My poor papa is positively pursued by such things. Everybody who reads a book on some religious matter brings it along in case he'd find it useful for sermons. Some funny outdated and narrow books too. Now he pleads lack of time and the need for using that time for selective reading. Oh, you said your brother was a surveyor, but it seems he was running the farm?"

"Because I said Ninian would follow his father's footsteps? Eric didn't finish his course, found he hated university life, town life, even as a means to an end. He couldn't get back to farming quickly enough. The main thing was, he'd had his chance and knew then where his bent was. It meant a lot to Dad to have one of us at home. I helped with shearing and harvesting at times, but I went into journalism in Dunedin, then Auckland, Sydney, London. I found what I wanted to do, came back here to write books. I'm glad I did, just then. Dad failed, so I pitched in, wrote in my spare time—well, a bit more than spare time. I can make do on very short rations of sleep. Mother was quite a bit younger than Dad, but she didn't survive him by long.

"I was a bit restless—after my engagement was broken. I went off to the South Pole where I wrote—or got the material for—*The Winter of the Darkness*. I stayed down there for the whole sunless season. I'll never forget it. It's something to see the world come back to light. One night someone broke into this house. Eric and Jan had the manager's house. A lot of stuff was stolen. This chap made a meal, was careless, and the house was burnt to the ground. Fortunately Eric saw the glow in the sky. They saved most of the furniture, but the house was just a shell.

"We were well insured and my books were doing better than I'd ever dreamed they would. I rebuilt, having it designed on the old, even to dormer windows. I felt I owed that to my great-grandfather who'd built, he thought, for keeps. I saw the framework up, and departed for Orkney. The situation I was writing about could date. The Watsons had the married couple's cottage then, but they practically camped over here to keep an eye on builders and prowlers for me.

"Then," he paused, and Jocelyn heard him swallow and take a deep breath, "Eric and Jan had a business trip to Christchurch. They were killed coming home—instantly, both of them. I couldn't be reached. Looking back, it seems incredible to me that I shouldn't have known. Eric and I were so close. When it happened, I was just revelling in being

51

on that remote island, even in being isolated. I was living my hero's adventures, not just imagining them. And while I was having the time of my life, my twin brother and his wife were being buried. And I wasn't there to be chief mourner. I couldn't even touch Eric's coffin to say goodbye to him. But the worst of all was that, by the time I was back in communication, the children had been whisked out of their own home by Ina and Harold. However, it's all in the past now. Ninian and Una are back on Isbister land. And there they stay."

"I can imagine how horrible it must have been to return to news like that. It's hard to know what to say, but I'll see you through till you can make more suitable arrangements. Things could wear a very different complexion in a year or two. The situation could resolve itself."

"Are you saying that because it's the sort of thing that ought to be said . . . soothing syrup . . . or do you really think this situation could be resolved permanently? If so, how?"

Jocelyn wouldn't allow herself to be stung by his tone. He was a strange man, and evidently not a highly moral one, but he'd suffered great loss recently and had been under strain the last few days.

She said mildly, "I was thinking, as most people would, that life has a way of providing the answers. It's always happening. You'll probably marry and, from then on, won't have a thing to fear from Ina."

He gave a short laugh. "Not likely! I cut marriage out of my scheme of things when my engagement was broken."

Jocelyn said hesitantly, "Manses see a lot of problems— broken engagements, marriages, the aftermath of suicides, sudden loss, sometimes betrayal. One of my father's recurring problems is trying to make either a man or a woman see that the world hasn't fallen apart because of a broken tie. Even if you feel now you could never marry anyone else, someone may come into your life in a year or two and change the whole course of events for you."

His voice was harsh as if he resented this. "It's not a question of my vowing I'd never marry anyone else. I was fed up with her whole attitude . . . can't stand people who put on holier-than-thou airs. Wouldn't risk it again."

Oh, the lordly male . . . he said the girl had broken it off because of a scandal he'd been involved in. He must have expected his fiancée to overlook it. But there were always two sides to things. A girl might have been afraid that this sort of thing would recur. Who could blame her if she lost trust in him?

Surprisingly, when he spoke, his voice was quite kindly and held no resentment, but a trace of amusement. "I expect as you're a daughter of the manse, it's a temptation to trot out stock solutions. Now, don't spark off, I like people who try to help."

She said, "I'm afraid it is a family trait, though heaven forbid we should think of ourselves as acting Providence. David, for instance, is a social worker, and Robert's a solicitor who has the name for helping folk who can't afford large fees."

"Tell me something. I've often wondered about this. I heard once of a marriage guidance counsellor whose own marriage was pretty rocky. In a minister's household are there sometimes family problems which a minister finds himself unable to handle—because he's too closely involved?"

"Can be," said Jocelyn. "In fact I've known of it. Sometimes strangers—other ministers—have to sort things out for sons and daughters of the manse, but not in ours, we've been able to take all our troubles home. Why, even just lately—" She came to a full stop. Goodness, where was she heading?

He gave her a quick sideways glance. "How provoking you should stop right there, Cousin Jocelyn. I'm as curious as the next person. It could make me feel better to know that other folks' lives don't pursue an even tempo. What happened just lately?"

She said slowly, "Oh, just that my own life turned upside down. I can't tell you about it, because it concerned someone else. I'm picking up the bits. I'll be glad of new scenes, of something that might provide me with a challenge. Like looking after a household in a remote area and providing some sort of mother-substitute for two orphaned children."

"Did your parents advise you to get away from it all?"

"Yes. They didn't want me at home where they wouldn't be able to resist tempering the wind to the shorn lamb." She laughed. "Another stock solution . . . change of scene. But my mother also provided me with an instance out of her own experience. It was painful to her to resurrect, I think, but she didn't hesitate. And she quoted something that really said, in a way, that time heals, that you never know what's just round the corner." She chuckled, and this time there was real merriment in it. "And I didn't know, did I? This very morning, when I'd thought to hear no other voice but my own, you catapulted into that kitchen and involved me in a whole family—a connection by marriage I didn't even know existed. Mind you, for a few hot moments I couldn't have imagined myself being even remotely thankful for your appearance."

He chuckled with her, then said ruefully, "Of course your parents will have to know. Pity, because the fewer who do, the better; but they'll be so used to the secrets of the study."

"Yes, they must know."

"How will they regard the deception we had to practice?"

Jocelyn dimpled. "They'll just regard it as another of my harebrained, unorthodox adventures that they've been used to from my kindergarten days up. They'll realize it had to be done for the children's sakes."

Again the hint of something grim in his tone. "Then, by heaven, don't let any hint of that old scandal come to their ears. We'd better just say Ina is a suspicious sort and she'd pounce on the idea of having a strange woman in my house overnight."

How safe and short this score of miles seemed, with no mist making everything featureless, no lack of visibility to make an unknown road a way of dread.

54

The lake lay to their right this time, and under today's cloudless skies it gleamed forget-me-not blue, though Magnus said it was rarely as blue as Wakatipu and Wanaka whose waters were sapphire and cornflower. This was often sea-green in the shallows, pewter-silver in the depths, still and mysterious. Sometimes great waves white-crested, were whipped up, when gales played havoc on the lake. In winter, when the mountains were blanketed in thick muffling snow, reflections stood out so sharply and clearly, slides could be projected upside down and nobody could notice. "My mother used to call it her lake-of-a-thousand-moods," he said with pride, "and every one had its own beauty and charm."

They came into Te Anau. Now for Aunt Clarissa . . .

THE MOMENT Jocelyn met her, the butterflies in her stomach subsided. Aunt Clarissa didn't bat an eyelid—said straight out thank heaven they'd had the gumption and the time to grab a heaven-sent opportunity by the tail, like a comet, and proceed to paint the lily in dazzling purity. Jocelyn blinked at that, and Magnus roared, giving his aunt a hug. "Oh, Aunt Clarissa, still mixing your metaphors. You really are a gem! A lily, painted, would have lost its purity, you daft thing. How marvellous to have you in the house with me. One of my characters can be a mixer-of-metaphors, and I'll not need to strain my brain to think them up—you'll produce a fresh one every day."

He looked at Jocelyn and chuckled. "This poor girl, Aunt, is feeling bewildered. She's got herself into a mad family all right. Pitchforked into a sticky situation, lots of relatives thrown at her, and I'm sure she expected to meet an Amazon in Ina and met a Dresden china shepherdess type instead . . . with the heart of a Borgia. Pure poison, that woman. But Jocelyn was magnificently quick on the uptake, seeing I'd just about blasted her out of the kitchen into the hall, with my first reaction to finding a female in diaphanous garments sitting at my table. Imagine if dear Ina had got there twenty minutes earlier! No amount of explanation could have excused that. What ammunition it would have made for her! She'd have marched upstairs to see the sleeping arrangements. That would really have been something . . . feminine gear strewn all round my room and only one bed slept in!"

Aunt Clarissa succumbed to the giggles at the thought. Jocelyn surveyed aunt and nephew rather appraisingly. It *was* odd to have two beds in a bachelor's room. Aunt Clarissa wiped tears away. "Eh, but it does me good to see you laugh like this. I've not seen you helpless for so long, Magnus."

He raised a red eyebrow at it. "Of course not. I've been overseas a year."

"I didn't mean that, and well you know it. You've not laughed quite like that since that business in Albertown."

For a moment that strange look which was more a steeling against woe than a hardening passed over the craggy face. Then he shrugged and said lightly, "Well, as our newly-found cousin here lectured me coming in from the Downs, life has a way of providing an answer to these things. Time heals and all that."

Aunt Clarissa shot him a quick glance. "Oh, so you told her about that?" She paused, then said, "And about your broken engagement?"

"Of course. Or she'd never have understood why it was that Ina mustn't know she'd spent the night at Ronaldsay. We had one narrow shave when Jocelyn thought I was a farmer. I just about broke into a rash, but I countered it and she caught on superbly. The next moment she was talking about polishing phrases and whatnot to the manner born. Can't think how she did it."

"Oh, I heard an address by a woman novelist, and she said just that," Jocelyn explained. "Odd how these things flash into one's mind when needed. I think we'd better get weaving. The children will feel better when you're back home with them."

Clarissa Archer said, "We'll have some afternoon tea first. You can pour, my dear. It takes me so long."

It seemed incredible to Jocelyn, who at this time yesterday would have imagined herself exploring the lakeside with the Ronaldsons by now. Yet here she was, filling in a strange woman with details of her family, so that if the cunning Ina rang and got her on the phone, she might not get bowled out.

Magnus, looking less like a warring Viking in this mood, even referred to her mother's queen cakes. Aunt Clarissa said, "I feel I know Ingrid already. After you've rung her, dear, I'd better speak to her. She'd better know her ewe lamb hasn't fallen into the clutches of a wolf."

Her nephew said, "You disappoint me. You didn't mix that up."

Clarissa had all her things packed. They took her out to the station-wagon, one each side of her, and got her into the front seat. The wheelchair fitted into the back compartment.

She had all the impatience of a young girl to get there now. "You don't know what it's been like, Magnus, fretting there in Invercargill, about the children, and feeling a prisoner in the flesh, shackled by my own stiff joints—all I could do was keep writing them every week, and sending them pocket-money. Ina's letters disturbed me, and what the children didn't say in theirs—because she read them over—was worse. Though I knew once you were off that wretched island, you'd be home and with them.

"I had to be very guarded, just saying once or twice that 'once your uncle Magnus is home, all will be well.' " She turned to look at Jocelyn. "It also meant a lot to me when Magnus rang me to say he'd need me at the Downs. My daughter's family are off her hands now. She was widowed so young, I felt I could help her then by baby-sitting, but it will be lovely for the whole family now not to have to worry about amusing a not-too-mobile grandmother."

Jocelyn's apprehensions about Mrs. Archer dissolved completely. She said, "I think you're a kindred spirit and I'm very glad to have you for an aunt. Not only that, but—" She paused, not sure how to go on.

Magnus looked into the driving-mirror when she didn't continue. His eyes were keen. But his voice held a teasing note. "Do I detect a blush on my cousin's maidenly cheek?"

The faint warmth became hot. Then she shook her head—
"It's an infantile thing to even think, much less say, that's why
I felt embarrassed. Sounds so babyish for a nursing Sister
who's been out in the world on her own for a long time."

"But we're still waiting—come, Jocelyn, when two people
have roared each other's heads off within seconds of their first
meeting, they should know no subsequent embarrassment."

"Goodness," murmured Aunt Clarissa, "you sound like one
of your own books, dear boy. But, Jocelyn, we're all infantile
at times, and you've made us curious."

Jocelyn chuckled, "Okay, if you don't think it stupid to say
I feel that having you in the house will give me a feeling
of——"

Magnus's tone was taut as he broke in, "I get it. You'll feel
safer. You like to think there'll be a chaperone about."

Jocelyn sounded completely exasperated. "I thought nothing
of the sort, I meant I still like the feeling of having a mother-
type in the house. There! I may have ushered people into the
world . . . and out of it, and have seen some pretty ghastly
sights in the operating theater, but sometimes I don't feel
much different from the time I was a diffident teenager, and
I love an older person around. Now call me babyish . . . it
is, but I'd rather you thought that than——"

He and Aunt Clarissa were laughing again. He cried, "Pax!
It's okay. It's just that at present, when I feel Ina would bring
all the big guns to bear upon me if only she had the
ammunition, I'm touchy about my reputation."

Aunt Clarissa's laugh stopped immediately. She said, "We
don't want to hear about things that were over and done with
long since, Magnus, and anyway, reputation has nothing to do
with character."

An odd thing to say. What could Mrs. Archer mean?
Perhaps she didn't like spineless people, those who never
became involved in anything, so therefore never had the finger
of scorn pointed at them. Did she mean that the things that
had happened in Magnus's life had shaped and made him as
he was? He was too dynamic a character never to have become

over-involved with someone. With *women!* Don't minimise it, Jos.

THERE WAS NO DOUBT Aunt Clarissa was a great favorite with the children. They stopped their play and tore to the car, talking at top speed. How they'd not played all the time, but had got the Watson children to help them sort their things. Gee, it was good to have *all* their books again. Aunt Ina hadn't let them take any tattered ones and they were the ones they liked the best, that was how they'd got that way. Mrs. Watson had even kept all their boxes of rubbish for them, all Ninian's spare bike parts and all his lake-stones, and his trolley and notebooks. And for Una, her Royal Family scrapbooks and her stamps. "Aunt Clarissa, have you brought yours, because I can peel the stamps off the envelopes for you if your fingers are too stiff."

Clarissa waggled her fingers at them. "See that? A new tablet. And no side effects. But I'm slower than you'd be, of course, so we can work together. And up here in this glorious bracing mountain air I may improve out of all recognition."

Meg Watson stayed just long enough to show Jocelyn she'd put a leg of hogget mutton in the oven, and the potatoes and carrots and pumpkin were ready to go beside it. She had a banana jelly in the fridge and some fruit salad. "No, my two can't stay. It's enough trying to get used to a new family, Miss Alexander, without having to look after the neighbor's children too. Come on, Kitty and Errol, I've a few chores for you to do."

"Oh, make it Jocelyn. And don't worry about the children. My mother used to say that two extra children could bring harmony with them—that we were more polite to guests than to each other. Let them come over whenever they want to."

"Fair enough, but not today. And let Ninian and Una come over to our place more for the next few days till you get settled in. By the way, will they be starting school Monday?"

"They will. I'll take the first week in the mornings, Meg, if you do the afternoons. Okay?"

59

"Yes, but as far as you're concerned, won't it cut into your working hours too much? Your mother once told me that what you got done in the morning was worth twice all the other hours. Colin and I could do both trips, now."

He shrugged, "Different circumstances make for different timetables. Plenty of authors have to make it by working at night after their other jobs, Meg, till they earn enough to make it full-time. I'm Eric's stand-in, so I'll take on his usual tasks. We're talking about the school bus, Jocelyn," he explained. "We have to take them three miles to the nearest pick-up. It's a long day for them, but worth it to be home every night."

Jocelyn reflected that he mightn't be much as far as women were concerned, but he surely was a good uncle. She said, "I suppose Jan drove, and took her turn?"

Magnus said, "Yes, but you don't have to."

She said, "None of that. I'm family too. I'll take my turn at the mornings. I have much respect for authorship!"

They proceeded on a tour of the house. She found it had all the charm of an old style and up-to-the-minute convenience of a new one.

One large room upstairs was as yet unfurnished. "That was my parents' room," Magnus's voice held sorrow. "So much furniture was saved, but nothing from here. We lost some things that were more valuable, but I miss this room's contents most of all. It's associated with our—my—earliest memories. It was shabby, but had a sort of patina of generations of living that enhanced it.

"The walnut bed had round wooden knobs at each end, paler than the rest, because a whole cavalcade of children had swung on them as they talked to their parents. On the inside of the chest of drawers, Eric once carved his initials trying out a new pocketknife. Oh, he got walloped for it. You can't let kids get away with things like that, but it was just one more bit of him that disappeared. And Granny's rag rugs were here."

Jocelyn said, "A fire is such a deadly, consuming thing. It's a ritual in our house every night for two people to check that all switches that can be switched off are, all heaters checked, and nobody's allowed to smoke in bed. Some things would be irreplaceable—like Dad's sermons and scrapbooks and his library. Oh, he rewrites a sermon completely if he preaches again on the same subject, but all the references and illustrations are there. And to lose one's letters must be cruel."

Magnus nodded. "And ours were at the mercy of someone who broke in. What he stole was recovered. What was burnt is gone. At first, looking at the scorched earth, and the belongings piled in filthy stacks in the sheds, it seemed as if we could never create any architectural beauty here again, but once the blackened stones and charred timbers were bulldozed away, I saw, one day, with delight, delicate ferns and beech and *totara* seedlings springing up. This was land the first Ninian Isbister cleared, you see. I felt reproached for my feeling of despair. I knew then that I too must regenerate the past and build as near as possible the Isbister home that had been here before."

Jocelyn felt moved. This man had done a lot of rebuilding in his life. Certainly some of it, the crash of his engagement, for instance, had been caused by his own folly, but at least he'd taken on a terrific task, and word by word, from his imagination, had pounded out, in long hours at his desk, when possibly work outside would have relieved his stress more, that which made it possible to create a new home in the image of the old. In these days of inflation, the cost must have far exceeded even the insurance. He'd mentioned raising a mortgage. Now he was committed to paying it off. She guessed that the farm, in these days of changing overseas markets, would do little more than pay the wages of the men, and keep the children.

Well, she'd wanted something to fill up the blank in her life; this was certainly it. She realized with a sense of shock that she'd thought of Leigh only once today, when she had spoken of him, indirectly, on the way to Te Anau.

By the time they had had dinner, they had settled into

something approaching normality. Jocelyn began to lose the sense of incredulity that had possessed her.

As they finished, Magnus said, "The children will wash up. You must ring your parents, Jos, to let them know we're in and settled, and that they must spend a weekend here as soon as possible. Oh, how stupid of me, you don't get weekends in manses. Well, whenever they see a fairly clear week, they must come down on a Monday and spend a few days."

Aunt Clarissa's eyes met Jocelyn's with a wicked twinkle. "Be sure to give Ingrid and Niall my love and tell them to take that little break as soon as possible. I'm dying to talk over old times with them."

Magnus's lips twitched. "Aunt, you can supervise the washing-up—it may keep you out of mischief too. I'll go upstairs with Jos to show her how to get through to Te Anau for her call. It'll be quieter on the study phone."

Yes, and well out of the way of little pricked-up ears!

As they mounted the *rimu* staircase with its smooth, gleaming reddish bannisters, he said, "Tell them in as much detail as you can, but leave out my reputation. Just say Ina is a poisonous creature, possessive and mischief-making, and she's said if there's any way at all to prove this is no place for the youngsters, she won't hesitate to use it. That's why I was so alarmed when I found you here in your negligée."

He got the number for her. Jocelyn felt a return of trepidation. She had to put this over in a way that didn't either worry her parents to distraction, or cause them to tell her she ought never to have got involved like this. Come to think of it, though, they never had reacted like that.

CHAPTER FOUR

Nevertheless she didn't plunge till she felt certain preliminaries would lessen the coming shock. She asked if her father was free and would like to listen in on the study phone, and added, "Neither of you must 'ooh' and 'aah' too loudly or you'll deafen the other."

She said she wasn't ringing from Kamahi Point, because the Ronaldsons had dashed off to Wellington to see Ian, but that she was very fortunate; she'd found a private case, very light nursing, at some neighbours of theirs. Magnus was nodding approvingly. It established a friendly, respectable background.

Jocelyn went on. Oddly enough, the chap was an Isbister, and guess what, he was a sort of cousin! Well, he was, Sarah Isbister's cousin, and he and his mother had actually been at that wedding. Pity *they'd* not been able to make it, or they'd have met him too. Yes, wasn't it a small world? He wasn't unlike Sarah to look at. His twin brother and his brother's wife had been killed while this chap Isbister was in Orkney and he was now guardian to their children. He had an elderly aunt in charge, but she was arthritic and needed a certain amount of attention from time to time, plus regular massage, so she'd offered to take it on. Actually, it was as much to look after the children as Aunt Clarissa. She added, to give it a family touch, "She's already asked me to call her Aunt. Isn't that nice?"

Her mother's voice was warm. "Indeed it is. Honey, I think this will suit you down to the ground, and it's just magnificent for this man to take on the guardianship of his niece and nephew. I take it this man is single, or a widower, or something?"

Magnus had dropped on to one of the packing-cases, facing the desk at which she was sitting, and had folded his arms across his chest. He was regarding her intently, one of the fiery brows raised.

She said, "Yes, he's single, has been single a long time, I'd say. All the more credit due to him, don't you think? A wife would make it so much easier. What did you say? Oh, yes, provided she was the right sort. If I'm not, he can sack me. How old?" Over the phone her hazel eyes gave him a saucy, appraising look. Then, "In his late forties, I should say, or even a little older."

Magnus Isbister looked startled, then indignant, then caught on and grinned. Better make him old enough to sound safe. As if any age was safe!

Jocelyn said, "But now I've got to tell you how I got the job. I made a frightful blue and nearly put this poor man in the soup. You know what I am for unorthodox adventures. I've told you about Sybil's measly children and my deciding to come on. The Ronaldsons told her I'd find the key among the plants on the back porch. Well, I got here very late—I was delayed by fog. Some vandals had turned the signpost at the crossroads round and, all unaware—and mainly because this place is called Ronaldsay Downs—I thought it was their house. I found a key under a pot-plant and let myself in. I was desperately tired, so I just went off and slept in the first made-up bed I came to. I was finishing breakfast when this man arrived. He took me for a lady burglar. It was dreadful. You know, just like Goldilocks and the Three Bears. 'Who's been eating *my* porridge?' Only it was grapefruit. He took it very well really, after the first few moments. He must have a lovely nature!" Her eyes met Magnus's and at the look in his she nearly choked.

"No, my dear Papa, it was *not* hilarious. But listen, here's the crunch. It involved a very delicate situation. A perfectly horrible woman, the children's aunt on their mother's side, had snatched the children away from the farm—the manager's wife wanted to keep them till their uncle got back from

Orkney—and she's possessive and mischief-making—had once nearly split their parents' marriage up—and she'd do anything to wrest the kids from him.

"Now listen. I'll explain it in detail, and don't interrupt, till I get it all out. Please understand we couldn't do anything else because we only had seconds to work in. I'd no sooner explained how I'd got there than the manager rang to say this woman was on her way; she'd called there first. And Mother, I was in that diaphanous garment you gave me in a moment of frivolity and extravagance. Imagine how that would have looked to anyone who had a reason for wanting to believe the worst! So I shot into a uniform, and plaited my hair in earphones like in that play I was in, and we pretended I was the nurse he'd engaged for his aunt. We played up the cousin angle like nobody's business. Now, pin your ears back, here are the details you must remember, because it's a small world, and we never want any of this to get back to Mrs. Chester's ears. She's Presbyterian you know, and ten to one she'll ask her own minister if he knows you." They were good listeners.

When she came to explaining how at the time of the tragedy Magnus was marooned on an Orcadian island, her father suddenly caught on, gave an amazed ejaculation and said, "You're talking about Magnus Isbister, the author, aren't you?"

"Oh, do you know his books? I'm afraid I'd never even heard of him."

"Good grief, girl, you know I always read Hammond Innes and Alistair Maclean . . . he's right in that tradition. D'ye mean to say you've not read his *Winter of the Darkness?* Just imagine, I'd never dreamed he'd be connected with Grant Alexander's wife. This is fascinating. For sure we'll come up for a few days some time. I'm tickled pink to be even remotely connected with him.

"We'll certainly go along with you, child. I can't see you could do anything else in the circumstances. In fact I'd say it was sheer inspiration engendered by desperation and being pressured for time. Main thing is for these children to get adjusted again. But, Jos, you'll have to take the Ronaldsons into your confidence when they come back. They'd think it mighty odd that we'd never mentioned the Isbisters when we're claiming relationship with them now."

"Yes," said Jocelyn unhappily, "we've thought of that. The fewer who know the better, but that's a must. Ina might run into them. Anyway, this position will suit me very nicely for a while. It's a nice change from the regimented hours of surgery life. Yes, Mother, I've a few cooler things with me, but you can send up my summer wardrobe later. Now, Magnus would like to speak to you, and tomorrow I'll get Aunt Clarissa to ring you. She feels it's your due. Oh, what did you say, Dad?"

He said, "We'll have to ring you back later, Jos. We've just got visitors. Don't know who it can be, though, I'm sure none of our parishioners owns a red Jaguar. Only one person . . . your mother can talk to Magnus if you like. I'll see to her. She may not want to come in—I could get back to the phone. She's a perfect stranger, a little woman, in blue."

A dreadful suspicion struck Jocelyn. She shrieked into the phone, "Dad, don't go yet . . . it sounds like Ina Chester. Red Jag . . . blue suit. Oh, surely not; but Dad, if it is, watch every word you say. It's vital to the children's welfare. Mum, don't you go yet."

"Simmer down, darling," advised Ingrid's voice. "Whatever it is, Niall will handle it beautifully. What did you say?"

Jocelyn shrieked, "Before Dad gets her to the lounge, scoop that photo of me off the piano. Now scram!"

She hung up the receiver, turned, looked at Magnus, and sat down on another case. Her legs felt too shaky to support her a moment longer.

"Magnus," she implored, "you guessed what was happening. Oh, do pray it's sheer coincidence. A red Jag, a little woman in blue."

He looked grim. "It could be; but knowing Ina, I'm pretty sure it's her. What she can hope to achieve is beyond me. She said she was going to a friend at Gore. I don't remember hearing about a friend there. That could be to account for her taking the road to Dunedin—not that we could have known that. Oh, in case Harold rang here, I suppose. Normally she takes the Crown and the Lindis."

Jocelyn said, "Perhaps she didn't feel like those roads so soon again. They're so high, so tough."

"Oh, she's an excellent driver, no nerves. Odd, isn't it, when she looks like a bit of porcelain. I'd find her interesting if it wasn't she's a threat to my peace of mind."

"I hope she doesn't strike my parents favorably," said Jocelyn. "They're pretty discriminating, but on first appearance she's anything but a battleaxe."

He looked grim. "I'm afraid that's only too true. She'll do it so delicately. Although she'll think they know me, as a relative, she might make them feel uneasy notwithstanding. She could insinuate that it's just as well we're cousins . . . then she'll retract, appear magnanimous. She'll say she mustn't hold his past against him, but that it's bound to be all right, with Aunt Clarissa there. And say if only Magnus had left the children with her and Harold, they could have had the setting of a natural home life."

"And it could sound all right at that," said Jocelyn. Suddenly she decided on frankness. "Magnus, if she comes back here and gossips she might expect me to know—" she found her cheeks warming but gave him a level look. "This isn't just curiosity. But surely it wasn't—I mean, anything more than being rather a gay bachelor?"

His lips were a thin line and this time no expression of woe crossed his features. He wore a don't-care-a-damn look.

"All right. Can you take it? I'd rather tell you than have you go in for any of the devious means women employ when they want to find out the juicy bits."

Jocelyn stood up. "Hold it! Then you *do* think it's curiosity. Thanks for the compliment. It was merely so that if Ina came back, or rang, I could counter any snide remarks she might make. She might even hint that it had been hushed up in the larger family circle, but I really ought to know what had happened. But now I couldn't care less. If I blunder, I blunder. I'll just assume that you're rather notorious for affairs, so much so that if you had a young nurse in the house, not related to you, it might be pointed out that you're hardly the person to be the guardian of young children.

"All I'll say if the dear Ina hints at such a thing is that I believe you to be a reformed character, otherwise my father wouldn't have allowed me to come here. Having a father a minister is a great help in this situation. I hope you appreciate that. Now, I'm going downstairs, and while I have to be outwardly friendly in front of Aunt Clarissa and the children, and will appear even to have respect for you, inwardly I'm as distant as the South Pole. Remember that, Magnus Isbister. I am *not* devious. I don't relish gossip and I couldn't care less what you've done or are going to do with your life!"

She was halfway across the room in a splendidly dramatic exit when the phone rang. She turned back, then said, "You answer that. Heaven knows who it might be. Possibly even some of the women in your life. I don't want to do any more explaining this day!"

His "Wait!" halted her again. "It could be your mother ringing back to say it was only a small parishioner in a blue outfit in a red Jag."

The amusement in his tone flicked her on the raw. He picked up the receiver, said, "Oh, hullo, Aunt Ingrid. Yes, Magnus. How are you? I sincerely hope Cousin Jocelyn came up here armed with your queen cake recipe. They're my favorites."

Even from here Jocelyn could hear her mother's chuckle. She could have smacked Magnus. He continued, the amusement dying out of his tone. "Oh, it *is* Ina?" He listened, then said, "Oh, good show. I can't thank you enough. The whole thing browns me off. I find all this deception most distasteful, but I can't risk anything. I don't want the children to feel they're a bone of contention. She'd have no hope of getting them, but even threatening to try would upset Una and Ninian. Oh, thank you. I'm sure you'll handle it beautifully—I hope for your sake she doesn't stay long. Jocelyn is just here—oh, I see, yes, perhaps you'd better get back to Uncle Niall and Ina. Goodbye."

His mouth was wry. "You heard. Your mother rang back so we'd know, and when Ina is gone, if they don't get other callers, she'll ring back. If they do, she'll make it tomorrow morning instead. I think I'm going to like my Aunt Ingrid very much. Not all ministers' wives would take it like that."

"Perhaps you've not known many," said Jocelyn.

He looked at her sharply, then said suavely, she thought, "You think I'm not a church man because of my reputation. Let me tell you, our minister and his wife are very close and dear friends."

She curled her lip. "What makes you think you can read my mind? I happen to be a daughter of the manse. Do you imagine all our parishioners are models of rectitude? It's for publicans and sinners, the church, Magnus Isbister. I think you've got a chip on your shoulder about women. You'd better get rid of it. It's not a healthy atmosphere in which to rear children. Just because one woman—your fiancée—sat in judgment on you over some scandal it doesn't mean all women will. I suppose the poor thing was only jealous."

"She wasn't. That I could have taken—but she condemned me out of hand. I wouldn't want to live my life out with a woman like that."

Jocelyn had no idea why she felt driven to defend this unknown girl. "There are two sides to every problem. Dad always had to tell people that who came to him in righteous indignation over some marriage partner who'd erred. It wasn't always black and white. And the so-called innocent party wasn't always blameless. You might feel she condemned you and ought to forgive. But she may have seen something of the havoc unfaithfulness can cause and decided it wasn't worth risking. Better a broken engagement than a broken marriage."

He looked at her keenly. "Then you've made up your mind that it *was* unfaithfulness? The ultimate?"

"Anything less would hardly be likely to affect your custody of the children. And it explains the conniption you had when you found me in your house. But if it wasn't as bad as that you'd better tell me rather than have me think the worst of you if it isn't deserved."

A look of extreme distaste crossed his face. He seemed to be considering what to say. Then he assumed a stolid look. "Ina has every right to doubt that I'm the person—morally—to bring up these children. It just happens I know they'll be happier here. And for their sakes there'll be nothing in my life from now on that could affect them in any way. But you'd better know that I was having a weekend with a girl in Central Otago and, as we left the motel, Ina spotted us. Now if you don't like it, you can just play things along here till I can get some older, sensible body to take charge. Though—" he looked at her appealingly, "I'd rather have someone your age, they need someone with whom they can have fun, go picnicking with, swim with, boat with. Jan, their mother, once she matured enough to shake off her sister's domination, was great fun. She finally managed to put first things first. Marriage, for instance, as against other affections. Well, now you know what sort of a chap you're working for, Jocelyn Alexander, what about it? Do you want to opt out, or were you really sincere about the church being for the sinners? Perhaps it's one thing to be impersonal about it, and another to be living here with me? But make up your mind before—before the children get too fond of you."

Jocelyn drew herself up. "You might as well call me hypocrite if you expect me to rat and run. It was Dad who said the church was for the publicans and sinners, and he's never impersonal about his parishioners—not even about the difficult ones who never err. They're part of his flock and sometimes he feels he loves the lost ones best." Suddenly she grinned. "It's easier than loving the others very often—they are warmer, more human."

She couldn't read the light that leapt into the intense blue eyes. Then he said, "Then despite your scathing remarks just now, although you deplore my morals—you might find me more approachable than some of the sterner characters?"

She grinned again. "I'm pretty certain I'd find you easier to get on with than the nittish Harold!"

He laughed. "Right; on the lighter note, let's go downstairs."

They returned to a family scene. Una was finishing the washing-up; Aunt Clarissa in her chair, drying; and Ninian putting the dishes away. Clarissa said, her brown eyes alight, "We thought if we got these done we could go out for the traditional sunset viewing." She added, for Jocelyn, "It's been a custom here, from pioneer days on, to take a last long look at the mountains before nightfall. The very first Ninian decreed that since their lot had fallen amidst lines of beauty, it should never be taken for granted."

Jocelyn didn't know how her own greenish-brown eyes widened and shone. "That's one thing we've never had, as children of a succession of manses, continuity like that. I'm all for keeping up the family traditions. Let's go."

Magnus said, "And, Aunt, you're not to hurry. We'll saunter. Sunset and twilight aren't bustling times, they're leisurely. The day is over."

The path was shadowy enough to make the white azaleas and rhododendrons outshine the pinks and purples. In the sycamores, a thrush was singing his mating song, pouring out his ecstacy of love in cadences repeated over and over.

The children ran here, there, and everywhere, darting into little mysterious paths among the bushes, laughing, exclaiming over all the things that belonged to their happy yesterdays, finding new delights, rediscovering old ones.

Magnus said to his aunt, "Darling, would you like to walk down to the lakeshore, or has it been too big a day?"

Aunt Clarissa's voice was the voice of a young girl in its eagerness and lilt, suddenly. "Oh, Magnus, I was so hoping you'd offer me that when you said time wouldn't matter. Jocelyn, this spot is particularly dear to me and he knows it. See where that line of willows extends from that clump of poplars almost down to the edge of the water? The dividing line that shelters the private beach? Beyond there is where my husband proposed to me.

"There was such a crowd of us here that Christmas. My sister, Magnus's mother, was just a bride. She asked all the relations up to celebrate her first Christmas here. That big mown paddock over there was just dotted with tents. I'd been secretly in love with James, one of the men on the farm, for months, and was terrified he'd think me too young. I made such a fool of myself trying to look and sound older than myself. By the time our last night came, I was desperate.

"There was a huge orange moon over what he always called the Delectable Mountains. I was plain miserable, thought James must be laughing at me. He was fifteen years older than I was. I kept right away from him, losing myself in the crowd of others dancing in the big barn. Suddenly he got hold of my elbow and said, in a whisper, 'Lassie, if we dinna get away frae this crowd soon, I'll go mad. Come on.' I went like one in a dream. I was so terrified I'd open my silly mouth and put my foot in it again, so I never said a word; neither did he. He just kept hold of my elbow to guide me over the tufty grass. He said afterwards that my silence had given him the courage. He thought that if I hadn't wanted to go with him I'd at least have asked where he was taking me.

"We went to the far side of the willows into the little bay. There was a rowing-boat drawn up there. James said, "If that daft crowd up there saw us sneak away, they'd likely follow us and turn the whole beach into a party. So we'll away off on the water, lass, till I've had ma' say.'

"I was afraid to hope, told myself perhaps he'd just wanted to get me to myself to tell me not to be so daft about him next time I visited my sister. We rowed right out into the track of the moon, shining across the water from Middle Fiord, and James said to me very directly . . ." She paused, savoring the memory.

Jocelyn said imploringly, "Go on, Aunt Clarissa, go on. Please don't stop there. Or is it too private?"

The older woman chuckled. "He said: 'Clarissa Mount-joy . . . I'm hoping all your wise cluckings and older airs were for one reason and one alone . . . to show a daft man of thirty-five, who's been captivated by a lassie of twenty, that he's no sae daft after all. Tell me, Clarissa, were you trying to grow up to me?'

"I said: 'Why, James? Why do you want to know? You've got to tell me why?' and he said, 'Because if you were, then I'll dare to tell you I love you and——' "

Magnus began to chuckle in an anticipatory way, only Jocelyn didn't recognize that. She rounded on him. "Don't laugh! It's just beautiful. Don't you dare!"

His laugh petered out, "Oh, my spitfire of a cousin . . . I'm not scoffing, believe me. It's just that I know what comes next. It's our favorite family story. Go on, Aunt."

Her laughter rose then too, but the mirth was tinged with rue. "Jocelyn, I cast myself into his arms, knocked the oars clean out of his grip. He tried to steady me . . . the boat turned over and in we went. We were both good swimmers, fortunately, but even though it was a warm night, the lake water is always cold after sunset.

"James got more of a scare than I did. He plunged for me, but I'd bobbed up on the other side of the boat, and we clung to the keel, one on each side. I thought he'd be furious, that I'd ruined his proposal, that he'd think me far too much of a harum-scarum to consider as a wife, but he started to laugh and said: 'I suppose you realize you've ruined our first kiss? *We can't even reach each other across the boat.* I wont risk swimming round to you, because it will keep steadier if I don't. When we get our breath back, if you think you can hang on, I'll go after that oar and then try to right the boat.'

"I panicked and shrieked, 'No, you won't, James Archer! You might get cramp and disappear in the bottomless depths and I'd be haunted with remorse the rest of my life . . . We'll have to yell, it's a very still night.'

"Yell we did, but the concertinas and the fiddles were making too much noise. We tried to right the boat, but

73

couldn't. Then James realized there was a faint drift over towards the right-hand Gate of Lilliput. It just had to be the farthest away, and it took a fair time—we sort of paddled over with one hand each—and James was much too anxious to think about keeping on proposing. He was afraid I mightn't make it if we abandoned the boat, though it would have been quicker. Finally we got into the shallows in the lee of the Gate.

"What a way we were from the homestead! I'd lost my foolish silver evening shoes the moment we went in and I had on a stupid sheath-like evening-dress in black satin that I'd thought might make me look older. Oh boy, was that some walk back to the homestead! James had taken off his shoes in the water . . . what with sharp rocks, and slime and bits of gorse washed down by the streams, to prick our feet, it was a real endurance test. By the time we got to the beach below the homestead, they were streaming out across the paddocks looking for us. I'll never forget when they shone a hurricane lantern on us and saw us looking like something cast up by the sea. Magnus's grandfather, old Francis Isbister, said, 'The saints preserve us . . . what have you been doing to the lassie, James?' And James replied: 'Asking her to marry me, sir.'

"He peered down on us and said, 'Well, some of my own Norse ancestors were a funny lot, but I never heard o' any of them holding their women under the water till they promised to wed them! What in the world's the matter with the men today?' "

When their laughter subsided, Aunt Clarissa said, "Poor Magnus, he's heard that story many and many a time, they resurrect it at every family reunion."

Jocelyn interpreted the slight shadow that crossed Magnus's features correctly. At every reunion, no doubt some face would be freshly missing, in the natural order of events when someone ripe in years would be no longer with them, but this family had suffered too many bereavements too recently. James, evidently, had been gone some years, but Magnus's parents not so long ago, followed by the more poignant cutting-off of two young lives, Jan's and Eric's, who ought to have been spared to see their children and their children's children grow up.

He didn't let it last, said teasingly, "I may have heard it often, but when we have a new audience, it loses nothing in the telling. But I find it frustrating. Never, in all the years they've recounted it, did Aunt Clarissa or Uncle James ever reveal the most interesting bit of all . . . what they said, and did, when they reached the shore." He looked expectantly at his aunt who might, at last, have told all.

She only gave him a saucy look and he said mischievously, "Oh well, I daresay neither of you caught a cold despite your immersion . . . there's more than one way of keeping warm!"

The children came running up in distress because they'd found a nest on the ground. Magnus examined it. "Not to worry. It's a last year's nest."

The sun dipped a little, quite suddenly it seemed, and it sent great beams of light raying up above the cardboard cutout edge of the mountains across the lake. It was for all the world like a miniature Aurora Australis.

Magnus paused to look. "Wouldn't it be wonderful to be in a helicopter at this moment, looking over the rim of the world into the far west? Right beyond all the mountains, the arms of Lake Te Anau and the deep fiords of the coast running in towards us from the Tasman Sea? We'd see the sun going round from one side of the world to the other. Whenever I felt very far from New Zealand and home when I was in Orkney, I told myself that it was only the distance from sunset to sunrise, even if sometimes I did long for the wings of the morning, and the sandals of the wind."

Jocelyn felt a tremor pass over her. She'd felt like this at high school when she'd be listening to some loved teacher read a poem that had in it some magic quality of phrase and word. Of course this man was a writer. He would feel all things passionately. *All.* Yes, he would know an intense love for beauty in the contours and colors of the world about him. *And* for beauty and response in women.

The sunset deepened to violet and indigo and finally into a featureless purple so that the angles and valleys and peaks of the mountains across the lake became haunts of mystery. Here, over the open water, the twilight lingered on, and the gentle lap-lap of an inland sea unstirred by wind, murmured against the countless glacier-polished stones of the shore. "The most peaceful, soothing sound in the world," said Aunt Clarissa.

She and Jocelyn sat down on the keel of an upturned boat and talked now and then, or in silence watched Magnus and the children playing ducks-and-drakes, selecting the thinnest, smoothest stones for expert skimming.

Clarissa said, "I wonder how many generations of children have done just that, in all the waters of the world? They probably did it in prehistoric days, and built dams with rocks and driftwood for the sheer pleasure of doing it, and dabbled little bare feet in sun-warmed pools." She looked at Magnus, balanced on a rock, pointing out something to the children. Possibly a stilt, seeing one rose from over there, flying low over the water, calling raucously, its long, graceful legs stretched out behind it, a poem in feathered grace and symmetrical line. She said fondly, "It's so good for him, this. It's hard enough at any time to lose a brother, but to lose a twin! And he feels things so deeply. All the strong passions of the Norsemen are let loose in Magnus, I'd say. Eric wasn't a bit like that. Odd, when they were identical twins in looks.

"Magnus seemed to be born with an awareness of his Orcadian ancestry, but Eric lived in the present. He didn't have Magnus's ebullient, extrovert nature. But the bond was almost frighteningly strong. Laura, my sister, used to say she hoped the strength of that tie would never cause them any anguish. But when Eric married young, Magnus didn't fret at all. He was glad for his brother's sake, and he loved Jan too, even if at times he wished she'd have more strength of will and not let her sister rule her. Well, it's over now. I hope some day Magnus will find true satisfaction in life. I don't want the second-best for him."

Jocelyn felt a warmth of affection for Clarissa. She knew what Clarissa meant. Some things in Magnus's life had been second-best, cheap, shoddy, clandestine.

Clarissa added, "When Meg told me on the phone to Invercargill one day that Magnus had arranged the room that was the duplicate of the one he'd always shared with Eric, just as it had been before, I knew he must have felt that if he didn't, it would be like shutting Eric out of his life."

Jocelyn felt ashamed of her previous thoughts about the two beds. She looked at her watch, said, "Mother said not to expect her to ring back before nine-thirty, but I expect we'd better go back now and get the children to bed. It's been a long and gruelling day for them. I expect their aunt kept at them about the situation all the way down."

"She would. Give me both your hands, dear. I can always get down, it's the getting up bothers me."

By mutual consent as the five of them left the daffodil-sprinkled sward of the shore, they swung round. Now only a faintly silver glimmer revealed the presence of the mountains.

Jocelyn said, "I can see the darker smudge of St. Ringan's Isle, but for the life of me I can't pick out St. Olaf's. Where is it?"

Ninian laughed. "It disappears at dusk, because it's got only dark trees on it. St. Ringan's has lighter willows to circle it."

Una added, "And St. Ringan's has that little white sandy beach, see . . . dead center. St. Olaf's looks from here as if it has no landing-place at all, because this side its bluffs rear straight up out of the water. But we can beach our boats on the other side in a tiny, tiny bay. That's why we call it The Secret Island."

"Oh, like Enid Blyton's *Secret Island*. I used to love that." She looked slightly amazed as both children promptly stood on their heads.

Magnus said, "That marks sheer delight . . . you're of the-race-that-knows-Joseph."

She blinked. "Race-that-knows-Joseph? Oh, I remember, it's a quotation from *Anne of Green Gables*. How clever of me!"

"It would be more clever if you realized it was first from the Bible, daughter of the manse."

Una, right way up again, said rapturously, "You *like* Enid

77

Blyton? Aunt Ina wouldn't let us take any of hers—said she was going to see we got into proper reading habits, that we were going to read things that helped our education and not as much as read one book over again, that it was just wasting time."

Jocelyn looked horrified enough to please them. She said hotly, "I can't think of anything worse than not being allowed to read a favorite book over. Of course a lot of people had a kink like that about Enid Blyton. It's quite stupid too, because the very writers those rigid critical people *would* approve of, in the literary world, like Samuel Johnson, for instance, and somebody else . . . oh, I know, Somerset Maugham, believed children should be able to read what they *want* to read, not what adults think they *ought* to read."

Magnus looked interested. "Did they? I didn't know that, Jocelyn."

She nodded. "I've got a couple of clippings in a scrapbook. I never travel without my scrapbooks. When we get ourselves more organized I'll hunt them up and read them to you. Mind you, it would be awfully foolish to read nothing but Enid Blyton. You'd shut the door on a world of delight otherwise. You've got to adventure with books."

"In fact," said Magnus, "you ought even to try Magnus Isbister some time. Now, kids, you've had a long day and a fair go. You can go to sleep knowing you're here for keeps. So as soon as we get inside it's showers and bed. I'll come and tuck you in."

Una said instantly, "Could *she* tuck us in too?"

Jocelyn didn't bat an eyelid. This meant Una was remembering Eric and Jan had done it together.

Una added, "I know you aren't supposed to say *she*. Sorry. We don't have to call you Cousin Jocelyn, do we? Can we just say Jocelyn?"

"Of course. I used to get so tired of being Sister Grant. Up you go, and we'll come up when you call out."

The house seemed warm and welcoming and when the children were in bed, Magnus put a match to the fire Meg had set in the living-room, whose far windows looked out on to the lake from the patio that seemed more an extension of the room, because it was divided only by a wall of bubble-glass panels, with two wide doors in the middle.

"The old place had had a patio like this added, with double-hung windows like these, because it faces west, and sometimes the storms sweep in from there, from the first Elsbet's mountains of the mist."

Aunt Clarissa began to knit, Magnus turned on the television. It was a familiar program she'd often watched in Auckland. Jocelyn knew a sense of unreality. Was it only last night about this time she was enquiring where Ronaldsons' turn off was?

Just imagine, if those vandals hadn't turned that signpost round, she'd have been in the blissful solitude of Ronaldsons' house, quite unaware of the needs of this family, and wouldn't have suffered the embarrassment of being caught as an intruder in a stranger's house!

Her feeling of unreality jolted into something definite. *She wasn't sorry she was here.* Oh, well, perhaps that wasn't so strange . . . wasn't it true most people needed to be needed?

CHAPTER FIVE

As they mounted the stairs when the children called out that they'd finished reading, Magnus said, "You caught on, didn't you, that Una wanted not only just a father substitute at tuck-in time, but a mother substitute too?"

"Yes, but how astute of you, as a mere male, to catch on."

"Perhaps I've extra-sensory perception."

"God forbid! I can't think of anything more trying—or dangerous—to live with."

"Oh, I don't know," said Magnus. "Some couples develop it to a remarkable degree. Mother and Father could read each other like an open book. They anticipated each other's needs. Mother knew, even when Father was most poker-faced, if he was offended or deeply moved by a remark someone had made."

"Yes, but they were married. My parents are like that too. I meant it would be uncomfortable to live with a stranger who could read one's thoughts." She looked at him sharply. "I hadn't thought of this—it's because you're an author, isn't it? You enter into people's feelings so acutely, you get under their skins more than most people could."

He pulled a face. "Could be, I suppose. I hope not, though."

"Why?"

"It would be like picking the lock of a person's mind and heart. I'd rather just imagine things for my characters. People could resent it . . . a certain nurse, for instance, who's been propelled into our lives against her will, but who is going to tide us over an awkward time in our lives."

Tide them over? Then he looked on her as only a stop-gap. He must think the first nurse he'd engaged might come after all, later. She mustn't get too fond of this family.

Would Una want to be kissed goodnight? One must never take too much for granted with a child. It was resolved for her by Una flinging up her arms as she bent over during the process of tucking her in, and giving her a neck-straining hug. But she was greatly surprised when Ninian said, "Did you kiss Una?" and at her nod, said nonchalantly, "Then I expect I'd better let you do the same to me."

His uncle merely said goodnight, then his eye fell on a candy wrapper beside Ninian's book. "Ah, a stickjawette. Well, you know your mother's rule, lad. If you eat in bed, then it's back to the bathroom for more tooth-drill."

Ninian grinned and got out. "I ought to have hidden that. Gosh, grownups don't miss a move! Dad was a stinker on that too."

Before he came back Magnus said, "Another hurdle taken. Ina said she'd found it best not to mention their parents, that they shut up like clams. I don't think that's healthy. The loved dead have to be with us, always. My grandfather used to say that. He made the first Ninian and Elsbet as real to me as Aunt Clarissa."

What a mixture this man was! A hint of ruthlessness that probably came from Viking forebears; a man of passionate feelings not always, it seemed, disciplined; a man with whom it would be easy to clash; a man who could take words and fascinate one with them. What a good job she was twenty-seven and that what she felt for Leigh, stifled though it had had to be, armored her against that sort of charm.

That night Aunt Clarissa said, "Now, Magnus, you'd given Nurse Belgarde a run-down on what you expected of her. You'd better do the same for Jocelyn. Tell her how much Meg is prepared to do."

He nodded. "It won't be easy, Jocelyn. But first of all, it won't be Meg, Aunt, who'll be coming over. It's the wife of the new couple in the cottage—Gail Whitton. She's rather eye-catching. Meg and I thought Ina would raise her eyebrows if she saw her and wouldn't scruple to throw a spanner of suspicion in the works. She'd probably hint to Reg—the husband—that he'd better keep an eye on us. You know, say Aunt Clarissa rarely climbs stairs and who's to know what they'd be up to when she's doing the bedrooms and that loose-living author is supposed to be at his desk.

"Anyway, Meg's got too much to do. The Whittons' house is much smaller and they've no family yet. Gail said she'd love to make a bit of extra money till such time as they decide to have a family. She's not got enough to do over there, and this will give her an interest. Despite her glamorous appearance, she's very domesticated. She was brought up on a farm.

"Aunt Clarissa can manage the dishes most times, and she's brought up the specially-fitted ironing-board that goes over her chair. There's an automatic washing-machine, though Gail will do the washing. We'll all make our own beds and she'll clean those rooms. I always see to my own study, and Meg had promised to do the baking over there and send it over. We can always buy extra cake in Te Anau if it's needed. Nurse Belgarde said she didn't mind meals but she hated baking. And of course she'd keep up with Aunt's massage. How about this, Jocelyn? Suit you?"

She went over it, then, "Well, surely I could manage that, and I certainly won't expect Meg to do any baking. I had a look in that deep-freeze. She must have worked like a Trojan to stock it up like that. There are biscuits, scones, cookies and pies galore. It would give me a flying start. I'm not the sort of cook she is, but I like cooking, and I'll have more time for it now than since I left home. We all used to help, even the boys, when garden parties and parish visitors were in the offing. And honestly, few people would engage a nurse for anyone as mobile as Aunt Clarissa, so I'll expect to do more than just the invalid cookery that goes with most private cases. You won't get ritzy meals, but they'll be wholesome."

Aunt Clarissa said, "Good for you. I dont like a diet of pavlovas and rich curries. Plain everyday foods, with a party flavor now and then to satisfy the children. Don't argue about that offer of hers, Magnus, just thank the saints that she broke into your house. You're going to have to get at that study and concentrate on it. That's your bread-and-butter and you've been away from it too long. You've still got to finish the Orkney book. Get your books unpacked tomorrow."

Magnus looked younger almost immediately, and hopeful, as if some cares had left him. "I'm like Jocelyn. You make me feel secure, Aunt Clarissa. I know I'm a thrawn de'il most of the time, but sometimes it's good to have decisions made for one."

Jocelyn felt happier. Planning a routine made her feel less strange. If only that phone would ring and her mother's voice would assure her that they'd got Ina speeded on her way with no suspicions.

Magnus said, "I reckon they'll manage it. Ina is more given to wily ways than direct questions such as might put your people on the spot. I'm pinning my faith on them. They seem such sports. They'll last out for an hour or two. Surely she wouldn't have the nerve to stay longer! I expect they got parish visitors in, or were called out, so they wouldn't be able to ring as soon as she left, and if they don't get in till late, they'll decide we'd had a big day and are probably sound asleep."

The phone kept a maddening silence. Magnus lifted it once to make sure they were still connected. At midnight they retired, Jocelyn to the room off Aunt Clarissa's. She was sure her mind would come wideawake as soon as her head touched the pillow, but blessedly it didn't, and she knew nothing till her alarm went off.

It was quarter to seven. She rose, slipped on a dressing-gown more adequate than yesterday's, made Aunt Clarissa a cup of tea, with a slice of thin bread-and-butter. The others didn't stir till she'd showered and dressed.

She'd done both at great speed, sure her folk would ring early. But still a silence. After breakfast Magnus announced that he'd start unpacking his books. "You children can help

83

if you do exactly as I tell you, and treat every book with care."

Jocelyn sought him out privately. "You don't have to take them out of my way. I'm sure you'd rather unpack them on your own. Dad wouldn't even let Mother help with his."

"Well, perhaps I would rather do it on my own, but the very nature of my work, which demands solitude for clear, swift thinking and appraisal, means there'll be many hours in the future when I'll be shut away from them, and children on farms are used to being with their parents a lot. So this is something that may make up for it. If we get all the books on the shelves today, I'll get back to my routine in the study. I like to work nine to twelve, and one to four when I'm actually engaged on a book. I have fairly big chunks of time in between books when I can indulge myself in other activities, golf and so on, but I'll skip golf for a bit. The youngsters will need family life at the weekends."

"Don't drive yourself too hard," urged Jocelyn. "Children are adaptable. They won't expect what they had from both mother and father, and I've an idea Ina fussed them so much, they'll quite like being on their own. You'll need the occasional break."

"Oh, yes, I suppose I'll need the occasional weekend away, or bust, but apart from that, their time away from school will be in the main more my responsibility than yours."

Jocelyn wondered what form of relaxation those weekends would take, then shut off the thought. It was nothing to do with her.

He added, "And you'll have to have your times off, too. I'll look after my aunt on your days off, and you'll go up to Dunedin sometimes for a weekend."

She laughed. "I've only just got here . . . and this is a tourist's paradise, every day with views like that will be a holiday. By the way, if that phone rings, get to it in the study, before the children do, and if I've not already answered it downstairs, call out to me. I'd like you to come down if possible, in case I want to ask you anything."

He nodded. "Good idea. I don't want them to suspect we're up to anything. It could make them uneasy. They've accepted you as my cousin and if they don't know the whole thing was cooked up, they'll be more natural when Ina visits us—heaven save us from frequent ones, though."

"Amen to that," said Jocelyn. He looked at her in a more personal way than he'd done before. As if she were a woman, not a nurse and a cousin. As if he rather appreciated the look of her. She'd forsaken the severe white uniform of yesterday. Aunt Clarissa had made it plain she couldn't abide starchy white. "It makes me feel an invalid, and as Ina doesn't live in the neighborhood, thank goodness, you don't need to."

So she was wearing buff-colored trews with a smock-top in lime-green with big splashes of orange and brown patterned over it. She had tied most of her hair up on top with a lime-green ribbon, but a tendril hung down each side of her face. Her creamy-brown skin was glowing with health and she looked happier this morning, not strained.

Magnus said, "I thought yesterday your eyes were brown, the color of dry sherry, a pale brown, but they're really green."

She shrugged. "That's the effect of wearing green. I'm a bit of a chameleon, most hazel-eyed people are."

"And you look about nineteen." He chuckled reminiscently. "I'll never forget how you looked with your hair coiled round your ears like that. It not only convinced Ina you were an old-fashioned staid kind of nurse, I found myself accepting it. Then I'd have a confused flashback to the glamorous female in the diaphanous garments who'd been sitting at my table when I burst in. You looked more like Nell Gwynne then. You seem to be a lass o' pairts, as they say in Scotland. But now you look just a kid."

She looked him straight in the eye. "I'm no kid, believe me, and no wish to be again. I think twenty-seven is a much nicer age than nineteen. One's so unsure of oneself then."

He looked serious. "Are you sure of yourself *now*, Jocelyn?"

She considered it. "I don't know, but surer than I was. Is one ever really sure of oneself? But of course you will be because you've achieved so much at a comparatively early age, become an author, held down jobs in the big capitals of the world, seen life. So——"

He held up a hand. "Do I give that impression? Perhaps I do, but I'm not. Maybe that's why I still go seeking. It will do me good now to be rooted here, like my forebears, to have a family for responsibility. Rebuilding this house has stabilized me. Goodness, what a conversation to have at this hour of the morning! Hope that ring comes through soon." He bounded upstairs.

She stared after him. She pondered one phrase he'd used: *"Perhaps that's why I still go seeking."* Seeking and finding what? Temporal pleasures that gave satisfaction only fleetingly, like taking a lemon drop to try to quench your thirst when what you wanted was good well water?

She gave herself an impatient mental shake. She was being far too introspective, too heavenly-minded. She'd taken the mixed bag of hospital staff quarters in her stride . . . hadn't been too condemnatory of some things that happened . . . at least she hadn't condemned the people, had only been sorry because they had tarnished the best in life, and it so seldom added up to happiness. Then why be so wistful about this man? Why wish his standards were higher? That he had a better reputation?

It was so stupid. She was a romantic twit, wanting him to match up to his looks . . . she could see him as a Viking of old, with hair matching the sunset over the sea behind him, a winged helmet on his head, broad-chested, sturdy-thighed, eyes as blue as the sea, and one who would know and repeat by heart all the Norse sagas, because he belonged to an ancient race of story-tellers. Oh, looks . . . Jocelyn, what did they matter? Leigh, now, was very ordinary-looking, not very tall, not a man to stand out in company, but a giant in moral stature, in endurance, never openly resentful of the portion life had dished out to him. For a moment she was shaken with

86

the old impotent longing to be able to help him. Some time he must, surely, think it was hardly fair to go on paying for the rest of his life because he'd made an unwise choice in his green and salad days and married an unstable woman? Yet he'd said, so simply, so beautifully, "She needs me." So even if Eloise hadn't given him joy, she'd given him purpose. God knows what it had cost him to keep his marriage vows.

Jocelyn gave herself another shake. Here was the task to her hand . . . making a home for two orphaned children. Vacuum the lounge, Jos, think about what you'll make for lunch. The phone rang.

Magnus came down, having set the children a huge case to unpack. He got there in time to hear Jocelyn say, "What?" then, "Just a moment. Magnus has come in. I'll tell him." Her hand covered the mouthpiece, said, "Ina stayed the night. She didn't feel very well. She's just gone. She woke up quite all right this morning."

"I bet she did! She's the best I ever knew for playing the old soldier, to get her own way. Sheer fake, I'll guarantee."

Jocelyn made her answers illuminating enough to relieve Magnus's mind somewhat. It was apparent her parents had coped very well indeed. The Reverend Niall was on the second phone. He said, "I admit that at first we were puzzled. She's such a dainty thing it seemed incredible she was so possessive. Then I remembered someone we knew in our first parish. Everyone—at first knowing—thought how sweet she was, how helplessly appealing, and all the time she was as dangerous as a boa-constrictor. When Mrs. Chester began to drop hints that Magnus was an undesirable character, I knew it must be false. I've read every book he's ever written, and they're not like some of these thrillers where the hero hops into bed with every woman he meets, and at the earliest possible stage in their acquaintanceship. I mean his books are full of vigor and feeling, but they've a high moral tone. The love scenes are romantic and idealistic. He doesn't inject sex as a sales allure." Jocelyn was glad Magnus wasn't on the other phone.

Her father continued, "So I said very coldly, 'Mrs. Chester, if we hadn't the utmost confidence in Magnus, we wouldn't have allowed our daughter to take this position, even if they are cousins. Even with Clarissa there. You must be mistaken. The children must grow up on their father's property, in the care of his twin brother, their appointed guardian.'"

"Oh, Dad, you absolute darling! It must have been terribly difficult for you and Mother to carry this off, knowing so little. We were a bit scared that you wouldn't see through her."

"Your mother thinks it was about then that Ina decided to pretend the upset had made her bilious I hope we're not doing her an injustice."

"You aren't. Magnus says she's a past master at that. But how clever of Mother to twig it. Then how did you get on?"

Her mother came in, chuckling. "I got all solicitous and fussy. I was certain this was to prolong her chance of going on insinuating things. She said how terrible she felt, but she couldn't face an hotel feeling queasy like this and she knew manses were renowned for keeping open house. I thought it would seem strange to rebuff her, but I had a feeling that we were going to sit up till the early hours while she tried to persuade us it was no house for a daughter of the manse. That, of course, would have put Magnus into a hole.

"I was really rather dreadful. But I was overcome by an irresistible temptation. I switched on the electric blanket in the guest-room, insisted she'd be better lying down, and I said I knew exactly what to do to settle queasy stomachs and I mixed up that fizzy stuff I used to give you children when you ate too much at parties. It has salts in it. She had quite a busy night, believe me, and was glad to get away from us in the morning. She wasn't risking any more doses. She ate a very good breakfast—the manse phone rang practically non-stop, there was hardly any chance of consecutive conversation, so she gave up and went home.

"Mind you, your father was very kind and tactful with her, till she tried to run Magnus down. Earlier he'd said to her he quite understood what it cost her to part from the children, but the legal position was very plain and he was sure they would get over their loss sooner if they were in their old familiar surroundings. Then, of course, she started in on the other tack. Said pathetically it was because she and Harold had such high standards which she knew were outdated in this permissive society, but she so wanted the best for her dead sister's children, no undesirable influences.

"She tried to make out that perhaps we'd not heard of one particular incident, seeing we'd been in the North Island and that probably the family down here had hushed it up. It was a sticky moment, Jos. We dared not say too much. Your father said weren't we told we weren't to cast the first stone, unless we ourselves were without sin, and that Magnus's books were proof of the fact that he now lived a very upright life and that he'd be a fine father substitute for the children. Do you want to tell us anything about this, Jos? Oh, you can't, he's in the room, isn't he?"

"Yes, but it doesn't matter, Dad and Mum. He's been very frank with me about what happened." Over the instrument she met his eyes and for the first time saw him look apprehensive. She grinned at him and said into the phone, "Dad, it was merely a bit of youthful folly Ina will never forget. The sort of thing that ought to have ceased to matter long ago. It's only important to her because it's positively the only thing she could use against the children's guardian. It's so far in the past it's incredibly stupid of her to imagine it could matter. I think she's a bit emotionally unbalanced, not fit to look after children. But you can now imagine that had she caught me here at breakfast time, with Magnus, and in that super-frilly garment you bought me, Mother dear, she might have had something to go on.

"I mean, things can look so black. Look at Eloise catching me with Leigh—you two believed me about that and so did she, eventually, but someone like Ina, with an axe to grind for herself, wouldn't have. It must have gone against the grain with you, my darlings, to embark on such deception, and terribly difficult when you were so in the dark about it, but it won't be a black mark against you, I know. It will be a very bright star in your crowns. Magnus, will you speak to them now?"

On the phone he sounded so sincere and unperturbed, which was as well for her parents' peace of mind. He begged their pardon for involving them in such a tangle, and thanked them for being such sports. He expressed a wish that they should come up here for a few days as soon as possible to get acquainted, he laughed, with their new relations-by-marriage.

He put the phone down and drummed his fingers on the table. Jocelyn hoped he wouldn't probe into what she'd said about Leigh. But he said slowly, "It was to ease your parents' minds you said it was purely a bit of youthful folly that Ina would never forget, wasn't it? That it was the sort of thing that should cease to matter. You surprised me, because you were rather censorious earlier."

"Yes, I was, but—"

He said, when she paused, "I hate people having second thoughts. First thoughts are more honest."

She nodded. "I agree. I was trying to assess, honestly, why I'd said it. It wasn't, I find, to ease my parents' minds."

"Then why was it? I'm interested."

"I did sound censorious earlier, in fact, possibly smug. That was merely because I was pitchforked into this situation too quickly to be able to analyse it, to form judgments about what kind of man I'm to work for, in whose house I'm to live. It's not like a nine-to-five job. So I felt it was best to state my views."

He nodded. "I can understand that. This tangle has meant we've had to get into discussions on topics that would normally take months of knowing each other to reveal. You were right. But you've not gone far enough."

"Why, what else is there to explain?"

The blue eyes became a little guarded. "Did you mean that about it ought to cease to matter—that bit of youthful folly?"

90

"If it *was* youthful folly? If it's not in the past?"

His hand came to his chin, consideringly. He had to think deeply. What did that mean? That it had been one weekend among many?

Then he said, "Oh, yes, of course. Ninian was four, Una was two, therefore it was seven years ago."

How odd. Why was it marked by the children's ages?

But there was work to be done. She said, "Seven years. Then it should cease to matter, Magnus."

"Right," he said, and his expression gave nothing away. "I feel the decks have been cleared for action. I'll get back to the study."

CHAPTER SIX

Suddenly it became fun. They all worked flat out to get the house in order, even Aunt Clarissa. It was amazing how much she accomplished.

Certainly the main rooms had been set out with their basic furniture, but the pictures had to be hung, boxes of china sorted into cabinets and cupboards, books grouped for the downstairs rooms. As far as possible Magnus wanted them where they'd been prior to the disaster.

The children had the furniture they had in the other house, and in one of the dormer-windowed rooms at the top of the house, he stored all of Jan's and Eric's treasures that the children might love to have in future years.

Anent this, he said to Jocelyn, "I told you my parents' furniture was destroyed. That leaves that room bare. I wondered if I should set up Jan's and Eric's beds there. Their suite isn't so fiercely modern it would look out of place, but I wondered if, seeing that room will be empty except when we have visitors, it might be too poignant for the children. What do you think?"

She considered it. "I think it might. If you'd been married and it had been constantly used, it might have been different, because the pair of you would then stand in as substitute parents, and your presence would overlay the sense of loss. But if we set it up as it was before, we might find one of them slipping in from time to time to brood. I'd say stack it in the junk-room and cover all with some old sheets. In years to come when the sting has gone, one of them might like to have it."

He nodded, much relieved. "Thanks. I appreciate a woman's viewpoint on so many things. They don't seem to be fretting much, do they? Yet that worries me too—what if they are bottling it up? I don't want them to have any complexes, but how to handle it?"

He was standing at the far window under the eaves, looking out unseeingly, she thought, across Lilliput Bay to the Mountains of the Mist. His face was etched against the light in the angular lines, she had come to recognize even in this short time, that meant he looked back in sorrow. It always moved her. She herself knew Ronaldsay Downs as inhabited by Magnus, Aunt Clarissa, and the children, but for him it would always be ghosted with dear ones of the past, his mother and father, his twin brother, his sister-in-law.

She said now, "Magnus, a thought occurred to me when I was thinking on these lines too, wondering how much we were making up to the children. I thought they were remarkably adjusted in a very short time. Then something hit me. I think perhaps their stay with Ina and Harold yielded *some* lasting benefit. I felt, at first, that the most terrible thing of all was that you'd not been in New Zealand, or even accessible overseas, when Eric and Jan were killed. But suddenly I realized that the youngsters were so miserable with Ina and Harold that being restored here was such a felicitous happening for them that it took the edge off their personal grief. They're so happy to be here with you.

The profile became a full face as he turned toward her. He took a half-step, then stopped. "And with *you*, Jos. Thank you for saying that. I believe it's true. I must stop grieving that I can't—ever—give them back Eric and Jan." His face creased into laughter-lines. "Jocelyn, I thought you were a disaster when I first beheld you, but now I'm believing it was providence. You understand the children so well. What with your nursing experience and being a daughter-of-the-manse, you take everything in your stride. The children like you as a friend, as well as the one who looks after them. You're so like my mother. She was a good housekeeper, but never made a god out of tidiness or herself a slave to routine even if she stuck to it six days out of seven. If a day was glorious with sunshine, she'd go tramping or swimming with us. If it was wet and we were bored, she'd make toffee with us, or sit down and play childish games. She wasn't afraid to spank us, but she didn't do it too often. And if she thought she'd treated us unfairly in the heat of the moment, she'd apologize, admit she was in the wrong. I saw you do just that with Ninian the other day. She didn't have breakfast moods. And neither do you."

She burst out laughing. "What about the breakfast mood the morning we met?"

"Oh, but there was a reason for that slanging match. I mean people who are surly and moody till the day gets under way. There's nothing more calculated to do harm in family life than that. Admittedly we all feel better when we've got food tucked away under our belts, but to start the day with a scowl, I canna abide, as my granny used to say."

Jocelyn laughed, to hide her pleasure at his praise. "Well, I was prepared to be a mother substitute to the children, didn't realize I was standing in for your mother too! But as for them, I guess I'm near enough to Jan's age for them to accept me."

"Oh, you're not like Jan one bit—she was too sweet, too gentle for—now what are you laughing at?"

She was helpless. "It's just that you're doing so much for my ego! I do know nobody could ever call *me* sweet and gentle!"

He looked appalled. "Suffering saints, what a clanger!" Then he considered it. "Jos, perhaps I said that only because of my first impression of you—when you flew at me like an enraged turkeycock—oh, gosh, that's hardly a compliment either. Stop laughing. You've got me floundering, and I'm apt to pride myself that I'm skilful with words . . . stop it."

"Yes, but you go on. Dear Cousin Magnus, your facility with phrase and epigram has given me an inferiority complex till now . . . it awes me . . . but this is revealing. I'm enjoying it. You're usually too assured by far."

He looked serious immediately. "I have a lot of things that undermine that seeming assurance, if you but knew," He strode to her, caught her by her shaking shoulders, said, "Pax. I cry mercy. You've got me all tied up, you little devil," She subsided, but he kept his hold. "And you interrupted my train of thought." He adopted the reflective look again. "Our dealings have all been in the domestic strain, or caught up in high drama, trying to outwit the crafty Ina. So I've not seen you in any other light save as to how useful you are to me."

The blue eyes looked deeply into the hazel ones, probing, assessing. "I take back that remark. About what I thought you weren't. I think in some moods you could probably be very sweet . . . very gentle. Did anyone ever tell you that you have a very tender mouth, Jocelyn Grant? That you have a short upper lip given to easy mirth . . . and a full, passionate lower one?"

She stood transfixed, then blinked, and said quickly, moving out of his grasp, but not as if disturbed or angry. "Goodness, cousin, how very analytical! No wonder you got yourself involved in emotional situations in the past. Some women would take that as very personal, but not me. I've too much sense. It's just because you're a writer. You notice things that no other man would. Or if he did, he wouldn't comment on them."

He didn't look abashed, he simply said, "But it's true, isn't it?"

"What's true?"

"The tenderness, the passion . . . that you're capable of both?"

A warning light flashed in Jocelyn's awareness. One must be careful with this man. Magnus Isbister was vital, compelling, very male . . . and at present he was tied here, by family loyalties, to a domestic situation where no emotional release was possible. And she was under his roof. She must warn him off.

She put her hands together, palms and fingertips meeting, and looked at him squarely. "Yes, Magnus, I am. But those things are there for only one man. Only one man has ever stirred me, and he doesn't need me, but no one can ever take his place. But there are other things in life, like finding a job like this, for instance, which satisfies my love of keeping house, of tending people, and to find it in beauty of surroundings such as these is a whopping bonus."

He stared back. "I think I'm being warned off. Why?"

"Perhaps that was vain of me, but a cousinly relationship suits me very well. I don't want you to overstep that in any way. Otherwise I wouldn't be able to stay."

He said shortly, "It's my reputation, of course. I thought you might have been sincere about it no longer mattering. Don't worry, Jocelyn Alexander. You'll never have to fend me off. I'd an idea that conversation in your father's household wouldn't be tame, that you'd give a writer a little bit of licence. I can see I must watch my step." He shrugged. "Pity, because I was rather enjoying most of my verbal encounters with you . . . You're fun to discuss things with, just as Eric was."

Jocelyn put a hand to her mouth in a rueful gesture. She ought to be mad with him for setting her back, but she wasn't.

He said impatiently, watching her hesitation, "What is it? Lash out if you want to."

She shook her head. "Not wanting to lash out, Magnus. Rather that I'd kept a bridle on my tongue. I haven't lived with an author before." She looked up at him frankly, appealingly. "I've been clumsy. This isn't an ordinary situation and I'd like to keep it on a very domestic footing so that we present a united front to the children, with never a hint of tension."

The stern lines went from his face. He took a step nearer, caught her hands, said, "Very nicely put. Sorry if I made it awkward for you. Let's just be natural with each other. Forgiven?" Before she could answer, he looked down on their hands and laughed. "There I go again! I've got no reserve. You'll have to get used to me. It goes with the hair and the Viking temperament. I'm an extrovert—or I was. Lately I've gone in on myself a bit. But I soon revert to my old impulsive self.

96

"I'm demonstrative. There, I've let your hands go. Cousin Jos." he went on. "sometimes Jan's sweetness and gentleness got on my nerves. It encouraged Ina's possessiveness and undermined her marriage. Then it came right. She developed a strength of character and put first things first—Eric before Ina."

"You don't mean she ever put her sister before her husband? But what about Harold, didn't Ina put him before Jan?"

"Jan was married first. I think Ina was pipped over that— stupid really, because it's largely a matter of chance when people destined to marry meet. Their parents were both dead, and Ina played up merry hell. Loneliness, the fear of being unwanted, blood being thicker than water—oh, the lot. I felt sorry for Eric. Not that he talked about it much, he was too loyal. The only time, in the first years, that Jan stood up to her was when Ina wanted Ninian called after someone in their family. Jan said Eric must have the naming of his son. To placate Ina she made Una's name as near her sister's as possible—said it wasn't to be exactly the same or there'd be confusion. But Eric and Jan drifted further and further apart.

"Then, after a really bad quarrel, Jan fled to Ina. She was soon disillusioned. She'd been too long mistress of her own household to live under Ina's dominance again. Most of all she couldn't stand the way Ina was infiltrating the children's minds with malice and jealousy and selfishness. She came back—almost too late—but not quite, thank God. Because now I've the comfort of knowing that for the last seven years or so, Eric knew true happiness. Ina married within the year, so the pressure was off." He smiled. "Well, we got ourselves into a snarl, but we seem to be out of it again. Where do we go from here?"

She knew he didn't mean practical things, but she said crisply, "I think you should go back to your study and finish settling all your books."

"Haven't you been in it lately?" he asked.

"Of course not. You said you'd look after it yourself, and I don't wonder. Dad only suffered us to tidy his. We weren't

97

allowed to shut up books in case he was delving into them for a reference, or to shuffle sermon notes round."

"I thought so. I've noticed how extremely careful you are not to disturb the children's things, whether it's homework or models, or even just jigsaws. I'm no more fond of cleaning my study than most men, so—would you take it on?"

"If you'll do your own desk, yes. I mean dust it. You've a lot of correspondence. You must have privacy in that."

"Why, I'd never suspect you of prying into anyone's letters. I can recognize integrity when I see it."

She shook her head. "No, thanks. I'll do it if you keep your desk right yourself."

When Jocelyn had last seen it, the study had been just a broad expanse of Persian-patterned carpet wall to wall, with bookshelves all higgledy-piggledy, packing cases pushed to one end as they'd got in the way of the workmen, files and cabinets and maps and photographs, piled in great confusion on the desks.

"Did you just finish it last night?" she asked. "It looks all shipshape and Bristol fashion now, so workmanlike."

"It won't always be as tidy, but I can't stand a study with stuff piled on the floor."

Magnus took a longing look at his desk. Jocelyn said, "How about pinning up your maps of Orkney on that peg-board? That's what it's for, I guess? I'll get this carpet fluff cleaned up and I honestly think that by tomorrow you ought to get down to your usual writing routine. Oh, is that shelf devoted to your own books? Now I'll start reading some."

He sounded off-putting. "Well, as long as you find you want to, and if they're not your cup of tea, don't worry. Must be shocking to feel obliged to read someone's books. I'd have liked it better if you'd been a reader of them before meeting me."

"Okay, if I don't then I won't make a penance out of it, but if you—" she stopped, saw the glint in his eye and went on, "but if you write the way you speak I'll enjoy them. I only stopped because it sounded like flattery."

"And I *am* flattered. This is great. Ever since you've been here I've felt your attitude towards me has been that of a very censorious maiden aunt. Keep this up, and soon even Ina's barbs will cease to worry you."

"Well, I can't imagine her coming all the way here again before long. Oh, dear, when she does she's going to find me changed. You ought to have let me keep my hair that way."

"Could you have stood it?" he queried. "I couldn't. If I'd not seen you first in what Herrick described as 'sweet disorder' I'd have put you down as uncompromisingly plain! Besides, Aunt Clarissa knows what to say if Ina suddenly appears and comments. She's going to say she can't stand that sort of hair-style and that you ought never to wear a center parting—too severe by far, and that she'd persuaded you to let her try her hand at a different style."

At her look of surprise he added, "Aunt Clarissa was a hair-stylist in her day. Ina knows. She's been studying you; Aunt, I mean. She'd like your hair shorter, barely shoulder-length. You ought to let her do it some time. That is, if you can bear to part with it."

Jocelyn remembered why she'd grown it . . . an idle remark of Leigh's one day as he lifted a few strands of his little daughter's hair, "I do like long hair on women."

Now she said, "This is the first time I've had it long. I like the feel of shorter hair far better, especially with the bathing season near. I'll get her to do it."

They worked with a will and when it was done, brought Aunt Clarissa up to 'ooh' and 'aah' over it. The Orkney maps were fascinating, marked with names Jocelyn had heard from childhood at her grandparents' knees. There were Antarctic ones too, done by hand by one of the Americans from down there, with trails and mountains and huts sketched in, penguin colonies, seals, ice floes.

She stood longest at a sketch done by one of the men marooned with Magnus in Orkney. It was stark and grimly attractive in its simplicity. Not a tree on this headland to soften the severity, but in the tempest-sculpted rocks, the arching drift of the spume and the water-worn curves of the bays, was all the symmetry of tossing branches and rounded trunks.

The old fireplace stones had been reincorporated in this new room because when winter storms lashed Fiordland, power might fail, and Magnus would still have a warm study. His mantelpiece held a piece of polished greenstone from the Martin's Bay area; some fossils from Orkney; an ancient fish hook found there, and the model of a Viking ship carved by the first Ninian. There was a photo of his parents and one of himself and his brother.

"Can you tell which is me?" he asked Jocelyn.

It was colored, a head and shoulders portrait. Oh, how alike. Jocelyn wasn't sure she liked seeing two of them. How absurd! How could it matter? She took it down, went to the window. Feature by feature they were so very much alike. Yet suddenly and with great conviction in her voice, she said, "This is you."

Magnus laughed, "Oh, well, the chances were fifty-fifty. Sheer luck."

Aunt Clarissa said curiously, "Was it chance, Jocelyn, or . . . ?"

Jocelyn said cautiously, "It could be chance, but I did think the expression was different. But with a likeness like that you must have played the fool on people often. It would be irresistible."

It seemed to her he paused before replying, then said lightly, "Oh, we did, I'm afraid. At times it served us very well. We were little stinkers. If there was any doubt about who could be blamed, we played it up for all we were worth. Till one day Dad tumbled to it and walloped us both. That way, after that, the guilty one always owned up. Mother, now, was rarely deceived."

Aunt Clarissa nodded. "Laura always said it was something in Magnus's voice, which she vowed had a more mature sound. He *was* the older by some twenty minutes! But it was mostly the difference in expression."

Magnus chuckled. "I felt very stupid once. I was in a large

restaurant in Invercargill. It had pier-glass mirrors. I was just going out when I thought I saw Eric coming in. I hurried towards him, started to say, 'Hullo, Eric, I didn't know you were coming to town today,' when I suddenly realized I was marching toward my own reflection. *Was* my face red? People just stared at this man who was not only talking to himself, but beaming!"

Their laughter subsided. Jocelyn said, "My father will love this room . . . the glorious mixture of new and shabby books, those beautifully bound books of poems, your range of paperbacks, the books on Orkney. Now . . . we've finished. Work for you in the morning, Magnus Isbister."

When Meg brought the children back from the school bus, she collected the mail. She handed Magnus a package of galley proofs. They must be dealt with pronto and returned airmail to London.

Jocelyn had quite a bit of mail herself. One gave her a bump of the heart. It had been face down among the mail Magnus had been sorting for distribution. He said, "Sender: Mrs. Leigh Worcester . . . I don't remember anyone of that name—must be a reader—oh, sorry, Jos, it's for you."

She thought he looked at her curiously the next moment. Was he remembering the name she'd mentioned on the phone to her parents? She slipped it into the big pocket of her smock-top. "I'll read it later. I'll read Mum's letter first."

She slipped away to her room to open Eloise's. She sent up a swift prayer that this letter might not be upsetting; news that would make her unhappy about Leigh.

Eloise Worcester had written a very straight-to-the-point letter. She wanted to tell Jocelyn her change of heart had lasted. For the first time she'd seen herself as she really was. It was a wonder Leigh hadn't left her long ago. She'd resented everything . . . the fact he was a good mixer and she wasn't, resented the long surgery hours that kept him from her.

The letter went on:

"I know now that it was ridiculous. I'd never have enjoyed this standard of living if he hadn't worked so hard.

101

I blamed him, Jocelyn, for the state of my nerves . . . pretended the births of the two children had affected them. It wasn't true—it was a horrible sense of inadequacy and I had to find a scapegoat. I even resented the fact that Leigh was so patient with me.

"These last few months whenever I visited the surgery, I used to envy you, your calmness, your way of dealing with patients, the fact that you counted for something in life, had completed your training, used it well. I never, in my whole life, ever finished anything I took up. I wondered if I could offer to help in the surgery, knew it was impossible, that Leigh just couldn't risk having anyone as unstable as myself in it. Then the other week his new nurse damaged her hand badly. Leigh just couldn't get a substitute, so I offered to help.

"All sorts of things happened with which, to my surprise, I was able to cope. A woman in a highly nervous state came in, and because I'd so often been that way myself, I understood her and seemed to get her soothed. Now Nurse is back, but would prefer shorter hours, and Leigh has asked me to do a morning and an afternoon a week in her place.

"Now I'm with him I can see what crowded hours he has and I'm only too grateful for what time he can spend at home. These people need him so much. We've been down to see Marguerite. She walks a little more every day. Her people made me as welcome as Leigh.

"I feel you left Auckland mainly because of my foolishness, but I do hope this attraction down South has made up for this. I think you'll make a better fist of marriage than I did. But now, so help me God, I'm out to make a good thing of it, and a lot of it is due to you. Forgive me for those wild accusations that day. I'll send this to the manse, and your mother will forward it if you aren't actually working in Dunedin. If ever you'd like a holiday in Auckland, I hope you'll stay with us. We would so enjoy it. Regards from Leigh and myself,

Yours, Eloise."

No, SHE'D NEVER go to stay with them, that was over. She would probably never see Leigh again, never see that dear head bent over some report, that familiar gesture of hand to chin, when he was trying to decide between advising surgery or treatment, the nervous tensing of his jaw when he must tell someone their time on earth was short indeed . . . never see him look up with thanks in his eyes when at some moment of extreme exhaustion or worry, she would quietly place a cup of coffee at his elbow.

She found she was crying, in a quiet fashion, tears just rolling down her face. As she hunted for her handkerchief, she heard a tap on her door and Magnus's voice.

"Jocelyn," it said, "Jocelyn, are you all right? May I come in?"

She didn't want him to find her like this, to ask questions. The French windows were open to the lake breezes. She rose quietly, gained the patio, and fled, losing herself quickly among the bushes.

This path took her down to the bed of the Swift, crossed it by a bridge formed of three willows felled, and bound by strong fencing wire. She gained the sanctuary of the mountain beeches that clustered here. The path took her round the lower slopes of Brobdingnagian Hill, so named in the early days of the Isbisters, because the rocks on its summit were steeple-sharp.

She went on till she came to the sight and sound of the Jonathan Falls, where they leapt from a high cliff that looked as if it had been sheared off by some calamity of eons ago.

Till now Jocelyn, in moments of stress, had always sought release beside the sea till its restlessness, contrariwise, had stilled her inner tumult and she had found peace again. She had instinctively sought this substitute, feeling that in the sight of the myriad gallons of water that dashed over the falls, flinging a bridal mist of spray far into the air, her revived longings might be stilled. All round these green pools were tossed great boulders that must have been brought down in time of flood and hurled violently over the cliff.

One formation was curiously like a hooded, cane swinging

garden chair, because a hollowed-out stone like a seat had had two curved stones flung upright against it, leaning together overhead and the ferns and mosses that flourished so luxuriantly in that area, had filled in the cavity at the rear.

The children had told her it was called The Pondering Stone. It gave a sheltered and wonderful view of the Falls. Here she would be hidden, sure of solitude.

But not for long. She leapt, startled, when Magnus suddenly appeared before her. "Sorry. I did call out, but you couldn't hear me for the Falls." He looked at her, closely. "Why did you run from your room, Jocelyn? I know you must have heard me. I saw you just vanishing." He looked at her sharply, said, "You're upset. I thought you were. It was that letter, wasn't it? You've been crying."

She put up both hands to her cheeks, said, in simulated surprise, "Oh, it must be the spray from the Falls."

"Oh, come, the spray never reaches this far, even in flood. Jocelyn, you've entered into our troubles. Can't we enter into yours?"

Her lashes fell swiftly, giving her a moment to think. Then she lifted them, said, "Magnus, the less anyone knows about this the better. It's private, and it's . . . finished. I was foolish enough to cry, to run. It's something that can't—that doesn't—matter any more."

He leaned against the rock, his thigh warm against her knee, looked at her penetratingly. She added, because he waited, willing her to explain, and silence made it more imperative to answer than a question would be, "It's something that has a happy ending and it might so easily have been otherwise. These were happy tears."

His eyes remained keen. "Were they now? You know, I thought when I first saw you here that you looked forlorn—desolate." When she didn't answer he said, "I get it. It's a happy ending for everybody else but you?" When she didn't speak he said, "And for you, what?"

She filled in the answer. "For me, Magnus? Just an end. Finish."

104

She was grateful he didn't probe any further. He said, instead, lifting his head to listen and identify, "That's the *riroriro* singing, the little grey warbler. Listen . . . you can just hear it above the sound of the waters. Let's continue on . . . you can climb the hill here, Jos, and cross the Jonathan tributary by a little bridge well beyond the cliffs. You come round again into the bush on the far side. There are almost always warblers there. They sing beautifully after rain. So they sing sweetest of all in this area where the sound of waters never ceases."

She wouldn't spurn this gesture of comfort. Magnus put out his hands to her and she sprang down.

When, from the far side of the Jonathan, they heard the tiny voice of the *riroriro* braced in an endeavor to rise above the music of falling water, Jocelyn felt there was a message in what Magnus had said. It sang its sweetest song after rain. Who was to know what life might yet hold, if she could succeed in forgetting the dear memories of the last two years?

CHAPTER SEVEN

They went on among the trees so tall and close you could scarcely see the sky. Magnus gave her a hand to steady her over the mossy stones, over roots, pushed aside lawyer vines that would have scratched her, supplejacks that would have entangled her, but his touch was only a solicitous one. It never ventured too far, or lingered.

He said ruefully, "I think no one has come this way since I went to Orkney. It's only use that keeps the bush from encroaching. This leads to a beach that's entirely our own and gives us a different view. We look away from the mountains of the mist down lake towards the cove of Glade House where the Milford Track starts."

As he spoke he pushed aside, at the end of the path, a curtain of cascading white clematis, and Jocelyn stopped dead from sheer enchantment. "Oh, I haven't realized that this lake went on and on . . . all those indentations!"

He said, "Of course, taking in the fiords running off it, and both shores, it has a shore line of three hundred miles."

"Three hundred magic miles! Oh, Magnus, why did you have to go to Orkney for material for books? Why not here? Isn't there enough mystery and adventure and practically unexplored country here?"

He burst out laughing. "There speaks the perfect example of one who is *not* a fan of author Magnus Isbister! You'd better ask your father. All my books, till now, with the exception of the two South Polar ones, have been set in New Zealand's Fiordland! And the Orkney one is only just started, you nit."

She clapped both hands to her mouth in rueful dismay. "It

would be just like me to come out with something like that in front of Ina. She'd wonder that a cousin had never read any. Oh, Magnus, what beauty here at our feet!" she exclaimed.

"Look how still it is . . . look at the reflections. It doubles its charm. Every tree has a twin. I've always loved paintings that have reflections in them as well as the actual scene. It seems to add another dimension and, in a lake scene like this, makes you aware of the great depth of the waters, gives you an impact of the knowledge of how still the day must have been. I mean you can convey the force of a gale in a picture by tossing branches, or *manuka* scrub on some wild coast, leaning away from the prevailing sea wind, but to convey a stillness takes more skill, and it's portrayed best of all by reflections."

Magnus gestured to her to sit down on a fallen blue-gum that had been brought low so long ago, all its bark was gone and its bole was as smooth and bleached as if it had been ivory.

He said, "You draw, then, I take it? I often wish I could. That's something that was left out of my make-up. Art was my worst subject."

"But you paint in words, Magnus. Don't forget that reaches more people—the printed word—than any other gift does. Art lovers can buy prints, and masterpieces if they're wealthy enough, I suppose, but never as many as they would wish. So many of the world's art treasures are in galleries not accessible to everyone. But books go into thousands and reach all corners of the globe. Words retain the originality and freshness of whoever first thought them."

He looked at her in amazement and delight. "I've never thought of that before, Jocelyn. Thank you. What an analytical mind you have!"

Magnus took a notebook out of his pocket and scribbled away. She said, "What are you doing?"

"Noting your use of reflections to enhance a picture," he told her. "I'll never forget those sunsets over Orkney. It's not enough for an author to retain them in his mind's eye, he's got to describe them in words not too hackneyed, so that everyone who reads them, say someone in the middle of a continent, far from any ocean, can see for a moment the fiery ball of the sun sinking into a northern sea. What you said made me realize it was the reflections that made those sunsets so spectacular, the fact that those changing lights painted the sea as well as the sky. Have you any other ideas like this? I've never had an artist for a friend. This could add another dimension to my own work."

She gazed out over the lake, but the eyes of her mind were turned inwards as if she held a brush in her fingers, stroking in what would make a picture. "Well, reflections can also suggest what isn't actually there. My favorite picture in the Wanganui Art Gallery was of a panelled room. A firelit picture. You look at it a long time before you realize that there's no fireplace, no logs burning in the picture itself . . . yet the leaping tongues of flame are everywhere, reflected in that polished panelling.

"So it is with landscapes. I like to paint scenes about four in the afternoon, with long shadows slanting across vivid green turf. A canvas is so small. It's within the confines of a snap-shot, a slide. The artist knows that all around her are other hills, mountains. The person viewing the picture doesn't. A patch of deep shadow on one side can indicate a towering peak that's cutting off the westering sun. A long shadow across a sunny road suggests a tree out of vision. Have you used shadows descriptively?"

"Yes, a sudden darkening of the sun to strike a note of fear in someone's mind, that someone threatening is behind, unseen. Or dappled shadows to suggest the moon shining through the pines. But go on, Jocelyn, what else?"

She grinned. "You're doing things for my ego. Can this be me? Never in my wildest dreams did I think I'd have the nerve to advise an author!"

He shrugged, swinging one long leg freely. A big fisherman-knit pullover in green heather-flecked wool made a vivid contrast to the bright hair. She thought it was the first time

108

she'd seen him fully relaxed since she had erupted into the life at Lilliput Bay. "What do all authors do, Jocelyn, but reflect the things we all experience, feel, taste, see? . . . and every author can, at times, feel limited. Particularly, I think, a bachelor one. Any more?"

She said slowly "In music, now, some of the most haunting melodies are because of the use of echo. Isn't that a lovely word on its own, echo? Echoes of the surf in sea-shells, of birdsong ringing back from canyon walls, valley walls. What scope there for describing. Scents . . . for a reader to remember with nostalgia, a drift of lilac perfume, of roses, or gorse blossom with the sun on it, must, I think, evoke a picture of it before them. Oh yes, and the shape of things. Not long ago I was reading a book that kept mentioning trees. It was good in action, tension, dialogue, but I couldn't quite imagine the setting. Then I tumbled to it. It was featureless. There were clumps of trees, rows of trees, a lone tree . . . I wanted to know if they were tall and tapering like Lombardy poplars, or whispering like aspens, or sheltering and secret like weeping elms; were they weeping willows that dipped down to dabble in streams, or rowans, bright with berries?"

She chuckled. "Perhaps as a family we have a thing about this. Rob's keen on cars—said once a book annoyed him all the way through because cars didn't have names. He wanted to know the makes, and when I said not everyone was as mechanically minded as he was, he retorted that it could save the author a lot of explaining. If the chap got into a Mini, or an old bomb, he'd know the hero wasn't exactly plutey; if it was an Aston-Martin he'd know he was rolling."

She thought of something. "The other night—in fact the first night I was here—I read an article about Orkney in one of those magazines. I read only part of it because I was so exhausted I fell asleep. This man had used the contrast of noise and silence most effectively. He told how all day the gales had scourged the islands. He managed to describe the cessation of each sound . . . the battering of the waves as they lessened, the rattle of stones dislodged from the cliffs gradually ceasing, the keening of the sea-birds dying away as night fell, the rustle of the grasses at last immobilised as the wind dropped . . . I swear in the end you could positively *hear* the silence!"

He didn't answer. She looked at him and found him grinning, said—"I know that's a stupid thing to say, but that's how it struck me."

He waved a hand, denying that. "And you said you'd never read anything of mine, Jocelyn Alexander! You have, you know, and that's the best compliment I've ever had . . . liking what I wrote without noticing my byline under its title. Yes, that article was mine."

Below them the bay shimmered greenly, and two paradise ducks rose from the marshes at the far end. Magnus said suddenly, "Oh, Jocelyn, for the first time since it happened, this last half-hour I've forgotten Eric's tragic death. I felt as if life could never be the same again. But if I can forget it for even that time, I feel hopeful now that I can take death the way one should take it."

She said, "It's a strange feeling. I know. I've not said till now, but we lost a little sister. And the first time Rob and David and I had a completely happy time at the beach after it happened, and we forgot for a little while that Evot wasn't with us, we were upset. Dad realized it, and though his loss was even greater than ours, he said we were in good company. Wordsworth had known what it was too, to be suddenly jolted. And he quoted what he wrote when he lost his little daughter Catherine,

> 'Surprised by joy—impatient as the Wind
> I turned to share the transport—Oh! with whom
> But Thee, deep buried in the silent tomb . . .'

"Don't ask me, Magnus, why knowing someone else felt the same helps, but it does, it does. I always hope that some day one of my brothers will have a little daughter to give her that Orcadian name my mother so loved."

"Perhaps *you* will," said Magnus. Their eyes met and

110

suddenly this discussion of theirs, this interchange of ideas, became too intimate. She rose, said, "I feel extremely guilty, Magnus. You've those proofs to do. We must get back. Thanks for distracting me. I feel better now. Good job I'd left a casserole in the oven. We'll have dinner early and you can retire to the study. I'll take the children to the bus tomorrow. How long will it take you? Are you a fast reader?

"Yes, very. It's a sizeable book. If I burn the midnight oil I might finish the first reading by midnight tomorrow."

She looked horrified. "You mean you correct it twice?"

"Twice at least . . . if they aren't pushing me for its return. Thanks. I'll be glad if you can cope with most things the next few days. But promise me this—that you'll not hesitate to call me if you need me."

"I will, but Aunt Clarissa is a great moral support in crises affecting the children's behavior. You ought to be free of that."

"It's very understanding of you."

"Well, a wife would do that for an author husband."

"Not all wives. Some. Others, I believe, resent the time spent at the desk, the absorption in the plot, the characters."

"That applies to other occupations too. It's the daftest thing. Oh, some men may get totally absorbed in their work and neglect their families, but in the main it seems daft to me. A man carries the responsibility of earning his family's living all his life. As long as he makes life worth while for a woman when he's not actually earning a crust, a woman needn't resent his work. And in these days of labor-saving devices, women can have enough interests of their own, surely, to keep them happy."

"And what of the ones who haven't other interests?" She knew that once again he was probing as a writer, not personally.

She thought, then, "They put their marriages at risk. There's so often another woman ready to step into the breach."

"That not only puts the marriage at risk, then, but also puts

111

the other woman at risk, puts temptation in her way. Must be the devil for a woman to see the man she loves getting a raw deal from his wife, don't you think?"

She wasn't to know he was thinking of someone who'd had such a deal. Who had been tempted because a woman hadn't put husband first. So it touched a tender spot in Jocelyn and she couldn't answer. Her indrawn breath, her air of flinching clinched it in his mind, for he said, "Was that why you came south, Jocelyn? Your letter today from Mrs. Leigh Worcester? I remembered you mentioned a Leigh to your parents that night."

She said stiffly, "Magnus, this isn't necessary. You don't have to know. Some things are private."

He said wryly, "You know plenty about me. You've had to, peccadilloes and all. It might even ease you to talk about it."

"There's nothing to tell. It was over before it began. Nothing to confess, anyway, if that's what you imagine. I found my feelings getting involved, so I cut and run, that's all."

They measured glances. She took his look for an unbelieving one. She said hotly, "*You* might find that hard to understand, Magnus Isbister, but it *was* all. Leigh would have had every excuse, I suppose, a neurotic wife who resented the hours that he spent curing or alleviating pain . . . no relaxation at home. Oh, it was far from the corny story of a wife who didn't understand him—but for his sake, because I admire him more than any man I've ever known, I won't have anyone thinking that in any way, ever, did he betray himself by look or word.

"In a moment of extreme jubilation over the almost miraculous recovery of a child we thought would never walk again, Leigh hugged me. He'd have hugged anyone at that moment, when he put his phone down. If old Marty, the char, had been there he'd have hugged her. In walked Eloise." She paused, remembering. She couldn't know how bleak her eyes were.

"And . . . ?" prompted Magnus.

112

She told him all, then said, "Nothing must ever be said against Leigh. One breath of scandal can ruin a doctor, even these days. So I want you to read Eloise's letter." She drew it out.

She half expected him to thrust it back at her. But he didn't hesitate. He read it, handed it back. "Thank you, Jos. I'll never mention it to anyone. After all, who should know better than I how it undermines your life, having your name bandied about? The way Ina goes on I'm always expecting it to crop up in a news item about me. Imagine one of the gossip rags getting hold of it . . . the women in Magnus Isbister's life, and so on. Bachelors of my age are extremely suspect—if not of one thing, of another."

Jocelyn said awkwardly, "I . . . thank you. I thought it might be best for you to know what really happened because . . . because——"

He held up a hand, said wearily, "I know, I know. You wanted me to know that, like Caesar's wife, you were above reproach, in case I thought you fair game . . . a girl living under the same roof as a man with a bad rep——"

Her eyes were flashing. "Stop this moment! What an abominable thing to think! How pharisaical do you think I am? It never entered my head. I wish you wouldn't try to read my thoughts . . . or to be so damned touchy. I've not lived a secluded life by any means. I've never found it hard to call the pace with any man I've gone out with. Now stop thinking about yourself and listen. I wanted you to know what really happened because if I'd played round a bit, especially with a married man, you could have all sorts of worries, wondering how many people knew, because if it came to Ina's ears she might think me most unsuitable to be looking after her niece and nephew. The other had never crossed my mind. I will *not* be made to seem a prude!"

He stared at her and burst out laughing, great gusts of laughter. "Talk about the lake of a thousand moods . . . you're certainly the girl to live beside it! All in the space of one afternoon you've switched from a little girl lost and in tears,

113

to analytical reader and hander out of advice to hard-working authors, to a firebrand. Now, who apologizes to whom? All right, we'll let it go. We are about to have a really splendid platonic friendship, how about that, Cousin Jocelyn?"

"Sounds okay to me. I'm tired of all this emotional guff. I'd like just to enjoy my job, and be at peace."

And she thought she meant it.

THEY WANDERED back through the bush. "We called this part The Enchanted Wood when we were kids, Jos," Magnus told her. "In our imaginations it was peopled with lions and tigers and elephants. We swung like Tarzan from tree to tree, dug animal pits—Eric broke an ankle in one, so that put paid to that little caper—I'm afraid we were broths of boys, what one didn't think of, the other did. Some people our parents' age wouldn't have been able to cope, but Mother reckoned she'd waited so long for children, she relished family life more, never made us feel nuisances.

"I'd like to think Una and Ninian did the same. Never to feel they're a complication in my life. They could have felt that, the way Ina poured poison into their ears. She even told them it wasn't because I wanted them I'd assumed their guardianship, it was because I hated her so much I wanted to hurt her through them. Una told me the other night after I'd heard her prayers. Fortunately she hadn't believed her. She's a spunky kid, said she looked Aunt Ina straight in the eye and said, 'That's just not true. Uncle Magnus loves *us*. Why, when he was home he was always taking us out—up-lake on the boat, camping on our own and everything.' " He paused and said, "And then that—that devilish woman said, 'Well, he loves Ninian because he looks like an Isbister, and I'm so afraid for you, honey, that you'll get left out in the cold. You won't understand, at your age, but you're a Sheldon. You're not like the Isbisters, you're like my father.' Poor wee Una, I don't think she let Ina see, but that *had* hurt. She cried out to me passionately, 'But I'm not, Uncle Magnus, am I? I'm an Isbister too, and you *do* love me just as much, don't

114

you?' Honestly, Jos, if Ina had been within reach, I think I'd have struck her. If there's one thing I can't stand it's favorites in the family."

Jocelyn said, "I should think so." She caught his arm. "Magnus, I hope you convinced her."

"I did. At times like that one is given a flash of inspiration. I said: 'Why, poppet, you're *more* an Isbister than Ninian. I mean, who ever heard of a sea-going Orcadian being sick in a boat?' Poor Nin is always sick if a storm beats up when we're out. It wouldn't matter how rough it is, Una revels in it. She bobbed up like a cork in her spirits when I said that. And I went on to say,'You do have Grandpa Sheldon's coloring, but he was such a fine old man, you would have loved him, and he'd have loved you. Grandma Sheldon was like Aunt Ina, very possessive. But Grandpa had a lovely easy-going nature like your mother. Besides, you also have the coloring of one of the Isbister wives, the very first to live here, Elsbet Irving she was. She had a round brown face like yours, and merry brown eyes, and even the same dimple in her chin.' I took her up in my arms and carried her along to the study to see that old daguerreotype of Elsbet. I've put it in her room now. She can look at it every day and it'll take the sting out of her aunt's words. I put the one of the first Ninian in Ninian's room."

When they got back Aunt Clarissa and the children were busy at the big homework table in the living-room, soaking stamps off. Aunt Clarissa beamed on them. "Well, if I wasn't glad you'd gone off for a walk. You've both of you had your noses to the grindstone far too closely, and it makes you dull."

Magnus chuckled. "It's supposed to make things sharp!"

"You know what I mean. All this work and no play. No sense to it. That's the trouble when you're young. Despite the fact you've all your life ahead of you, you want everything finished at once. When you're older, even though time's running out on you, you know that there are pleasures of leisure that must be taken when offered—they may never come again. How far did you go?"

"Beyond the Falls. To the Forgotten Headland."

"Why is it called the Forgotten Headland?" asked Jocelyn. "Magnus didn't tell me its name." She looked at the children. "Did you name it for another of Enid Blyton's books? I can't remember it."

Ninian laughed. "Sounds like one, doesn't it? But the Maoris called it that long before she was born. *Te Wareware Mata* The Forgotten Headland or Cape. You see, it's sort of tucked between two others that stretch further out, so when the mist was thick on the lake, the canoes had to remember only the two that jutted right out, the inner one could be forgotten with safety."

Una came in, "And there's a little forgotten house on it, tumbledown, and covered with creepers. A hermit lived in it. His name was Francis Thorkel, and they called him Saint Francis, because he loved birds and animals so well."

Jocelyn's eyes were wide with delight. "Living here's just like living in a storybook! Just think, three weeks ago I was homesick for Auckland, and now . . ." She stopped as she found Magnus's intent blue gaze upon her. He cocked a ruddy eyebrow. She felt a little warmth in her cheeks. Little laughter lines creased beside his well-cut mouth.

"And now, Jocelyn Alexander, you wonder how you existed before you came to our lake of a thousand moods."

"Well," she said, striving for lightness, "that's the way an author would put it. Let's just say I'd not dreamed I could be so happy away from Auckland."

Una got off her chair so quickly it went crashing to the ground. She flung herself on Jocelyn. "Uncle Magnus is right, though, isn't he, Jos? You'll never want to go away, will you?"

Jos's chin was resting on the soft brown hair. "Of course I won't want to. Who would want to leave Arcadia?"

She wouldn't look at Magnus. She looked at Aunt Clarissa instead and wished she hadn't. Aunt Clarissa was wearing a look Jocelyn recognized . . . a bemused, knowing, hopeful look, a matchmaking look. Oh, no, no, that would never do.

She let Una slide down, said crisply, "Well, that ramble will be the last for some time. Your uncle has his time completely taken up for the next few days, so we must spare him all we can. Magnus, we'll expect you only at mealtimes."

IT WAS A GOOD THING that Magnus was out riding to exercise his stiff limbs after too long a stretch at his desk, when Ina rang.

She sounded conspiratorial, asked was he within earshot, said she had worried over Jocelyn a great deal, that she was sure when she'd called at the manse, that they'd been up north so long, they couldn't really have known what sort of a man her cousin was, really. That if they had, they wouldn't have allowed their daughter to keep house for him.

Well, Jocelyn knew she was going to let it come clear and loud. She said, "Mrs. Chester, if you mean that business about Magnus's weekends all those years ago, of course we knew. Does a man have to pay all his life for what happened when he was young? That's in his past, and I assure you here and now that my cousin will never do anything again that could possibly affect his niece and nephew. And you have no business to bring up a man's past against him. I didn't have much opinion of you before, and I have less now. I hate tittle-tattle, and against anyone as fine as my cousin, however foolish he may have been in the past, it's a thousand times worse."

Even over the phone she knew Ina was panicking. She twittered, she stammered, finally implored Jocelyn to try to realize that it was only her concern for her beloved niece and nephew that made her want to warn Jocelyn.

Jocelyn said coldly, "I'm not sure that it *is* concern. If you'd had their welfare at heart, if you'd loved them truly, instead of just wanting to possess them, you'd never have thrown a little girl's beloved teddy bear into the dustbin. It's here, now, cleaned and restored to her. Ninian rescued it and posted it back to Mrs. Watson. That alone would convince me you haven't the faintest understanding of children. You took her teddy bear away and gave her that hard, huge, uncuddly doll, dressed in a ballet-dancer's tutu, and forbade her ever to remove the clothes. It was to sit on her bed so you could show your friends how indulgent you were, how fond an aunt. You know perfectly well, Mrs. Chester, that you have no legal claim to these children, and nothing in Magnus's life from this time forward will cause anyone to think other than that he's the right and proper guardian for them. As for trying to part the children, for only wanting Una, words fail me. They wouldn't have parted them even in an orphanage. How you could think of it, I don't know. Magnus is the nearest to their own parents they could possibly find, Una is like his own daughter, Ninian as his own son."

Ina Chester gave a strange laugh, it sneered. So did her voice, "Well, that at least is natural—about Ninian, I mean. Miss Alexander, it's only natural that your relationship binds you to Magnus's real nature. For instance, he blames me for the breakup of Jan's and Eric's marriage some years ago, but that's only to hide his own guilt. Magnus was always the same. Whatever Eric had, he coveted. He hated Eric getting married. He set out to break the marriage up, and very nearly succeeded. Eric forgave what many men would have found unforgivable. I loved my sister, Miss Alexander, she had no strength of character, but I loved her. She had no chance against Magnus's charm. Now do you understand why Magnus wants the children?—he's willing to take Una so he can have Ninian. Do you wonder that I would like to have Una under our care?"

Jocelyn had never known anger like this, cold, justifiable anger.

She said, "Mrs. Chester, *you lie*. I think you're going out of your mind. There just isn't the faintest chance of my ever giving credence to that abominable insinuation. Under no circumstances whatever would Magnus Isbister ever seduce his beloved twin's wife." At that moment she heard somebody's voice other than Ina's at the other end—an incredible voice, an angry voice. It must be Harold's. He said, "Ina . . . what

118

the hell are you saying—and who are you talking to?"

Ina said very quickly into the phone, "I've got to go now. My husband wants me."

Jocelyn said, "Don't you dare go . . . Ina, if you hang up I shall ring and ring till I finally get hold of your husband. If I can't get him tonight I'll get him at his place of business tomorrow. You must be ill——"

The next moment she realized Ina's husband had wrenched the phone from his wife and his voice said, "Excuse me butting in on this, but I must know to whom my wife is speaking. You must excuse her—she's overwrought. Her nerves are in a sad state—but what I heard her say is positively dangerous. It's also completely untrue. She's obsessed with trying to get charge of Una. Who are you, for God's sake?"

By this time Jocelyn's knees were shaking, but at least she was speaking to Harold Chester. She said, "It's Jocelyn Alexander here, cousin to Magnus Isbister, and nurse to Aunt Clarissa. Thank goodness she's lying down at the moment, and Magnus is out riding. I think your wife must be having a breakdown. Is she under a doctor? She *must* be stopped from uttering vile lies like these. This sort of thing could become public. It could follow Magnus and Ninian all their lives. I mean, it's slander and they could have redress for it in a court of law, but mud always sticks. Ninian and Eric and Magnus are all made in the same mould, but nothing could ever make me believe a thing like that."

Harold's voice was savage. "My sincerest apologies. I only hope that, as a nurse, you've come across obsessions like this. I think Jan dying must have been the last straw. I'll get her to a doctor tonight and a psychiatrist as soon as he can make an appointment for her. Look, I'll have to go after her—she's beside herself—but first let me say that of course it isn't true. Why, Magnus was in Sydney and then in London when Jan and Eric first met. He was never home the whole time they were engaged and he couldn't get home for the wedding because he was covering an assignment in the Middle East. He

119

never even saw his brother's wife till Ninian was—oh, I forget how old—but about six months or so. Don't tell Magnus, *please*. Are you any good at keeping things to yourself? I'd hate to think he suffered any more. I believe—according to Ina—he was a bit wild and amorous years ago, but she's battened on that, and cooked up this. Could you manage to ring me, on the quiet, at my place of business . . . it's Chester and Marriner . . . and I'll let you know how she is. I must run after her. Goodbye and thanks."

Jocelyn thought she'd like a stiff brandy and soda, but Magnus would be in soon and might smell it on her breath. She made some strong black coffee and put sugar in even though she hated it. Her teeth chattered against the rim of the mug, then gradually she got composed. She wouldn't tell Magnus. He was only halfway through those galley proofs.

BY THE TIME Magnus was in family life again, Jocelyn was able to push the horrible incident to the back of her mind. She'd rung Harold Chester at his office three days later. She'd known it would be of little use ringing earlier to find out Ina's condition.

When Magnus had announced that he was driving right to Invercargill to airmail his proofs because he'd missed the mail at Te Anau, and would Jocelyn and Aunt Clarissa like to go along, she had thought it a golden opportunity, had said how lovely if she could go over and have a whole day with the Ronaldsons, talking over Wanganui days.

She did, but rang Harold Chester first. She had known an immense pity for him. No doubt he'd be pompous and boring, and it could be he allowed business to loom too largely with him, but he was facing up to the situation in a most admirable manner.

Ina was under observation in a clinic, and strangers, expert strangers, were doing more for her than he or anyone else had ever been able to do. He'd said heavily, "I'm not looking for a miracle, but if we can get rid of this obsession, it will be something. I think perhaps I showed my disappointment at

120

not having a family too much. I didn't particularly want Eric's children and to hide it, I think I overdid things, was never really natural with them. Anyway, when Ina's had some treatment, I'm taking her off on a Pacific cruise. Before we go I'll drop Magnus a line to say Ina's nerves have been bad and I'm taking her away for a bit. I'll be no end grateful if you keep quiet about what happened."

Jocelyn was greatly relieved.

CHAPTER EIGHT

The days slid into weeks and what at first had been strange, a little frightening, because such feelings of malice and resentment existed, became the familiar routine of this lakeside family. As soon as Harold Chester's note to Magnus arrived, saying Ina hadn't been well and he was taking her for a long cruise round the Islands now she was recovered, Jocelyn noted a great lifting of the spirits in Magnus, and even in the children.

Gail did so much in the house it gave Jocelyn more time to be with them, to say nothing of spending longer hours in the garden. The snowy balls of the guelder-roses dropped petals like white confetti everywhere, pansies bloomed in every crevice, London Pride nodded carol bells, and catmint bloomed in lavender ribbons wherever it could get a foothold. The cats rolled madly in it, and came in every night to be nursed, as fragrant as an English garden.

All sorts of alpine flowers flourished in small rocky corners, and the dark spikes of the flax-flowers were hosts to the honey-eaters, *tuis*, wax-eyes, bellbirds, now that the flowering currant and the *kowhai* had faded. The weeds also ran riot from a year when they had known neglect, and seeded to full advantage.

Jocelyn, in faded jeans and an old khaki shirt of Magnus's, rose from her knees and glared at a dewy patch of chickweed. "I don't think I'll ever get this garden free of weeds so that I can just hoe the littlies down as they pop up!" she said to herself.

She leapt in fright as a voice beside her said, "Why try?

Nobody's ever succeeded in that in four generations. Isn't half its charm in its wildness?"

She chuckled, pushed a hand across her moist brow, leaving a streak of soil across it. "I've been trying to tell myself that. But I'm enough of a city gardener to want to have the beds round the house more formal, and weedless. Just look at Aunt Clarissa, moving round those beds snipping off dead heads. Isn't she a brick? But it's so good for her."

"You've done wonders for her—physically and in the matter of morale. She was thrilled when you told her that even if she was slow, she still moved with grace. But she's far more supple and mobile than when she first came here."

"Why, Magnus, it's only because she's had more frequent massage. And that keeps my hand in."

He scowled. "Keeps your hand in what for?"

"For my work. I am, after all, a nurse."

His voice became harsh. "I forget that. You do well to remind me. I'm so inclined to think of you as heaven-sent. I suppose it's selfish of me, we need you here so much—but you have other skills you might feel were being wasted. But it's more for the children's sakes than my own."

Jocelyn turned her head away swiftly, bent to pick up a heap of weeds, dropped them into the wheelbarrow. She felt exactly as if something had hit her between the eyes. She took an immense pull on herself, managed to say mildly, "Magnus, I'm not thinking of giving this up. I've never yet run away from any situation that needed me. I had intended to take on private cases. I wouldn't have taken them on for novelty, moving on when I wanted new scenes, new experiences. I'd have seen them through."

His mouth was wry. "Yes, but in most of those there would have been a definite end to it. A sad end, perhaps. But it wouldn't have stretched out without limit."

She said calmly, "Sometimes I think the very nature of the work you do prevents you from taking things more easily, Magnus. You sit up there at your desk, feeling like Providence, manipulating your characters till you have them arrive at some solution, often a happy ending, all mysteries unravelled, all actions explained, poetic justice meted out. So you want to tie things up at Lilliput Bay too. But this isn't a fictional situation. You've got to take a day at a time. And perhaps the greatest Author of them all will see to a happy solution."

"Sounds fine . . . Mother Siegel's Soothing Syrup handed out in large doses! Have you any idea how even the greatest Author could solve this? I mean, all *I* can see is a succession of nurse/cum/housekeepers for years."

She took his tone as a challenge, said, "Well, what's wrong with getting married? You might meet someone else any time. It's always happening to people. It would solve everything."

"Would it indeed? How naïve can you get. I'd have to pick someone not only ready to overlook incidents in my past, but take on two children not her own. Not even her husband's children. I wouldn't risk the children's happiness like that."

She said a little unsteadily, "You . . . love them as much as that? And they're just your brother's children?"

"Not just my brother's children. Eric's children. My *twin* brother's. Every time I look at Ninian I see Eric. And yet every time Una laughs, I hear him."

She turned her face fully towards him again and smiled. "I like that, Magnus. I don't think you need to worry. In the future someone may come into your life, who won't be looking for just a boy-girl affair, first love, and all that, and a home for two. She'll see the situation as it is, a family resident here, the children as your wards. There are women mature enough to accept these things, accept them—and you—as you are." She paused, made sure Aunt Clarissa wasn't within earshot, said, a little less positively, even diffidently, "And, Magnus, I—I do admire your attitude."

"You mean because I feel the children's happiness must come first?"

"No, that too, but not particularly. I meant that in these days some men wouldn't worry two cents about what had happened in their lives before—with other women—they'd not even tell. But you face up to things."

124

His mouth was grim again. "I'd have to tell. I know damned well that Ina would see any girl I was going to marry knew all about it, believe me. In fact I wouldn't put it past her to say: 'All right, Magnus, let me have the children, and I'll keep quiet.'"

Jocelyn said with intensity, "I could really enjoy wringing the fair Ina's neck!"

She was rewarded by seeing him guffaw. "Well, it's a relief to know someone feels the same about her."

She was aware that all sorts of feelings were stirring her. The laughter lingered, giving him that boyish look. "Anyway, I've come down to tell you that I've just typed those glorious words, THE END, at the bottom of the last page of my book. There's a lot of work still ahead, and all the retyping, but I always take a good break at this stage, because the work of revision benefits from it, and so do I. I've locked it away in my steel cabinet, and it won't come out for at least ten days, which we're going to fill to the brim.

"I've rung your parents and they're arriving here tomorrow night for four whole days. That gives us time to prepare for them—I don't mean in the way of more spit and polish on the house, or wearing yourself out cooking, because that's what deep-freezers are for, to take the sting out of preparing for visitors . . . I'm going to mow the lawns and cut the edges tomorrow, and go over the engine of the boat. We'll give them the time of their lives. I owe them something for the way they backed me up over Ina."

He pulled at her hand, "Come and tell Aunt Clarissa."

"You go. I'll trundle this stuff round to the compost heaps."

When Jocelyn came back she went over to where Aunt Clarissa and Magnus were stooping over a patch of tiny forest seedlings that had lake-stones set in a miniature path to divide them. "They're coming on, the gallant little things," she heard Magnus say.

Jocelyn said, "How in the world did those seedlings spring up just there? There are no native trees near enough to drop seeds. And who thought of putting the stones in between?"

125

Aunt Clarissa answered. "They're the little seedlings that sprang up in the ashes of the old house. The builders were going to bulldoze through them, but Magnus stopped them. He thought that if they'd lain there since Ninian and Elsbet and Francis Thorkel had raised the foundations, those seeds ought to be allowed to regenerate."

"All things ought to be allowed to regenerate," said Jocelyn, and caught Magnus's eye. She said hurriedly, "You did it before you went to Orkney?" He nodded. She said, looking at it appreciatively, "It will be such a tiny spinney. Children will delight in it. Imagine the games that will be played in there, the feet that will chase each other through that curving path, the birds that will sing in the branches. It ought to have a name all its own."

"Then name it, Jocelyn," said Magnus.

"Oh, may I? But what? It's so tiny. Oh, that's it—the Lilliputian Spinney."

Late that night, before dropping off to sleep, Jocelyn found herself thinking of the conversation she and Magnus had had the day she got Leigh's letter. He'd said, "What do authors do but reflect the things we all feel, taste, experience?"

Those weekends Magnus had spoken of. Had they been in that nature? Experimenting in human feelings, reactions, gaining experience? She had heard of actors seeking such things. She'd always thought it a pity, because it was still a limited experience, with nothing of the fullness and richness and security that fulfillment within the marriage bond could give.

The other thought was that if Magnus married, it might never be for love. Other considerations would come first. The welfare of the children, for one. He wouldn't marry for love. Someone would have to accept his wards as a sacred trust, a condition of marriage. A little tremor of fear shook Jocelyn. Some woman, if she loved Magnus, might take him on on those conditions, but what woman would be content with that? For instance, with their welfare at heart, and knowing that she, Una, and Ninian already shared a special affinity, he might ask *her* to marry him. Not because he would love her

126

as every woman dreamed of loving . . . but for security for the children.

Then she faced up to that moment of truth in the garden. She loved Magnus. Loved him with his faults, his past, everything. What she had felt for Leigh paled into insignificance beside this. It had been nothing but hero-worship, born of pity and nurtured by day-to-day contact and admiration.

But this . . . this was something she would have to guard against revealing every hour she lived in his house; a tide of emotion such as she had never experienced before, swept over her now.

SHE WAS fiercely glad her parents were arriving tomorrow night. The setup here was too intimate. Aunt Clarissa rarely stayed up as late as Magnus and Jocelyn, going off to her room after a cup of tea at ten. By then Magnus was ready to relax, and most nights switched off the television.

They sat and talked about every subject under the sun, sometimes agreeing wholeheartedly, at times arguing fiercely or goodhumoredly. Lately, because he had been leafing diligently through huge scrapbooks that had belonged to the first Ninian and some to Magnus's father and grandfather, for material that would link up the New Zealand family with the Orcadian ones he had met, he would come across verses that appealed and read them out to Jocelyn.

She loved these evenings best of all, and used to find herself praying no attractive film would be on the late program. Sometimes he made her bring her own scrapbooks in. One night, before the children went to bed, he said, "You've never read about that bit that Doctor Johnson said about children reading all and everything. Would you know where it is?"

Her eyes sparkled. "Not in the scrapbook—it would be lost among other bits and pieces, but just the night before last, when I was reading Boswell's Life of Johnson, I came across it. I marked it with a cross. I'll get it."

When she came back with the old volume, one published in 1903, beautifully bound, he chuckled. "I took a short cut through your room to the patio the other day, and thought I'd never seen such a conglomerate lot of books on anyone's bedside table! Romantic magazines and novels, a recipe book, a book on native birds, and textbooks on the flora and fauna and geology of Fiordland. You have catholic tastes, my girl. And of course, Dr. Johnson sat there very proudly. It was open. How do you manage to read such fine print, in those double columns, at night? And I see it has your father's name on the fly-leaf. What's he going to say when you return it to him . . . there's hardly a page you've not scribbled on?"

"He's just not getting it back," said Jocelyn, hugging it to her. "I told him he was a thumping hypocrite. He said in the pulpit that everyone ought to have read Boswell's Johnson. So I started to read it and what do you think?—I found half a dozen pages uncut! You know how books used to be . . . with the edges doubled. I just love Doctor Johnson. I'm going to miss him when I finish it. Well, here's the passage. Listen, children, this is why you're allowed to read Enid Blyton and all those other books you love to read: 'I am always for getting a boy forward in his learning; for that is a sure good. I would let him at first read *any* English book which happens to engage his attention; because you have done a great deal, when you have brought him to have entertainment from a book. He'll get better books afterwards.' "

"And that, children," said Magnus, "was said by one of the greatest literary men who ever lived, a magnificent Latin scholar, and the man who took on a Herculean task and provided us with the basis of all our dictionaries. Right . . . off to bed with Enid Blyton, and when you say your prayers, don't forget to thank God that Samuel Johnson existed two centuries ago."

THE CHILDREN were now wildly excited about the visitors. It was as if subconsciously it gave them a feeling of added security to have another uncle and aunt coming. Aunt Clarissa said she'd do nothing to make them think it was also the first time she had met them. "After all, a nod's as good as a wink to a blind cuddy, and what the eye doesn't see the heart canna grieve over." Jocelyn managed to preserve her countenance, but saw Magnus escaping to the kitchen. "What in the world," he said to her afterwards, "does a wink to a blind donkey have to do with that? Honestly, Jocelyn, she's getting worse. She's even mixing up the sounds of things. She told me the other day, quite seriously, that a horseshoe in the stable fell off its nail and missed her *by a mare's breath!* It was half an hour before I realized she meant a hair's breadth!"

Mother and Dad were entranced with Lilliput Bay, with the house, with the farm, visiting the Watsons and the Whittons, helping with farm chores, and, since both of them had grown up in the country, rode over through entrancing bush tracks, to the Ronaldsons' house.

It was only to be expected that Ingrid would want a private talk with her daughter. She took the opportunity when Magnus had to spend a couple of hours in his study with urgent correspondence. She asked Jocelyn to take her to the waterfall. Jocelyn knew her mother would ask her about Magnus's reputation and she shrank from it.

They were almost at the Falls when they heard Niall coming after them. "I guessed what you were up to, Ingrid, and thought I'd like to be in on this."

He instinctively made for the Pondering Seat. Jocelyn wished he hadn't. How odd to feel it betrayed Magnus and the tender understanding he'd shown her there, to discuss him here. The other two hoisted themselves on to it, but she stood beside them, one hand on the rock-shelf.

Niall said, "It's this business of his reputation bothering you, I suppose, is it, Ingrid? As it might concern your one ewe lamb?"

Ingrid said unexpectedly, "That was my idea in coming up, but since being here——"

Jocelyn grinned. "Since being here, pet, you've fallen under his Viking spell. You find it hard to think anything but good

129

of him. Oh, Mother, at your age! Don't you realize that that's exactly the effect all these charmers have . . . they have 'the power to stray, yet all the saints disarm,' as I read once. I'm surprised at you."

She was quite pleased with herself. Now Mother wouldn't dream she'd fallen, hard, for her employer.

Ingrid said tartly, "I just love it when people think they've got a sixth sense and presume they know exactly what one was thinking. If you'll let me finish, my darling daughter, I'm going to say that since being here I so admire Magnus Isbister's performance as a substitute father, I just wanted to know about the reputation he had once, so I can counter the wily Ina. She supposed we knew about it, and your papa handled it beautifully and squashingly, but I'd hate to get tripped up if ever she calls again. My opinion of her was that she was slimy, tenacious, and—though it may sound imaginative—utterly evil. And as I felt she might include you in that animosity, I'd like to know something about it."

Jocelyn said, "You were right—about the evil. Her mind is sick. Her husband, not a bad sort, took her away on a long cruise. They'll be back shortly. She was having psychiatric treatment, so she may be better now. I hope so, for Magnus's sake."

Niall looked at Ingrid. "For myself I refuse to believe anything but good of that young man. Not only have I been impressed while here, but I'd a head start on all of you because of having read every book he's written. There are some authors I'd not like my daughter housekeeping for, but not Isbister. He doesn't bring sex down to the level of still another appetite to be satisfied, *love* enters into his man-woman situations."

Jocelyn said cautiously, "Of course the love interest in his— the ones I've read so far—are wrapped up in adventure. Usually some girl the hero meets while involved in some escapade, so it's before marriage, merely the courtship stage. It's not to say he himself—" she checked herself.

Her father said crisply, "Oh, come, Jocelyn, don't be so

130

naïve. Hardly any of the big adventurer types are married—in other authors' writings. I mean. But there are plenty of amorous incidents inserted. I'd say that as a man writes so he is. I'll bet Magnus got himself mixed up in something quite innocently, and this Ina, in her possessiveness, is trying to use it for her own ends. Probably nothing in it, some silly scrape of long ago. I expect Ina's made a good deal out of some trifling incident." He was looking at his wife, but swung round and surprised a wistful look on his daughter's face.

"Jos? Was it more than a trifle?"

She said tonelessly, "You'll have to know, because if you take that line with Ina, ever, she'll pick you up on it and ask if spending weekends with lady-loves is trifling! There! It's out! But—" her voice crisped to his defence, "I don't care. He's just magnificent with those children, as you've seen. I believe he has their welfare so much at heart that he'll never put their guardianship in jeopardy by any behavior that could affect it, from now on."

Niall said, "Good, that's my girl. When you spoke about him being a charmer, with the power to disarm everyone, I thought it too cynical by far, and it didn't tie in with my impression of him."

Jocelyn hid an inward smile. Dad didn't want to believe anything of an author he liked so much. How sweet, a man of his age almost hero-worshipping! She said, "Well, now you've got that off your mind, my doting parents, back to the house. Magnus said have an early lunch because he's going to take us to the Forgotten Headland, Te-Wareware-Mata."

They went by launch so Aunt Clarissa could go too. She was all for it. "I've not been there since James died. Every time we came up here for holidays, he and I had a day off round there on our own." She turned eagerly to Niall and Ingrid. "Take your swimsuits. It's so gloriously sheltered, even better than Lilliput Bay. Thorkel's Voe was always our favorite spot."

Ingrid was struck by the name. "Why, it would have to be sheltered, with a name like that."

131

Three of them gazed at her uncomprehendingly. She laughed. "Magnus, you'd know, wouldn't you? I know you're not a born Orcadian, but having been there so recently . . . ?"

He nodded. "I knew before going. In the old days here our family was very isolated, so it became a community that retained many words from over there, that were Norse in origin. Voe, the sheltered bay. And of course old Thorkel himself was Orcadian."

"Of course," agreed Ingrid. "That's a family name of the Fletts. They were descended from one Thorkel Flett. He was a chieftain of Earl Paul's. He was slain in 1137, and was succeeded by his son, Haflidi. Gorgeous names, aren't they? There are Kolbeins and Cristes and Cristanes," her voice faltered a little, "and Evots, besides the ordinary ones that have been repeated right down through the years, the Williams, Davids, Roberts. And, as in your family, Magnus and Ninian."

"I'll show you Francis Thorkel's house," said Magnus. "Not all of it standing. When I can find the time I'm going to restore it. It's part of the history of the lake. He built it himself from lakeside stones. He was a magnificent old man. My father used to tell me endless tales about him. How they called him St. Francis. He lived the life of a hermit out there on that headland, yet his knowledge of the flora and fauna of Fiordland is the basis of much of the encyclopedic information used today. My grandfather knew him from the day he was born, and was called after him.

"He was a sailor and taught my grandfather all he knew about sailing, so that he was an expert lake navigator. He came out on the same sailing ship as my great-grandfather and deserted. That seemed to be why he became a hermit. When roads were built to Lilliput Bay, Thorkel retired to the headland from the farm." He looked sharply at Ingrid. "What is it? You look as if someone has handed you the treasure of the Incas?"

"Oh, you have, Magnus. I think you've restored that which was lost. I'm pretty sure this man was Francis Thorkel Flett. When my father came to New Zealand when I was ten, an

132

elderly and distant cousin charged him to find, if possible, any trace of his uncle, one Francis Flett, a seafaring man who was reported to have deserted from his ship at Port Chalmers in 1865. It was the *Lady Clyde*. Would you know what year your——?"

"Ninian and Elsbet arrived on the *Lady Clyde* on August the tenth of that year, winter in the new colony. They were given the chance to take up land here if they stocked it by a certain time. They came this terrific distance inland by bullock dray. When they'd been on their way five days, they became aware that they were being followed. Elsbet was terribly frightened and Ninian called to the man to come out of the bush, that he was armed.

"Out came Francis, whom Ninian recognized. He was in pretty bad shape, not having had much money to stock up with provender. He hadn't wanted to show himself to the traders in Dunedin anyway. He said he had reasons for not wanting, ever, to return to Orkney. This did nothing to reassure Ninian, but he took pity on him, fed him, and when he was strong enough, they resumed their journey. Francis thought he'd be looked for at the ports, or the goldfields, and had decided to strike inland.

"Whatever he was running from, he proved a sterling character, and when Elsbet was delivered of her first child, with great difficulty, Ninian said that but for Francis's help he'd have lost both child and mother. We've brought some of his gear, not all, over here. It's in the big barn, uploft. It's supposed to be sorted out for the museum some day. It would have been done long years since, but my people had the idea that if it were exhibited with his name on it, some long-ago and best-forgotten crime might be resurrected to tarnish a name that here, at least, stood for nothing but good."

Ingrid's blue eyes were a-shine. "It stands for nothing but good in Orkney either. Francis and his brother both loved the same girl, but it was his brother she loved. She came from a family much better off than the Fletts. Andra wanted to keep her in the style she was accustomed to, to win over her people.

133

He stole money. He was seen and described. Francis and Andra were as alike as twins. Only a year separated them. Francis took the blame and disappeared."

Jocelyn happened to look at Magnus then. He had a strange look on his face. Did he not believe her mother? No, it didn't look like that. More a look of wonder.

Ingrid, unknowing, continued. "It was thought he might have got on this ship. Inquiries led them that far. You can see why he deserted. Oh, how thrilled my father will be, after all these years!"

Magnus said, "Is your grandfather still alive, Jocelyn?"

"Yes, that was why Dad accepted a southern parish, because they're so old now. They live on the Taieri, in a little house my uncle built them when he took over their dairy farm."

Aunt Clarissa said in a tone of utmost satisfaction, "This will be one in the eye for Ina. A real link between the two families."

Magnus said, "Right, let's go. The children are going to Watsons' for tea, as you know. We'll take advantage of the twilight to stay out as long as possible. A quick snack lunch now. I'll pack the tea-basket while you get it Jos, and everybody can grab their own swimsuits and towels. Aunt Clarissa can dabble her feet in a rock-pool while we swim."

She nodded. "And while you're up on the headland exploring, I'll sit in the camp-chair and dream."

Sometimes Jocelyn felt she loved Aunt Clarissa so much, it almost hurt.

For Ingrid Alexander it seemed as if she walked on holy ground when she crossed the threshold of Thorkel's cottage. That same threshold was a lake-stone, perfectly rectangular, and grooved in the middle with the feet that had crossed it . . . Magnus's forebears' feet, and Thorkel's. Two rooms were still quite habitable. A lean-to that had been built of logs, not stone, for Francis's injured birds and animals, had crumbled

134

away, but the rest endured. Magnus told how all the birds of the wild would come to perch on his fingers.

The living-room was a good size and the fireplace had a swee for hanging kettles and cook-pots on, still in place. Ingrid could remember seeing similar ones in her Orkney childhood. Each side were bookcases made from native timber, each end carved with native birds, done with exquisite skill by the old hermit himself. "His books are stored in the barn at home," said Magnus. "You must go through them, Ingrid."

A big table stood at one end, thick with dust and cobwebs. Niall took out his handkerchief, made a clean swathe through the dust, said, "Southland beech. That could be restored beautifully."

Jocelyn said, "True to type. Magnus, that's Dad's hobby. He loves working with wood and restoring old furniture." The chairs were sturdy, hand-made, rather scarred with use. The rails at the back were carved intricately, the all-over background for the motif in the centers minutely done with a pattern of ferns. Niall swung them round, tested them for joints springing, said, "Sound as the day they were made. Of how much modern stuff can you say that?"

Suddenly he made an exclamation, examined a panel, carried the chair to the door for better light, called the others, said, "Can you see what I see? Those intertwined initials are three letters, not two."

He looked smilingly at his wife who traced them with a reverent finger, "F . . . T . . . F! Francis Thorkel Flett, so it's true, not just wishful thinking!"

A magic moment, when an old search had ended.

Magnus said, "Are there people back in Orkney who'll be glad to know? Or will there be no one left to care?"

Ingrid said, "That elderly cousin of Thorkel's who charged my father to try to trace his grave has a grandson with whom I correspond. He's never given up the hope. Thorkel's brother confessed to the theft, he'd felt so remorseful that it had sent

135

his brother to the ends of the earth. The girl stuck to him and the man who'd been robbed refused to press charges because if he did he said it would render a brother's sacrifice null and void. Oh, what a happy day this has been!" She reached up and touched the lintel of the door affectionately as she went out. "How really wonderful. Life is full of the most amazing coincidences—but it still seems unbelievable when one happens to oneself. It seems to me it was meant to be . . . Jocelyn coming here, getting held up in the lake-fog, signposts being interfered with, getting into the wrong house because the Ronaldsons had been called away . . . and now this. I'm sure it was meant to be."

Jocelyn and Aunt Clarissa and Niall were standing below Magnus and Ingrid on the rock-steps that led down to the shore. They were looking up at them. They had the same coloring, Ingrid and Magnus, pure Norse. Magnus said, "*I* think Jocelyn was meant to stumble into our lives too." Jocelyn caught her breath in. Then Magnus laughed and said, "Oh, Aunt Ingrid, I do love you," and kissed her cheek. A stab of envy shot through Jocelyn. She told herself as they retraced their steps to the Voe that it was quite ridiculous. It was all part of Magnus's demonstrative, ebullient nature. But she wished those words had been said to her in a deeper, closer meaning.

Yet Magnus would never dream that she could switch so quickly from thinking she loved Leigh, to loving *him*. She suddenly realized what she'd thought. *Thinking* she'd loved Leigh. Surely that hadn't been all? Yet wasn't it said that the naked truth was buried in the subconscious?

There was something in the way that she loved Magnus that eclipsed all that. Because she loved him in spite of the things in his life she found less than admirable. It was without rhyme or reason and beyond analysis. She realized once more that some day Magnus might ask her to marry him, out of his desire for the security he wanted for the children. Well, half a loaf was better than no bread.

She thought that when this girl he had been engaged to had given him up because of the scandal, something had happened to Magnus. Despite his natural demonstrativeness, there was a reserve deep within him that guarded that disillusionment. For the first time Jocelyn wondered about that girl. Had she ever married? Had she ever regretted her action?

They changed and plunged joyously into the cool waters. Jocelyn wore an emerald two-piece, her skin as brown as a nut against it. Magnus was ruddy rather than tanned, and water was his element. The future and its problems receded, the here-and-now was fun and to be enjoyed. "You look exactly like a seal," Magnus told Jocelyn as she came to the surface after diving through her father's long legs.

She burst out laughing as she swam away with him, when he said in the next breath, "Race you to the launch," and knew she wouldn't be the winner. They rested their hands on the sides, their legs reaching down but not finding bottom. She said teasingly, "For an author, you don't turn a neat compliment, Magnus Isbister. What girl wants to be likened to a seal?"

"I believe in truth, and it was one degree better than saying you looked like a drowned rat. When a girl's like that, you can hardly tell her she looks as ethereal as moonlight, or as sweet as a rose!"

She chuckled, then thought of something. "Yet that was a very romantic scene in your book about Preservation Inlet when the hero rescues the girl from drowning."

His blue eyes were alight with laughter, "True, but that was due to the measure of his relief and the upsurge of his feelings, at finding she was still alive no matter what she looked like. You don't have to have moonlight and roses for true romance. I daresay a husband can feel swept with love for his wife even when she's got her hair in rollers." A reminiscent chuckle took him. "Come to think of it, my grandfather proposed at what my grandmother called a hideous moment. The one who was named after your ancestor, Francis. His Janet was up here, helping his mother. They were still doing the washing on the bank of the creek. You can see the remains of the brick surround they'd built round the copper to keep the smoke away from the washing.

"Janet had had hopes of something happening at a New Year's Day picnic the day before and had lain all night with her hair in curlers and wore a beautiful blue dress. He'd hardly come near her. And she was down at the creek *in a sack apron,* and her face was covered with smut from the fire when he suddenly appeared and blurted out his proposal. But five minutes later she wasn't thinking about how she looked! Jocelyn, can you scramble over the edge into the launch?"

"With a bit of help, yes. Why?"

He wore the boyish grin that always made Jocelyn remember that once there had been two like that to get into mischief. "I thought it'd be fun to make them think we'd marooned them."

They were in in a trice, he cast off the mooring rope, roared the engine to life, turned to give an audacious wave to the startled three at the water's edge, and headed for the wider lake-waters beyond the Forgotten Headland.

Jocelyn seized a towel that lay on one of the lockers, rubbed the ends of her hair dry, pushed it back from her ears. Magnus said, "Give mine a rub, would you? The water's trickling down my back." She rubbed his back down too.

"I'm taking you into the mountains on the other side we call the Delectable Mountains. Eric and I loved it better than all other places when we were children. I've not been back since he died. But your own ancestor discovered it. Thorkel's Falls. Can you walk a bush path in your bare feet?"

"Yes, we grew up in a country parish outside Wanganui and we ran barefoot all summer long."

They edged into an inlet on the far side that was like a miniature fiord, with steep sides. They beached the launch, tied it to a tree stump. Few people came here, because the track was only just visible. Ferns lodged in the crevices of the tree-trunks brushed their skin as they climbed. Jocelyn was glad of Magnus's help, and not only because it was hard

138

going. Sometimes they had to crawl over fallen giants, sometimes under them.

Among the dark canopy of the various beeches, the *rimu* drooped its coppery-green needles gracefully, *totaras* and *kamahi* and the broadleafs flourished in abundance, *kotukutukus*, the tree-fuchsias, hung bright cerise-and-purple bells everywhere, much smaller than their garden counterparts, and there was a carpet of creeping plants, with tiny lantern-berries starring the mosses.

They came to a little glade. Magnus helped her over the last gnarled root, said, "We climb up on to this rock. I won't let you fall."

It was almost perpendicular and the one foothold was tiny. He said, "It's easier getting down . . . you just jump."

The rock ledge might have been formed by God in the long ago for just such a viewing-platform and overhung a vertical-sided cleft that plunged from an immense height, far above where they were standing. On the far side, from a mountain-top lake they could not see, spilled this narrow, foaming fall of water that Thorkel had discovered more than a century before. It disappeared into the forest far below on the narrow valley floor and eventually forced its way out to the lake.

"I'll hold you, Jocelyn, in case you get giddy. You mightn't have a head for heights such as these." She had a perfectly good head for heights, but why say so? She even clutched his hand tightly as he slipped his other arm about her.

She longed to turn to him, but mustn't let him guess how much this meant to her. No doubt he'd brought other girls here; perhaps people had been known to turn giddy, so she mustn't read anything into it, but the delicious headiness she was experiencing had nothing to do with the height.

She lifted her profile to gaze at the leaping wall of water. "I wonder how many thousands of years that water has spilled over the lip of that gash. It's a dwarfing thought, isn't it? And somehow immensely comforting as if all these problems that seem so real and daunting in our little lives can't possibly be as important as they seemed before we came here."

139

His eyes met hers as she turned to him. He'd been watching her rather than the fall of water. "Jocelyn, that's the most imaginative thing anyone I've ever brought here before has said. Most just squeal about the height, ask how many feet below, or how many gallons of water pour over in an hour."

They turned back, watched it in silence, which was its best tribute. His body was warm against hers—comforting, in face of that immensity of power and volume, yet too stirring.

Then he said, just as if there'd been no break in the conversation, "Do you really feel that, Jos? As if previous problems no longer mattered?"

Her hazel eyes were candid as they gazed into the blue ones. "I do. It was so true what Mother told me when I was leaving to come here and she knew I wasn't happy." She stopped. She mustn't quote that passage. It was too revealing.

He said, "Yes, Jos? I'll shake you if you don't go on. You know I hate second thoughts."

She shrugged. "Oh, just the usual guff. You know what parents are. Time heals and all that."

He turned her round to him and did give her a little shake. She put protesting hands on his shoulders. "Magnus . . . not here, nobody argues and shakes people up here. It's too dangerous."

"All right, then. *Don't* argue with me. I'm sure your mother never said anything as trite as that."

"Trite things can be comforting. Because they are tried and true."

"That's no answer, girl, and well you know it. What *did* Ingrid say?"

"Mother told me of an experience she'd had before she met Dad. I'd just not known there had ever been anyone else. She said she walked the floor some nights trying to conquer her sense of loss. Granddad gave her a quotation, and it helped. Then she met Dad. Now can we get down, please?"

"No, the quotation first. Don't be so mean. You know that such things are grist to the author's mill, and I treasure and note every one. Give!"

She looked away from him, back to the waterfall, and repeated in a tone that tried to be light: " 'Not by appointment do we meet delight or joy; they heed not our expectancy; But round some corner of the streets of life they of a sudden greet us with a smile.' It's by Gerald Massey. Oh, what's that?" A little scatter of fallen red blossom had dropped on her shoulders. Magnus picked them off. They were tubular petals, if petals they could be called. His mouth quirked up. "New Zealand mistletoe, of course. Haven't you seen it before?"

She said quickly, "Get me off this rock, I'm beginning to sway."

He laughed, jumped down, held up his hands to her, but he stood too close to the rock, so that she had hardly enough room to land. She crashed against him. He caught her, steadied her, laughed, and didn't release her. Jocelyn knew a blend of panic and delight as he bent his head . . . she realized she was now experiencing all she'd ever read about such moments. Other kisses she had known, but none like this. A wildly beating heart, pulses racing, a tide of feeling sweeping her whole being. She'd thought such descriptions exaggerated, but they weren't.

He kissed her as she had somehow known Magnus Isbister would kiss—passionately, yet tenderly, as if more was held in check. It lasted some time. He lifted his mouth from hers, looked into her eyes, and smiled. "Coming up for air?" he teased.

Ah . . . that was to be her cue. He didn't want her to take this seriously. It was to be thought of as just a mistletoe kiss. She took the cue, managed an amused smile back. She said, "Is that one for the writing too, Magnus? Shall I recognize this moment in a book some time?"

A look leapt into his eyes. A look of . . . what? Anger? She felt the hot color of embarrassment rush into her face. She said quickly, "Oh, sorry, that was a bit mean. It was rather stupid. I—" she stopped because she didn't know how on earth to go on.

Into the silence that resulted fell the unwelcome sound of

141

laughter and conversation . . . a sound that moved upwards towards them from the track below.

"Damn!" said Magnus violently. "We have company, it seems. All right, Jocelyn, I'll accept that apology. But *never* say such a thing again. I may be a bit of a cad, but not as much of a cad as that! Come on. I've no wish for them to catch us dallying."

He went ahead of her. They met the bunch of people on the way—not tourists, but folk Magnus knew, from Te Anau. He introduced her as his cousin. The encounter overlaid both the tenderness and the tensions of the last quarter of an hour. Magnus asked them the time.

He said, "My word, we must get going back to Thorkel's Voe. We left the aunts and an uncle there."

They were both silent as they headed for the other shore.

CHAPTER NINE

Although Jocelyn knew she had been clumsy in her reaction, and wished passionately that she had been otherwise, the rest of the day was so delightful, she hoped it would blot out her gaucheness. When they got back to the Voe nobody was to be seen.

Magnus gave a shout of laughter. "They've turned the tables on us—spiked our guns. Oh, listen to me, I'm as bad as Aunt Clarissa. They've scarpered! My goodness, it'll take them some time to get Aunt Clarissa back by the track. They must have had their tea first."

Jocelyn looked dismayed. "Oh, the mean things! I'm starving. Imagine leaving us without as much as a sandwich to allay the pangs."

"Don't be daft. They'd never do that. They'll have left the picnic basket; it would be too heavy to carry, anyway."

They heard laughter and looked up to see the three of them standing in the doorway of Thorkel's refuge. They were beckoned up.

The three older folk looked like children who'd prepared a surprise for their elders rather than the other way round.

They'd swept the floor with what Niall called a besom . . . a long branch with *manuka* scrub tied round it. The old table had been dusted off and the chairs had had the same treatment. They had even cleaned the windows roughly with the paper towels Magnus had packed round the mugs.

The blue-checked cloth was spread on the table and the viands set forth. The fresh pikelets Magnus called pancakes were spread with butter and mulberry jam, there was a stack

143

of club sandwiches, and the queen cakes Ingrid had made this morning, and which Magnus said were called fairy cakes in the Northern Hemisphere.

Magnus remarked as they polished off every last crumb, "Well, that'll do us till we get a proper meal back home." They all groaned.

He was sitting on a corner of the table, swinging his legs. He was still in his dark green trunks, and his skin was so ruddy the hairs on his legs stood out goldenly. Jocelyn realized afresh just how relaxed he was now from when she had first met him. She hoped she might be responsible for some of it.

He looked down on her, tweaked a lock of her hair. "Come back to us, Jocelyn. You're dreaming. It's no compliment to present company to go into a trance like that, *elsk-inne*. You haven't said you'd think it would be fun."

"Think what would be fun?"

"There you are. I knew you weren't with us. We were talking about Christmas, which isn't far away. Your folk can't make it to be with us, of course, because of your father's Christmas services, and they're having dinner with your grandparents on the Taieri, but I've asked them to travel on here after that. They can stay for about three days, then come back for three weeks in January. How about that?"

Jocelyn's eyes lit up. "That would be marvellous. But I thought you were going to Wanganui?"

"We couldn't get that beach house there after all. Besides, this will be a far more restful holiday for your papa. He'll only visit all the time up there. Imagine him fishing day after day! It's extremely kind of Magnus. I ought to be saying won't it interfere with his writing, but I'm afraid I'm getting selfish—I'm grasping this opportunity with both hands."

Magnus said, "I'm hoping to finish the typing of this book before Christmas. I'm amazed at the speed I've made. I'm full of inspiration—even if it still takes slogging at it. I'm surprisingly pleased with it. Half of it's due to your daughter."

This was sweet to hear. She tried to look as if this was merely praise from an employer. Though she hoped——

144

He continued, "She's an absolute wizard at keeping interruptions away. Colin was inclined to come to me almost as often as he used to go to Eric, but his demands grow less each week, with Jos guarding the study door. Her manse training stands her—and me—in good stead. She's got Gail creeping round in the bedroom like a mouse. She used to wear slingback shoes with plastic soles, that sounded like clogs, but now she wears rubber-soled slippers." He laughed. "But there's one drawback about becoming known. We aren't far enough off the tourist run through to Milford Sound. Scotty MacPhail is one of the local drivers. Grand fellow . . . we went to school together. He began bringing busloads up here to see where Magnus Isbister lives. Jocelyn managed to put a stop to it without giving offence to him. At first he just used to drive up to the back door, let his coach-load spill out, and lift up his voice to sing out to me. Jos soon put an end to that caper. She took the line that she knew the tourists were pressuring him into it, that she must save him from their importunity. It was adding too much to his day, and it was long enough as it was, she didn't know how he stood up to it. Oh, it was cunning. Not that I don't enjoy chatting to readers . . . or that it's the actual time that matters . . . it's losing the thread of your thoughts that counts."

When they were packing up, Jocelyn said curiously, "Incidentally, Magnus, what did you call me before? What language was that and what did it mean?"

He replied promptly, and she was sure he winked at her mother. "I'd better not tell you. It was mean of me. In as poor taste as swearing in a foreign language, at people who don't understand it."

"You make me more than ever curious. Come on?"

He grinned. "You might slap my face. It's Norske and—well, you know how it is with English idiom—you call people little devils and whited sepulchres and what-have-you and it doesn't mean a thing. Leave it, Jos. I don't want to translate that one."

She left it. Magnus wasn't much of a swearing man, but he

145

mightn't want to explain it in front of her minister father. At that moment she realized her mother was trying to subdue a giggle. Oh, well, it didn't take much to make Mum laugh!

Magnus said, "You're dying to take a couple of these chairs home to restore, aren't you, Niall? Would you have room in the back of the car?"

The Reverend Niall Grant looked as if someone had handed him a golden casket. He picked one up, ran his hand lovingly over the carving, carried it down to the launch. Magnus picked up the other. The day, with all its loveliness and its mistakes, was over.

SUMMER DAY after summer day succeeded each other. Magnus worked with terrific concentration. Jocelyn's admiration for him grew. She was always seeing some facet of his nature that made her understand even more that a man of his caliber must be forgiven the lapses in his past.

He must discipline his warm nature rigorously. He took no weekends off. He showed no signs of chafing at the bit, of resenting his lack of freedom.

The evenings spent indoors were shorter now. With the extra hour of daylight saving, it was light till after ten o'clock, and they rarely forewent the custom of watching the sunset and the afterglow.

Jocelyn thought that, feeling as she did about him, it was probably a good thing that they were rarely alone. Occasionally, he would flick her cheek with casual affection, take her arm on the scrambles they took with the children, was solicitous that she didn't overdo, but none of it was more than he would show to a cousin who had come to his rescue in a family crisis.

He laughed at her because she was so seldom away from the place. "All staff are entitled to regular days off, you ninny. I can manage things here for the occasional weekend if you want to go home for one."

Her whole love for Lilliput Bay was in her eyes as she said, "But why leave all this . . . beauty unstinted? Other people

146

have to pay to come here. A year or two ago I was thinking of travelling to Britain. Nurses find it fairly easy to get temporary jobs anywhere. I must, some day, I know. I must see Orkney."

He started to say something, then checked himself. "Go on," he said finally. "Do you mean you've lost the desire to go? Is it that you've got involved with us? That you feel you must stay to look after the children? Oh, I daresay I could get another housekeeper if you left us, though I'd never get one as ideal. But I often wonder if it's fair to involve you so deeply."

His words struck a chill to Jocelyn's heart. He was speaking quite casually of the fact that she mightn't always be at Lilliput. Did this mean that though she herself would never take any step that might remove her from here, he could look on her departure some day with equanimity?

She said dryly, "Don't ever let my papa hear you talk like that. He has a fine scorn of people who won't allow themselves to get involved in situations because it might cost them something in bother, in loss of dignity, inconvenience. He says few people can go through life without becoming embroiled in other people's affairs—sometimes even dragged in—when it might be wiser for their own peace of mind to stay out, and that he always hopes we'll pitch in where needed. That one is so often shown the way out."

"Or not. Sometimes one is shown that one must stay, see things out. Like me. I'm here to stay now. But I don't want you to feel tied."

It filled her with depression. It seemed then she wasn't as indispensable to him as she had hoped.

She said, "Magnus, if you don't resent the fact that you're tied here, why should I? You must at times kick against the pinpricks. I suppose you've done enough travelling in the last few years to satisfy you just now, but later you might feel the need of looking for other backgrounds. Won't you feel tied then?"

She couldn't read his face. He was so intent on reading her

147

eyes, she thought. Then he said, "But after all, the ties that bind *me* here are the ties of love."

That stabbed. Did he not think that she too loved the children?

She thought of something. "Magnus, you've not been sleeping, have you? Something bothering you? I've heard you pacing around upstairs. You came down last night and made yourself coffee, didn't you? I nearly came out to see if you were all right, but—"

"But what?"

She colored a little. "It always seems intrusive. Everyone's entitled to a wakeful night once in a while without too much curiosity on the part of his household."

He peered at her curiously, because the twilight was deepening. "I think you're blushing. Why?"

Oh, dear, she lifted her head, looked him straight in the eye, said, "I also think every girl's entitled to blush once in a while without having to give a reason for it, my dear inquisitor."

His laugh was so loud that Aunt Clarissa, in the lounge, looking at TV, smiled too, and wondered if she might be able to slip away to bed before they came in. They had so little time together, and hardly ever had the chance to go to any late entertainments on their own. She, Clarissa, wouldn't be much use in an emergency, and that fire had scared Magnus.

Magnus let the question go. He said, holding out his hand to her, "Come on down to the shore. It's much too warm to go inside yet."

When she made no objections, he cocked an eyebrow at her, said, with a smile in his voice, "From the way you've been talking to me tonight, Jocelyn, fussing about my missing a few hours' sleep, I'm inclined to think you now regard me as your father figure—rather than as a rake. So my conduct must have been exemplary!"

"I do *not!*" she declared, revolted by this idea. "Who do you think you are, Methuselah or someone?"

He kept hold of her hand as they walked down the little

148

winding path to the shore of Lilliput Bay. It had been too hot for trews. She was wearing a frock of some blue gauzy stuff, simply cut, sleeveless, with a low-cut, softly-draped neckline. Her sandals were little more than white plaited thongs, attached to rubber soles.

"I like women in blue dresses," he said. He added, "How old do you think I am, Jocelyn?"

She turned that lovely line of chin towards him, said with astonishment, "It's not a case of thinking, I know. So if you were hoping I'd make you younger than you are you're out of luck. You're thirty-eight. It's on the jacket of *Fiordland Terror*, you dope."

He chuckled. "I'd forgotten."

The grey of twilight on the waters deepened to purple. It made talking easier somehow. A little zephyr from the Delectable Mountains wafted across the waters to them, ruffling the surface into pewter-texture from the glass-like smoothness of a moment before.

Jocelyn put her free hand to her cheek. "Oh, how delightfully cool this is. Magnus, aren't we lucky? We live on the loveliest of all the bays of Te Anau."

He laughed. "Aren't you forgetting that its coastline is three hundred miles all told? You've not yet seen all the indentations. Wait till your parents come up and I take you deep into South Fiord, Middle Fiord, North Fiord. You may change your mind."

"Never . . . this is such a blend of the old world and the new. In spring when I came here, the daffodils were blooming under the *kowhais* and laburnums were drooping over periwinkles. Do you know what I love best of all? The way, when we come down to bathe after school, then lie here in the sun, the ducks come up from the shore, and even when we have no crusts for them, they come as close as they can, and tuck their heads under their wings and doze off, as if they liked human company and felt themselves more secure from other predators. It gives me an idyllic feeling, as if this was the way the world should be, all God's creatures as one."

She could hear the smile in his voice. "The lion lying down with the lamb?"

She said, "You beast . . . one can't imagine a duck an aggressive creature, so that means *I* must be the lion!"

He said, seriously, "Is it a drawback to be aggressive? Sometimes it's admirable, and I think I felt drawn to you most of all when you were wishing to wring Ina's neck!" They both laughed.

His fingers were warm round her own, but the little breeze blowing against them made his forearm, when it touched hers now and then, seem cool. The sense of touch, how delightful it could be.

He said, "In other lakes, you look across to the lights of occasional homesteads on the far shore. Here you don't. You're conscious that across there, beyond the Murchison Mountains where the *takahe* dwell, lie tremendous ranges, immense forests, deep chasms, cataracts, and even if you penetrated, you would only come, finally, to the deep Vs of the salt fiords of the west coast bitten into the land, remote, and some of them inaccessible. It's one of the most treacherous coasts in the world, much of it unchanged since Captain Cook first mapped it, and anchored there to refit his ships. It's possible to still find the stumps. It gets you, doesn't it? I feel I'll never want to leave it again."

Jocelyn said, "Nevertheless, Magnus, it could be that it might be good for you to take time off sometimes. Go to see your friends in Invercargill and Queenstown. Aunt Clarissa and I would be all right. Christmas will be on us so soon now and you invited the parents for three weeks after that, you rash man. Don't you need a break before all this descends upon you? You couldn't sleep last night. I don't wonder sometimes that you should feel restless. You ought to—Magnus, what are you doing?"

He'd swung her round and was peering into her face. "Jocelyn Alexander, now I know what you were blushing about—and no wonder. Good heavens, surely you're not suggesting I go out on the town!" He gave a short, unamused laugh. "If that's what you mean, I don't like it. I told you that was all finished and done with."

She got such a shock she couldn't be angry. He was touchy on this and she'd been clumsy again. She put out her other hand, caught his, said, "Oh, no, Magnus, don't think that. I'd think you were pretty weak if you did anything to give Ina cause to doubt you. Truly, I didn't mean that. The friends you have in those places are young marrieds, aren't they? I thought they might put on a dinner or two, rustle up a partner for you, take you to the theater. Believe me, that was all I meant."

He looked at her as searchingly as the starlight allowed. "I'm afraid I tied it up with the fact you blushed before. Jos, why don't you tell me why you did, then I'll stop being touchy about—about things."

Her eyes became grave. "Magnus, a girl can have her reasons and so often speech is clumsy. Will you let it go, please?" He didn't answer, so she added, "I was clumsy that time at Thorkel's Falls. I felt I'd rather. . . ." She couldn't go on.

"Shall I fill that one in for you, Jos, in case you're clumsy again?"

She tilted her chin inquiringly. "I'm curious enough to wonder how you'd fill it in. Though it's not to say you'll be clever enough to read my thoughts."

His mouth quirked up at the corners. "I probably couldn't. Instead may I say what I hoped you'd say?"

"Very well. Let's have it."

"I hoped you were going to say you felt you'd rather spoiled a . . . a tender moment. Was that it?"

She said saucily, because he was so right, "There are some things not good for you to know. It's very hard for a poor maiden to deal with a seasoned author. He's always putting words into the mouths of his characters . . . and it makes the maiden nervous. Magnus, that water looks so tempting . . ." She kicked off her thongs, turned to face the lapping water, ran into it on the smooth lake-sand, delighting in the feel of

151

its coolness. Her brief frock allowed her to splash in a fair distance before he joined her, since his own sandals had been buckled ones. The hems of his shorts were wet before he reached her.

"Hey, wait a moment, lass. You'll go in too deeply yet, and you'll be as wet as Aunt Clarissa the night Uncle James proposed. If we keep out as far as this while we walk along the beach, we'll go right into that channel where the Swift Burn deepens the waters. Let's walk in the shallows till we get to the far willows."

It was pleasant walking along, hands clasped and swinging. They sat down on a fallen willow which, after flood had undermined it, had rooted again and was green. At the far end were scoured-out pools. Presently Jocelyn said, "Magnus, shuffle along a bit, will you. That end looks smoother. This is rather rough to sit on—it's lost most of its bark along there, so it's smoother. Isn't it a wonder it regenerated, when it lost so much. How tenacious trees are!"

They talked of many things. One part of Jocelyn, her mind, was content. The other part, heart and body, was yearning. There were so many things left unsaid between them. The wound Magnus had suffered seven years ago had gone deep. It had been his own fault, of course, but he'd paid dearly. He wouldn't love easily again. What had she and Magnus shared? Everyday things, a few rumpuses now and then, little worries about the children, their schooling, their scrapes, their health . . . and long, kindred talks. Yes, they were kindred, never a doubt there, but what a waste to feel like this.

Jocelyn took hold of herself. This was ridiculous. How stupid to sit here, filled with longings. This was pleasant companionship and Magnus might never ask more of her. She sprang off the willow, began to say, "It must be terribly late, let's go in," but got no further than four words when she realized she'd forgotten the hollowed-out pool beneath them. It was deep . . . she clutched at all and everything. At the unsubstantial fronds of willow waving above them, a dead branch that broke, at Magnus himself, who made a wild swoop to save her, but it only succeeded in unbalancing him too, and the pair of them subsided in depths over their heads in a flurry of splashing water and thrashing limbs.

In a moment Magnus found his feet and was fishing her out. It took him just one stride to reach the edge with her. He was helpless with laughter yet concerned. "Oh, Jos, *kjele-degge*, are you all right? Good life, did you forget we'd shuffled along?"

She was helpless with giggles. "Oh, Magnus, and it feels horrible. We've stirred up all the ooze." She peered at him. "You've got lakeweed draped over your ear. Bend down."

He, in turn, fished some out of her hair. "I've never known anything like it," he complained, helpless and shaking. "You're so sudden, Jocelyn, like crashing off that rock at Thorkel's Falls, and getting into the wrong house in the first place. Still, I suppose it's all in the Clarissa-James tradition."

Jocelyn wished it was. But it had dispelled her megrims. You couldn't laugh to the point of exhaustion and still yearn mopily. They laughed in overcoming spasms all the way back along the beach. When they came to the boat-ramp, Magnus said, "Do you know what I'm going to do? I'm going to plunge off the far side. It will rid us of all this slime. It feels terrible. We can't get any wetter. Come on, in you go!"

She didn't hesitate. The gauzy dress was so light and short it hardly hampered her movements. Magnus had flung his shirt off. Suddenly it was gorgeous fun. They swam. ducked each other, rejoicing in the way the lake-water sluiced the twigs and silt out of their hair. Then they pulled themselves up on to the ramp and wetly padded it up to the shore.

Magnus said, "Don't bother looking for our shoes tonight. It's not like the sea with tides. I'll come down and get them tomorrow."

They were thankful that the path that led to the garden fence was clear of gorse. The little old picket gate had a rickety rustic arch over it, covered with the Seven Sister roses of another generation. Their perfume hung heavily on

153

the air. Magnus shut the gate carefully, turned to have a last look at Lilliput Bay. "Look at that, Jocelyn. The moon's come out from behind that one cloud. It's made a moon-path dead centre between the Gates of Lilliput. I've never seen it as symmetrical as that before. Perhaps we never shall again. It seems a pity to leave it."

So she turned back, clasped her hands about two of the pickets, gazed her fill. He disengaged her hands gently, turned her towards him, said, as his face bent above hers, "And a pity not to take full advantage of it, wouldn't you say? And listen, no dirty cracks after this one!"

Jocelyn's clothes were sticking to her rather unpleasantly now, and tickly rivulets of water from the rats-tails of her hair were running down between her shoulder blades, but what did it matter?

He stopped kissing her, but still held her, put his wet cheek against hers, and stayed there, like that, for some time.

She hoped desperately, that, wet as she was, he wouldn't feel her heart thudding madly against her side. How that wretched organ betrayed one! Then she realized something, he wouldn't be able to hear it for the thudding of his.

He lifted his cheek away, looked into her face, said, smiling, "Nice? Yes? Good." Then he added, "Thank you, Jocelyn, for the kiss, and for not spoiling it afterwards."

They didn't exchange any more words till they reached the back door. "At least," said Magnus, "we didn't have search parties out for us, like my aunt and uncle. Run off and have a shower. I'll have one upstairs. Goodnight."

She went with never a backward look . . . and didn't feel desolate any more.

CHAPTER TEN

Life was lived at an increased tempo in December. Just as well Magnus had finished his book, though business mail and estate management, held back until he'd done so, kept him at his desk for hours almost as long.

Then, when the fine weather was threatened with forecasts of summer thunderstorms, when shearing and hay-making was imminent, he had to forsake that to help in the sheds and paddocks.

They were fortunate to have the last sheep sheared and the last bale stacked before the weather broke in a series of spectacular thunderstorms that made vivid play among the mountains and filled the lake brimful. It wasn't as harmful as it might have been, and now they needn't dread the effects of the prolonged drought that had made them anxious about winter feed, and all the financial setbacks that that would bring in its wake.

Jocelyn did without any help in the house, and even managed to supply the other two women who were cooking for the shearers and the hay-makers, with baking for their substantial afternoon teas. Then she and Aunt Clarissa made joyful and early preparations for the Christmas and holiday time. Aunt Clarissa was looking extremely well, and could manage many things denied her long since. She used her chair only in the early mornings till her limbs lost their overnight stiffness.

It wasn't often that two women could work together so harmoniously in one kitchen. Aunt Clarissa beat eggs, creamed butter and sugar, while Jocelyn did the stooping over flour and sugar bins and weighed out ingredients, tended to the

155

ovening. Each day they proudly showed Magnus and the children the mounting pile of cookies and cakes that they hoped would carry them right through the festive season so they could revel in the long school holidays, live in the water and on it.

"How marvellous," said Jocelyn to Magnus, "to be able to holiday at home, and not have to pack and travel before reaching beaches."

He looked at her keenly. "You aren't pining for the Auckland beaches, then? No sweep of nostalgia for what your life revolved round just a few short months ago?"

They measured glances. She knew what he meant. "No," she said shortly, and turned away.

He put out a hand and arrested her. "Jos, don't take offence. I often wonder about you. I don't want you to think we take you too much for granted . . . as if only Ronaldsay Downs mattered in your life. People in the same household don't always live the same lives. They can have dreams of their own."

The phone rang—Te Anau Post Office. They read him a cable from his publisher, a very long one. He asked them to read it over again, slowly, and he took it down. It would involve him in much work for the next two days. "Just as well they don't need me at the farm now," he said happily, content to be back at his desk. "The usual formula, Jocelyn, as few interruptions as possible. This is very urgent." He went whistling upstairs.

Jocelyn was crushing store biscuits between sheets of waxed paper and adding them to beaten egg, vanilla, sugar, powdered chocolate and melted butter in a huge saucepan for the fudge squares the children loved. She was thinking dreamily of Christmas. Marvellous to have Mother and Dad here. Magnus was sweet about Mother and Father. He really did seem to think of them as his own kin. Perhaps that was how he thought of her? She'd come to be part and parcel of his household. Did that make for too great a familiarity, something that dulled the edges of any impact they might have made upon each other, had they met some other way? Was it less romantic? She remembered that wet, clinging embrace down at the picket gate, and knew it needn't be. But . . . had it meant as much to Magnus? She went on chopping the nuts, heard a tap on the open back door, a gay voice calling, "Anybody at home?" and a light step along the passage. Not a familiar voice. How odd. Only people like Gail or Meg came in so informally.

A girl—a woman—appeared, stopped in the doorway, said, "Oh, hullo. Who are you?"

Jocelyn felt herself go a little stiff. This was a bit much. No, wait a bit, don't get all uptight, it'll be someone from Te Anau who knows Magnus but—so she said politely but without warmth, "My name's Grant. I'm Mr. Isbister's housekeeper, and nurse to his aunt."

"He's home, I hope. I do want to see him."

This was a bit cool. Not: "Do you think I'd be able to see him? She said firmly, though quite pleasantly. "I'm afraid this is one of the mornings when Mr. Isbister can't see anyone. He's extremely busy at his desk. He just received an urgent cable from London concerning revisions and has given me orders he's not to be disturbed. If you're staying near here any length of time, it may be possible for you to see him on Friday. Today and tomorrow are quite impossible, I'm afraid."

The girl put back a head of shining dark hair, crinkled up her eyes and burst out laughing. "My, hasn't Magnus grown important! He has a dragon and all to guard him. Right in the tradition of the famous authors!"

As far as Jocelyn was concerned, no one was going to sneer at Magnus's talent, for talent it undoubtedly was. She lifted her chin a little, said, "Correct. He *belongs* in that tradition. He *is* a famous author. And now he's working against time."

The girl shrugged. "I can assure you he'll see *me*. I can well imagine a veto like that applies only to farm workers and tourists. I think the house is much the same as the old one . . . trust Magnus to pattern it on the old! I suppose the study's in the same place? I'll just go up. Not to worry, *my* arrival won't get you into trouble?"

Jocelyn hadn't been a receptionist for nothing. Part of her job had been keeping people at bay. She said, holding up a hand that had sheer authority in it, "I'm not likely to worry about that. I *would* worry about Mr. Isbister's urgent work getting held up. They don't cable unless it's a case of a deadline. I'll ring him first, then it's over to him. We've got a house system."

"Goodness, he must have gone places. That sounds most important. Tell me, does he have a secretary too? Because I want to see him in private."

"No, he prefers to handle all his work himself."

"Well, it won't make any difference which way I'm announced. He'll see me. Tell him it's Gillian."

"Gillian who?"

"Gillian Greymore. Not that he'd need to know that. Just Gillian will bring him running."

The phone was just inside the living-room door that led off the kitchen, so Jocelyn still had this arrogant caller in her range of vision. She saw her sit on the edge of the table, pick up one of Jocelyn's chocolate chippie biscuits, and begin to nibble. What a nerve!

Magnus's voice answered shortly, "Yes?"

"You've a caller, Magnus, a—"

"Jos! Not now for Pete's sake. Or is it really urgent! I must get this lot into Te Anau before three or I'll have to go right to Invercargill!"

She said sweetly, sympathetically, for Gillian's benefit, "I know, Magnus, but this caller insisted so strongly, I thought I'd better contact you. I explained how urgent your work is today. She told me to tell you it's Gillian Greymore."

"What. Oh hell! What a morning to pick!"

Jocelyn was surprised at the mean satisfaction she felt. That girl must have really put her back up. Next moment she was completely deflated as. he said, "For sure I'll come down. Pronto."

So it wasn't exasperation but ruefulness that he was so busy that had caused him to swear!

She managed to smile, say, "He's coming down."

The girl looked scornful, triumphant. "I hadn't expected anything else."

Jocelyn experienced a great desire to pick up the gooey mess in that pan and dump it on that beautifully set dark hair. She had a flawless complexion, and almost black eyes. She looked a trifle hard, though.

Magnus came through the door, unsmiling. That much Jocelyn was grateful for.

The girl slid off the table, went to him, both hands out, lifting her face towards his. Magnus put out only his right hand, shook Gillian's right, said, "I thought you were still in England. How long have you been back in New Zealand?"

"Oh, a very short time . . . of course."

He looked at her levelly. "Jos said 'Gillian Greymore.' But it isn't Greymore now, is it? What is your married name?"

Jocelyn breathed a little easier for some reason.

Gillian laughed, said, "Oh, don't worry, I've not got one. I didn't marry him after all. Not really my type."

To Jocelyn's surprise, little white lines appeared each side of Magnus's nose and he compressed his lips a little. Then he said, "Goodness, Gillian, you do make a habit of it, don't you? Jilting people, I mean. You ought to watch it. Some day someone will jilt you."

Gillian laughed as if it had been a compliment, turned and said to Jocelyn, spreading out her hands and shrugging, "See . . . what did I tell you? We're on such close terms, we can say anything we like to each other, and not take offence. Now, Magnus, we'll leave your housekeeper to get on with her chores and we'll have a yarn." She took a step towards the door.

Magnus said, "Wait. Let me get this straight. You told Jos we were on close terms? Why—"

She held up a finger, wagged it at him, "Oh, Magnus, you always did like i's dotted and the t's crossed. I mean, she had the quaintest idea you wouldn't see me, so—"

"And she was right. You couldn't have struck a worse

morning, Gillian. A cable from my publishers about some alterations which must be made, because the situation in Orkney—the setting of my book—has been subject to change by the Government. It was a sheer miracle that they were able to hold it up. It was past the proof stage. I've not only got to alter it, but it must be done skilfully, in as near the same number of words as possible, to avoid too much resetting of type for the printers. I'll see you this afternoon when I've got the first lot away."

Gillian pouted. All the lovely maturity of her face changed and she looked like a spoiled child. "Oh, Magnus, how you've changed. What a welcome after all these years! Why, I thought——"

"You ought to have rung, Gillian. These sort of deadlines occur in every author's life. This is my living, and I've a responsibility to my publishers. They're the ones who have to deal with the printers, have schedules to keep to. Have you come through from Invercargill? Oh, it's too early for that—where are you staying?"

"With my sister in Lumsden. She'd love to see you, Magnus. How about coming through for dinner tonight?"

"Sorry, it can't be done. I've got to get away the next lot by tomorrow's mail, and must be back here to do it. You can fill in time in Te Anau. I'll meet you on the lake-front there just after three. Just past the Fiordland Travel Office."

She blinked. "Oh, I quite understand, Magnus darling, about your work. That must be attended to, but I can fill in the time here, can't I? I'd love to renew old memories wandering round the bay. I won't upset your housekeeper's routine—they're too hard to get, so have to be studied—I'll just wander round. She looks so efficient with all this," she waved a hand at the array of cookies, "I'm sure one extra wouldn't matter to her."

Magnus said, "It's just not your day. She and Aunt Clarissa are going out to lunch. To Kamahi Point."

Gillian looked delighted. "Well, what could be more convenient? I'll cook your lunch, and we could talk then, and fix

160

a date for you to come to Lumsden when you aren't fighting a deadline."

"Lunch? I've no time for such luxuries today. Jos is going to leave me a slice of cold pie and a flask of coffee. Sorry, it's Te Anau at three-thirty for half an hour, or nothing."

Suddenly she took it with a good grace. "Silly of me not to have rung. I did so want to give you a lovely surprise. Didn't come off, did it? Never mind, three-thirty, by the lake. I'd not realized you'd be so tied to your desk. Life up here used to be so unregimented, so leisurely, with time for everyone and any-one." She sighed. "We were so young, and hardly appreciated the loveliness of life here. How different now!"

At that moment Aunt Clarissa appeared in the doorway from the living-room. "Ah, I thought I heard voices." She nodded to Gillian. "Hullo, I heard the other week you were back, how are you?"

Gillian didn't bother to say. She darted a look at Magnus, "So it wasn't a surprise after all. You knew."

"I didn't. Why didn't you mention it, Aunt Clarissa?"

She looked a little vague. "I don't know. Never thought of it. I suppose I didn't think it important. My daughter always writes a chatty letter about people we know, and it was amongst other items."

Jocelyn had a moment of panic. If Aunt Clarissa said to Gillian, "Are you staying to lunch?" then Magnus would be bowled out. She must say something very quickly, but what? She needn't have worried. Aunt Clarissa had been listening in. She said, "Jocelyn, I'm almost ready, dear. If you'd pop that fudge cake into the fridge, we could cut it in squares when we came home, couldn't we? I'll put those biscuits into a tin, off you go."

Gillian said, "I'll wait till this afternoon, Magnus, to tell you how I felt about you losing Eric. I didn't know till I got home or else——"

His face closed up. "Thank you, Gillian. It's beginning to recede a little now."

Jocelyn scraped the fudge mixture into a tin, put it in the

161

fridge, said, "Oh, thanks, Aunt Clarissa. Put the biscuits in that red tin."

Gillian said quickly, "*Aunt* Clarissa? Are you family, then?"

Before Magnus could claim her as a cousin, Aunt Clarissa said, "She's as dear as any niece by blood, of course, but she's no real relation. She's Grant Alexander's cousin—you might remember hearing about him. He has a sheep station, Challowsford, in North Canterbury, and married a sort of second cousin of Magnus's, Sarah Isbister. It's an ideal set-up here, of course, because Jocelyn is a trained nurse, and has done wonders for me. I'm here as a sort of temporary chaperone. Very amusing." Magnus managed to conceal his amazement at Aunt Clarissa's astonishing outspokenness before Gillian looked in his direction.

Then he said, "Right, now don't wash up those dishes, Jos. Go and put on your beautiful garments and away with you all. The sooner I get this house to myself, the sooner I'll be able to sort out an amazingly tangled situation in Orkney. See you in Te Anau, Gillian."

Gillian said, presumably in a natural desire to save face, "I really am impressed. I'd thought at first it was merely that you were employing an over-zealous dragon. I've heard of secretaries to business men acting like this . . . people practically having to have a permit before getting across the holy threshold, so I'm afraid I did you an injustice, Jocelyn, it really was a busy day." She turned to Magnus, who was looking impatient. "How naïve of me to expect to find myself on the same footing as of old, with the right to come and go as I pleased. Naturally, with you not knowing I hadn't married Roger, you hadn't realized the years have swung back."

Was Magnus being deliberately tantalizing? He said, "*Roger?* Good heavens. I've usually got a good memory for names. I met your mother in Invercargill when I first got back, and I was sure she said his name was Gawain or Galahad or something else from the *Idylls of the King,* and I thought good grief, fancy practical-minded Gillian marrying someone with a romantic name like that!"

A flake of pink that was surely anger showed in Gillian's

162

cheeks. She said, "Gareth . . . and *he* was just a flash in the pan, a shipboard romance. I had a cruise in the Mediterranean."

She might just as well not have spoken. He seemed to be considering something else. "And even now *I've* no sense of the years having swung back."

Gillian said softly, "Of course not. Clumsy of me, after such losses as you've sustained."

He blinked a little, "Oh, I see what you mean. I was thinking on another tack. I don't want time to swing back. I very much like the present—apart from the deep loss of Eric. As Jocelyn herself remarked the other day, our lives lie in very pleasant places. The homestead is rebuilt, with improvements, and will serve another four or five generations, and I found, on returning to New Zealand, that Jocelyn had grown up. I'd regarded her as a very pretty but very junior bridesmaid when I went up for Sarah's wedding. I came back to find her the answer to all my problems."

Jocelyn managed to keep her countenance and, so she believed for she dared not look at her, did Aunt Clarissa. Oh, the devil had got into Magnus Isbister this morning! Gillian was obviously his ex-fiancée. That wound had gone deep, so deep that when she had returned, unwed, and obviously ready to make it up, he'd not been able to resist lashing out.

There was an awkward silence. Jocelyn felt Magnus was waiting for Gillian to break it, and willing her, Jocelyn, to keep quiet.

It worked. Gillian said stiffly, "I see. But Jocelyn herself did say she was your housekeeper. Then you want me to cancel this afternoon's meeting?"

"No, I think it would be a good idea. Some things were never quite cleared up. We have so many friends in Invercargill, I think I should make it plain where I stand, otherwise we'll have a lot of well-meaning but bungling matchmakers thinking up ways and means of getting us together, at theater parties, or cosy little dinners. Three-thirty on the lake-front. Now, I'm back to Orkney."

Gillian said, in a tone Jocelyn found she had to admire, "I'm afraid I must have, after all, upset your concentration."

He grinned. "Oh, never mind. I've learned to shut the outside world out to such a degree that even thoughts of Jocelyn rarely intrude. Goodbye for now. By the way, you can go right round the poplars now, back to the road. Jocelyn, if you and Aunt Clarissa don't scram, Emmie and Cosmo will be ringing to find out what's happened and that'll be another interruption."

Jocelyn almost felt she should rush off to change as Gillian walked out of the door. Magnus stood stock-still till he heard the car drive off. Without the slightest show of apology he grinned at them both. "Both of you look as if, like Lot's wife, you've turned into a pillar of salt. Fun, wasn't it? Damned nerve of her! Thanks, girls, you both did well. See you later."

Jocelyn's voice halted him. "Magnus, she's not the only one with a damned nerve. Haven't you got a bit of explaining to do?"

"Not now I haven't. I'm in one hell of a fix in Orkney. Oil rigs to the left of me, oil rigs to the right of me, protesting Orcadians and high tides in front of me, volleying and thundering. I used you shamelessly, Jocelyn, but you're such a good sport, you'll go along with me, I know. But for the love of Mike, don't ask about it now. Even after I get back this afternoon, I've another twenty-four hours or so of intense concentration. In ten days Christmas will be upon us. That slice of pie and some coffee at one, please." And he was away, bounding up the stairs.

AUNT CLARISSA sat down and gave way to mirth. Jocelyn didn't. She had a line between her brows. "I think it would serve him right if I stalked upstairs and told him exactly what I think."

Aunt Clarissa mopped her eyes, "But you won't, dear child. You've too much respect for his work. Besides, this is the time to play a game of your own. Ignore it." She looked reflective and shrewd. "Sheer inspiration on his part. That business about Roger and Gareth was funny. She didn't terminate *that* engagement, Gareth did. She's extremely attractive,

164

but palls quickly. I knew far more than I let on. My daughter has this friend in London who also knew Gillian. They weren't close friends, but Gillian looked her up. Gareth was far too nice for her. She made trouble with his family, and he broke it off. She got engaged to this Roger to save face."

Aunt Clarissa went on ruefully, "It must be the original sin in me, but I was downright glad to see that one get her come-uppance. After all, she deserted Magnus when he needed her most. Still, it was a good thing and all. I'm not one for prating glibly about all things working together for good, I'm more a firm believer in the fact that God has the power to bring good out of things that are, in themselves, evil. The things that happen because man has a will of his own. But what happened saved Magnus from a lifetime of regret. So, Jocelyn, though you might well be angry with Magnus for using you like that, could you remember he went through a lot of heartbreak over that girl's lack of faith in him all those years ago? It did something for me to know she'd no longer any power to move him."

Jocelyn wasn't so sure. Magnus must have been rigidly, coldly angry inside, to behave like that. But she smiled at Aunt Clarissa and said, "All right. I want no unpleasantness in the house so near Christmas." Something struck her. "You precipitated that, you wily creature! If you'd not come out with that about me not being a real cousin, Magnus would never have thought of it."

Aunt Clarissa visibly preened herself. "I'm glad you thought of that. I had a feeling my stroke of genius was going un-noticed."

Jocelyn crumpled into laughter. She gave Clarissa a hug. "Oh, you are a wicked soul, but I do love you."

Clarissa looked as she might have when a naughty ten-year-old.

Jocelyn said, "I can't help feeling sorry for her. She came in so full of confidence. She went out so deflated. And it may have undermined that confidence when Gareth broke it off."

Aunt Clarissa looked scornful. "There's such a thing as

165

being too charitable. The only thing that's brought that one back into his life again is that she's just read that article Magnus was chuckling over last week . . . the one that grossly overrated his book sales. Don't worry that anything'll happen to soften him up when he meets her this afternoon. It won't. He was too completely disillusioned all those years ago."

"I wonder why he wanted to see her, then?"

"Now, my dear, don't make a problem out of that. I wondered myself, then realized the children hadn't been mentioned. She never as much as asked what had become of them. Knowing Magnus, I think he'll be telling her he's their guardian, that they're with him for always. That'll put that one clean off. And that *you* love them like a mother."

Jocelyn hadn't realized how much wistfulness her tone betrayed when she said, "Nice to know one is suitable. Magnus's bond with his twin extends even to the next generation, doesn't it? He'd go to any lengths to do what's best for them. Even to marrying for their happiness."

Aunt Clarissa sighed. "The young are so vulnerable. You're no exception. You're unsure of yourself, aren't you, Jos? If you knew Magnus as I know him, you'd realize how absurd that is. He has never in his life done anything for expediency's sake. At times he's been foolish, quixotic, impetuous to a fault, but never calculating. Now, don't force any issue at the moment by taking him to task. Just take what he did in a sporting manner—as a means of letting his former fiancée know he'd no wish to warm old ashes."

Therefore when Jocelyn took up the slab of cold pastry and the coffee, she just said, putting it down, "There you are. Hope that little scene downstairs has receded. I'll bring your car to the back door for you, and leave your keys in it. I'm making a curry tonight—that'll be easy for you to manage at your desk, so you can bash on, uninterrupted."

He looked most relieved. "Oh, thanks, Jocelyn. What a sport—especially considering how I used you."

"Oh, that. Don't worry, by the time you get this lot off your plate, you'll regard it as ancient history. Now I'm off."

PERHAPS it was his absorption with his revisions that made him seem so withdrawn when he returned from Te Anau, but nevertheless, she felt that the lakeside hour with Gillian had, in some way, stirred him deeply. Even when the last section of amended manuscript had gone, there was a reserve about him that hadn't been there before.

The Christmas rush was upon them, so there was no time for any discussion. She had a feeling Magnus was glad they were so busy. What a year it had been for him! Last year he'd had Christmas in Orkney, and the temperatures had been unbelievably low, with bleak winds sweeping down from the North Pole and ice-green waters smashing at the cliffs and swirling up the blow-holes. And he'd still had a brother, even if at the other side of the world.

Here, the wheat was growing tall in the paddocks. They needed more rain again. The garden was showing great cracks in the parched earth and, at night when it was cool enough, they spent their time hoeing and watering. Te Anau was thick with overseas tourists already, and each day saw more launches and sails on the lake. Sightseeing planes zoomed overhead, and amphibians landed with all the grace of water-birds on the ruffled waters. Only tiny pockets of snow were left, and though at times the condensation after heat caused mist to swirl down the lake in the very early morning, by nine it would have funnelled away in a peculiar action as if some giant vacuum cleaner was sucking it in.

MAGNUS WROTE the first chapter of a new thriller, put the cover on his typewriter and said, "That's all for this year. I take up again in February. January is our holiday month and in two weeks' time it will be Christmas."

Jocelyn was intrigued. "I'm constantly learning things about authors. I'd the idea that once you got a first chapter done you'd not be able to help going on with it."

He grinned. "Probably doesn't apply to all author's that. But me, once I get a book away, I'm restless till another's on the stocks. You must have noticed how I've been."

She had, but had put it down to being more disturbed than he'd admit, over Gillian's visit.

"But once I get that first chapter written, I feel it's on the way, and I have a really blissful time, mentally, in all sorts of odd moments, living with the characters, letting things happen to them. So if I'm absent-minded, understand and forgive. Normally, that first chapter is the easiest of all, but this one nearly drove me mad. I changed my mind dozens of times before I got it right. I tipped out three wastepaper baskets full of rejected pages."

"Well, hasn't it been said that an overflowing wastepaper basket is a sign of a discriminating mind?"

He burst out laughing. "I expect that's more from the inimitable Samuel Johnson!"

"It is not! I've no idea who said it. That reminds me, I must go out and pick some red currants."

"What reminds you? What's that got to do with an eighteenth-century lexicographer?"

"Everything. He liked them. He advised Boswell, when he was planning an orchard, to plant plenty of currants. That the fruit made a very pretty sweetmeat. And it does. It stimulates the appetite by pleasing the eye first."

He shook his head. "You sound a pedant yourself. Oh, Jos, you make me laugh. You could write a thesis on the good Doctor. And it'd be different from every one ever written. You'd bring out the homely touches that others ignore. I could have burst out laughing when you were giving Ninian that decongestant cough mixture when he had that chest cold a few weeks ago. You said doubtfully, 'This brand is new to me,' then you peered at it and said in such relieved tones, 'Oh, it ought to be all right. It's got tincture of squills in it. Doctor Johnson was a great believer in that.' I thought for a nursing Sister it was a quaint remark."

"Well, some of the old remedies are best. My mother used to swear by the ones that had the ipecacuanha as an ingredient."

"I'll come out and help you pick the currants, they take an

age, and I'll be glad to be free of desk work to give you a hand—you're looking thin and peaky. You work too hard."

Thin and peaky! How unromantic. Slim and pale would have sounded better.

He went on, picking up a billy-can, "I only hope we don't get too many people who take pre-Christmas holidays arriving in on us. It may sound inhospitable, but when one's flat out preparing, it's very disrupting. They can come in droves after Christmas and I shan't care."

Nevertheless, he was nothing but delighted when one visit was heralded. They were having morning tea when she rang and he answered the phone. His face lit up, his eyes warmed. "Edna! My dear, how marvellous to hear your voice again. When did you get back? Oh, and by ship. And you didn't as much as send me a postcard from any port! Or has one gone astray? You didn't? I'll have a few words to say on that when I see you. Oh, you wanted to give me a surprise? Then I forgive you. You're at Tapanui and coming through? Of course, we'll love it. Oh, no, you don't. No staying at a motel, you'll stay here.

"My housekeeping arrangements? Well, Aunt Clarissa is here, much more mobile than of yore, due mainly to my cousin, Jocelyn Alexander, who is an expert masseuse. She also keeps house for me. All right, I'll check with her." He put his hand over the mouthpiece, said, "It's a very dear friend of ours. Just back from Britain. You'll like her, everyone does. She won't accept my word for it that it won't put you out. I'd hate her to stay anywhere but at Lilliput Bay. Good. I knew I could rely on you, Jos."

He turned back to the phone, talked eagerly. Jocelyn gathered that the last time he'd seen this Edna was when she had seen him off at Heathrow Airport, London, on his sad flight home.

She said to him, when he hung up, "Is she married, or a widow, or anything?"

Magnus said, "She ought to have been married long ago,

169

but it—didn't come off. But she's a real charmer. Her name describes her perfectly. It means pleasure, or perfect happiness."

Jocelyn was aware of a mixture of feelings. It was the oddest thing. One hardly ever liked the people one was supposed to like, whom everyone else liked. Or paragons! Or beauties! Oh, dear, how stupid, to feel this aversion. Perhaps she was tired. February seemed a long time off, when they could return to their normal routine . . . the children would be back at school, her parents returned to Dunedin, and the peaceful silence of the house would mean that Magnus was in his study, working, Aunt Clarissa busy about her little loved tasks.

. . . She and Magnus would be almost alone again, would have time for their long discussions, walking in purple twilights and coral sunsets and long golden afternoons by the gentle shore of Lilliput Bay.

CHAPTER ELEVEN

Edna proved a delight. Jocelyn loved her from the moment she appeared . . . tall, like herself, with a spring in her step and a light in her eye; shoulder-length streaky-gold hair that waved back from a serene forehead, and candid grey eyes. She would be thirty-two or so, Jocelyn thought, nearer Magnus's age than herself, and it was evident they'd known each other a long time and closely.

They spent much time recalling teenage days when she and Eric and Magnus had spent most of their holidays on the lake, exploring fiords and islands. She and Magnus had been marooned on St. Olaf's Island for hours once, when they'd let their boat drift away; they had gone tramping in some of the remote areas across lake, with Magnus's father. They spoke of idyllic nights lying out in sleeping-bags under a canopy of trees, with only starlight to see by. Jocelyn found herself envying those memories, yet there was never a spark of real jealousy.

She gleaned from what they said that Eric had first invited her up here for a holiday. He'd met her at some high school dance when he and Eric and Scotty McPhail had been at John McGlashan. Scotty came over one night, with his wife, to renew acquaintance. They made Eric live again.

Jocelyn found herself studying Edna closely. Had she been a writer herself, she would have found her perfect heroine material. Did the little lines at each side of that full, passionate mouth indicate discipline? She had laughter crinkles at the corners of her eyes, noticeable more than usual, probably, because of the gorgeous tan she had acquired on board ship, in the Caribbean and the Pacific.

But sometimes, when she was silent, Edna's face had a pensiveness and yearning that made Jocelyn wonder if, in spite of her ready laughter, inwardly she knew a loneliness of spirit. Or was it that she was looking back to the days when there had been two copper-toned boys living here? Had she perhaps loved Eric? Calf-love perhaps, but sometimes it lasted. It might have for her, not for him. Life was cruel that way, sometimes.

Edna said to Jocelyn one day, "Ninian is so like Eric it hurts. Yet had neither of the children been like him, I'd have resented it. Oddly enough, Una's gestures are Eric's gestures, and there's something in her voice. However, Ninian has already more strength of character than his father. Eric always leaned on Magnus. What a pity it all had to end as it did." Jocelyn caught the glimmer of tears in the grey eyes, and put out a hand in wordless sympathy.

Edna smiled. "How silly of me! At least Eric knew happiness for the last seven years of his life. It seems so strange to me, Jos, that you never knew Eric."

Jocelyn said hastily, "Well, he didn't come to Sarah and Grant's wedding, and we all lived at such distances from each other."

"I didn't mean that. Just meant that for you, Lilliput Bay knows just one bright head. For me, it's always peopled with two."

Then she had loved Eric. A tremor of fear shook Jocelyn. And Eric's children were his twin's wards. His *identical* twin. In time might not Edna console herself with someone in the image of the man she had loved so long? Edna had been in Britain when Magnus was. They'd spoken last night of the time Edna had been in Orkney with him.

Edna said briskly, "I must stop this. Life is for getting on with. Eric told me that long ago, and I've proved it. Always another corner to turn, and who knows what's round it?"

Jocelyn said, "That sounds like a quotation my mother loves." She repeated it.

Edna said, shining-eyed, "Jos, that's wonderful. It's just what's happened to me lately. A sort of rebirth."

She didn't enlarge. Jos felt as if icy fingers had her heart in a vice-like grip. Reborn? What else could that mean but that in Magnus, who was made in Eric's image, she had found her lost love again?

Something struck her. Edna had said Magnus had always been the stronger of the two. Hadn't she known about Magnus's weakness, then? Perhaps Edna had gone to Britain long before that old scandal had happend. Anyway, if she did, Edna had enough strength of character, enough maturity, to overlook it. Just as she, Jocelyn knew that if Magnus had asked her to marry him, she would. But oh, how she wished Edna hadn't come home, even if, in spite of this new jealousy, she herself still loved this girl.

Magnus ran Aunt Clarissa over to the Ronaldsons to spend the afternoon. He got back to find Edna helping Jocelyn hull raspberries for jam. He said, "Edna, you'll be off home for Christmas tomorrow. How about coming for a long walk with me? I'm sure Jocelyn could manage on her own, eh, Jos?"

Edna protested, "Let's do the jam first, then we could all go down to the bay and have a swim. It's so hot."

"We'll bathe first. Jocelyn, would you mind if we took off now? When the children get home, you could have a bathe with them, couldn't you? I guess you'll want to cool off after that."

Well, she wasn't going to make an unwelcome third! She said, tipping the berries into the pan, "I'd be more than grateful if you'd take off on your own. I'd love to get my Christmas presents wrapped."

She saw them running through the garden just in their swimsuits. Edna's was a purple bikini she'd picked up in Acapulco.

The kitchen got hotter and hotter. If she left the back door open the wasps came in. Certainly the window was screened, but it wasn't enough this airless day. The honeysuckle scent coming through the gauze was almost too cloying. Jocelyn felt her yellow floral shift dress, thin as it was, sticking to her back. The phone rang three times. Every time she answered it she managed to transfer sticky jam from her fingers to the receiver. And she frequently dropped the spoon on the floor.

Just as she took the jam off the hot-plate, the phone rang again. She felt decidedly grumpy, but the sound of a voice she recognized steadied her. Ina's.

She must be careful. She said, "Oh, you'll be wanting my cousin. I'm afraid he's not in. He'll be back before long, though. Could I get him to ring you? Are you on toll?"

Ina said, "No, it's you I want to talk to, Jocelyn Grant!"

It sounded ominous. Jocelyn said, "But if it's anything to do with the children, only Mr. Isbister could tell you."

"I'm not asking anything. I just want to tell you something. I've tumbled to this cosy little set-up at Lilliput Bay. You aren't any more Magnus's cousin than I am. He's remotely connected with Sarah Isbister who married Grant Alexander, and you're only connected with Grant. It was all a hum to make me think it was a very respectable household."

Anger superseded fear in Jocelyn, "Mrs. Chester, you'd better be careful. It *is* a very respectable household. I'm merely Magnus's housekeeper and part-time nurse to Aunt Clarissa. There is nothing irregular here at all, and Magnus and I feel we're cousins by marriage."

"Really, then how come Magnus himself told his ex-fiancée he was in love with you? She told me herself, and believe me, if it hadn't been that she was still just about livid about the way he'd humiliated her, she'd never have let it out. It was magnanimous of her to look him up again, when you think he strayed off the strait and narrow when they were engaged. I don't think it's at all a suitable place for my niece and nephew."

Jocelyn said, "Ina, you've got hold of the wrong end of the stick, and you'll only make yourself ill again. It's an obsession with you. It's quite absurd of you to think you could upset the guardianship—any solicitor would laugh at the idea. A man has to have a housekeeper, so naturally Magnus took on his cousin's cousin, who he knew was out of a job at the moment. He brought his aunt into the household as chaperone. What! What did you say? Ina! Don't be ridiculous. Aunt Clarissa connive at an illicit relationship? Look, I'm afraid you've got yourself upset and off balance again. Now listen!

"Gillian called here at a very bad moment when Magnus was working against a deadline. He wasn't in a good temper to begin with—because Gillian insisted she see him. Magnus saw she was trying to make a comeback, and I'm afraid he suspected she was only too willing to overlook his peccadilloes of other years now he was a very successful man, and instead of blowing up and telling her what he thought of her, I'm afraid he went all wicked and pretended I was filling the bill! I assure you I'm not.

"I was about as cross as Gillian was. I was all set to tell him off, but Aunt Clarissa stopped me. He just had to get an amended manuscript off to London by that day's mail. He saw Gillian afterwards—briefly—in Te Anau, and from what you've told me, he must have enlarged on his spur-of-the-moment deception to get rid of her.

"If you're mean enough to tell her this, we'll know who it came from; and Magnus, I'm afraid, will take steps you might not like, to ensure you stop gossiping about us. He'll see his solicitors—and that means your husband will have to know again. I wish you'd leave poor Magnus alone. He's done a magnificent job in managing to settle back to desk work, help out in farming emergencies, look after the children, and do a hundred and one other things for which one can only admire him. If you don't promise me you'll let this thing drop, I'll have to get in touch with your husband."

Ina's voice took on a placatory tone. "Jocelyn, may I say I'm sorry? I . . . was much better . . . but meeting Gillian stirred all this up. She made me feel I was right to try to get the children."

Jocelyn cut in, "And for myself, as apart from Magnus, I'm furious to think you thought I was carrying on with Magnus. I won't have it. Neither will my parents."

There was a pause. Jocelyn could almost hear the wheels going round in Ina's head as she tried to salvage the situation. The attack had been carried into her own country by this irate and seemingly quite moral housekeeper of Magnus Isbister's.

Finally she came out with, "I suppose Aunt Clarissa has tried to whitewash his behavior of that time. He can do no wrong in her eyes."

"She hasn't tried to do any such thing. We've never mentioned it. And one weekend doesn't have to damn a man for ever."

"If that's all it was. Oh, dear, you'll think I'm not very charitable. But if you knew your cousin's cousin as I do you'd wonder if the leopard really could change his spots. Besides, Edna, that girl he weekended with, is back in New Zealand. They were together quite a lot in Britain. You wouldn't know that. In the Lake District, in the Highlands, in London, even in Orkney. She's bound to turn up at Lilliput some time. Better watch out for her. Before you know where you are, she'll be at a motel in Te Anau and Magnus will be coming and going. Well, you've been warned. By the way, I'd rather you didn't tell Magnus I rang. I'm relieved about the situation as far as you and he are concerned, and I daresay as a daughter of the manse you've a reasonably high standard of conduct."

Jocelyn was surprised at the sarcasm in her own tone. "Oh, yes, reasonably. My parents will be here for three weeks in January; they'll be here for a few days at Christmas too. That ought to reassure you. I'll go now, because Magnus could be in any moment, and I'd have to say who was ringing. No, I won't promise not to tell him, because, if I find you're still making mischief, or discussing this with Gillian, I'll certainly tell him, and he'll get his solicitors to act. Goodbye."

She sank down on the kitchen chair, put her elbows on the table and her chin in her hands. Her legs were trembling, and her heart thudding against her rib cage, it seemed. She felt slightly sick.

It was one thing thinking of an unknown someone with whom Magnus had weekended seven years ago, and another having her staying in the house. But *Edna!* Edna with her confident walk and candid grey eyes. It seemed impossible.

176

Thoughts buzzed madly in Jocelyn's brain. It *could* add up, but *did* it?

Edna herself had talked openly about spending time with Magnus in Britain! Jocelyn made up her mind to disbelieve it. Ina might have heard Edna was here, and was making capital out of this. She was hardly responsible for her actions. Why let those actions have any effect?

She finished bottling the jam, labelled the jars, washed up. She went upstairs to shower and change. She liked that shower best. She slipped into a thin tussore-colored dacron dress, tied her shoulder-length hair back into a ridiculous inch of ponytail, because it was cooler, with a coral ribbon, and slipped her feet into white thongs. The coral lipstick she used had a touch of gold in it. It did things for her coloring, lifted the morale. She *wouldn't* believe that of Edna and Magnus!

The phone rang. She answered it in Magnus's study. Another phone call, this time from Auckland from his publisher's agent. He was to ring them back before four-thirty if at all possible. She explained that he was showing a visitor round the estate, but she'd do her best to locate them. The agent explained that their Sydney representative was with them, had intended flying down to see Magnus, but now had to return to Australia by the seven o'clock plane and would like to speak to him if at all possible.

What a day! As she put the phone down, she saw Magnus's binoculars on his windowsill. She went across, pushed the windows wide. She swept the terrain with them. The beach was bare. They were probably walking in the bush near the Falls. They hadn't taken a launch out.

The trouble was, the bush was so dense, but even a glimpse of Edna's bright blue sun-dress, or Magnus's orange shirt, would give her a clue, and she could then run to get them.

Ah . . . the blue dress. They were in the sunlit glade where the first Ninian had planted a ring of hawthorns. Jocelyn focused the glasses properly, then froze. They'd turned to face each other, and Magnus made a gesture of gladness and held out his arms. Edna laughed, ran right into them.

The binoculars crashed from Jocelyn's nerveless fingers. She gazed with uncaring eyes at the detail of the scratch they had made on the new windowsill. Then she stood them up exactly as they had been standing before, drew the windows back, and ran downstairs.

She had done Ina an injustice this time. Magnus was a fool. Edna wasn't what she seemed. She, Jocelyn Grant, was a loser as far as men were concerned.

By the time she got to the picket gate, she could see them coming over the swing-bridge. She "cooeed" a couple of times before they located her. She wasn't going to wait here with the message, Have Magnus lope off to the house with that long-legged stride of his, and have to chat with the lovable but deceitful Edna all the way back to the house. She made gestures which would make them understand they were wanted. She didn't much care whether he got there in time or not, anyway. She was fed up.

She looked down on the pickets, absently caressed the two she'd clung to that lighthearted night they'd fallen in the water, and had kissed. She had read a whole future in that, and had decided to be mature and overlook his past. How many women had done just that, only to find the deceit went on? She was being made use of. She was a good housekeeper, a good gardener, the children loved her. Magnus had used her shamelessly when Gillian arrived, and now he was dallying with Edna again.

She wished desperately that Mum and Dad weren't coming for Christmas. That she and Magnus weren't going to the children's school breakup tomorrow night, that the season of peace and goodwill wasn't just two days away. They would go together to the darling church on the lakeside at Te Anau, a little modern building under its age-old trees, and sing all the lovely hymns of Christmastide together, and she would know it was a hollow mockery.

It seemed incredible to her as the day wore on, and the evening, that no one knew how she was feeling, what thoughts tormented her. All she could think of was that tomorrow Edna

178

was leaving . . . Edna kissed Magnus goodbye, oh, so lightly. She kissed Aunt Clarissa and Jocelyn too. Jocelyn felt she flinched. Magnus said, "Come back about March, or the end of February, Edna, and if you've a friend you'd like to bring, we'd be no end pleased, of course." Very clever. Who did he think he was kidding?

They waved her off, came inside. Magnus went upstairs to his study. This was Jocelyn's chance.

SHE WAITED for about a quarter of an hour She went upstairs, tapped and entered without waiting for a reply. That in itself was unusual. But Magnus swung round, smiled at her.

She came quite close to his desk. To her fury he caught at her swinging hand, said, "Well it was good to have Edna here, but how nice to be on our own again. Thanks for——"

Jocelyn interrupted as if she'd not heard, but stepped back so his arm fell to his side. She said, looking him straight in the eye, "I had quite a day yesterday when you and Edna were out rambling. You'll probably be furious with me that I gave the show away to Ina, but I don't care. You brought it on yourself."

Magnus stared, his chair scraped as he pushed it back, and he stood up. She wished he'd kept sitting. His height dwarfed her. She went back another couple of paces. "I hate the way you tower over me," she said.

The blue eyes narrowed. "I believe you're in a bad temper, Jocelyn, and it's only the second time I've ever seen you in one. Out with it. If I've done something I oughtn't to have done, I'm sorry. But I want to hear what it is. Or is it just that it was too much for you, having Edna here at a busy time?"

"Of course not. I've been wanting to have this out with you ever since Gillian was here. I didn't like being used like that. I was furious. Aunt Clarissa begged me not to say anything to you then, and I agreed not to. I shouldn't have agreed."

"Of course not. I can't stand people bottling things up. They get magnified with brooding over them and out of all proportion. Let's have it. You mentioned Ina too."

"You involved me in that scene with Gillian for nothing more admirable than a desire to get your own back on a girl who jilted you long ago . . . and with good reason."

She saw him whiten and was sorry, then the next moment was furious with herself that she could feel sorry, and she rushed on. "You enjoyed it—setting her back. I didn't like her myself, but it was cruel. Now it's bounced back on you. She told Ina, who rang when you were out with Edna. You ought to be very grateful to me. Even feeling as I did about the way you used me, I won hands down in hot defence of you. And then . . . oh, I could . . . no, I'll leave that. Back to Ina. It was charming, I can tell you. I don't feel now I can altogether blame Ina, but she accused us of having an irregular relationship. I knew it was your own stupid fault, but tried to save things by saying it was nothing but a pack of nonsense, because you'd been furious at Gillian turning up and trying for a comeback.

"That out of sheer devilment you pretended we'd fallen for each other. Gillian had told her we weren't really related, of course. I saved that by saying that naturally, when I was a cousin of your cousin, and was looking for work because I'd come south to be nearer my parents, I'd stepped into the breach to look after the children. I was proud of myself, because I convinced her. But I'm warning you, Magnus, never use me that way again!"

She paused for breath. She was now about to tell him that she knew Edna was the girl who'd caused the original trouble. But her courage failed her. He could just think she was angry over his nerve. She turned to go. It wasn't a bad exit line, but she was caught and held. His hands were like vices about her wrists. She felt a tremor of fear because Magnus's anger would be a Viking's anger. But when she looked up into his face it was all tenderness. How ridiculous! He was even laughing.

He bent over her so that she shrank back. "It's no go, Jocelyn, you aren't going to get away from me. You aren't going to stay mad with me. I'd lock the door sooner than have you run away. An awful lot of trouble is caused by people not talking things out at the right moment . . . and this is it. Pride gets in the way otherwise . . . yet if those things didn't happen, what would poor authors have to write about?

"Darling, darling, none of what I said to Gillian—in front of you, and later, on our own, was make-believe. It was what I felt. Only I thought I was jumping the gun. I was sure I could make you love me, if I gave you time to get over Leigh— and I'd another reason for soft-pedalling too. I thought if I gave you long enough and you came to care enough you might . . . thunder and turf, what's all that noise? Brakes! Oh, Jocelyn, why did you pick this morning for a confrontation? I was waiting till February when we could get away by ourselves to Thorkel's Voe and I could have time—what the devil *is* it? It sounds like a truck. They've come here instead of to the farm, I suppose. I'll soon get rid of them, because this must be cleared up here and now. Just a moment."

Cleared up? He was in for another shock. She'd tell him exactly what she thought of him. What Ina had revealed. What she had seen for herself.

He spun from the window. "Damn and hell! Look what's arrived!"

She rushed across. It was Scotty McPhail and a whole bus-load of tourists. They were spilling out in all directions.

Jocelyn felt as appalled as Magnus. She wanted to finish what she must tell him. She'd add a bit more to it now. Tell him it was no compliment to be proposed to because you'd make a good housekeeper and foster-mother to his niece and nephew. While he had his fun on the side. Oh, no. Now they'd have to be polite to a busload of tourists wanting his autograph. She was worked up to a fine pitch of anger and she didn't want to lose it.

Magnus Isbister wasn't going to be so confident, so aggressively and triumphantly male when she'd finished with him!

He grabbed her hand . . . "Come on, we're going to escape by the patio. I must delay Aunt Clarissa in answering the door. Praise be she takes a while to get there."

There was no releasing her hand. He had her going helter-

181

skelter down the stairs. They almost collided with Aunt Clarissa. He seized her, said, "Aunt, there's a busload just arrived. I'm in the middle of proposing to Jocelyn and finding it hard going. Tell them I'm not in. We'll go out here. Tell them we've just left on the launch for a trip on the lake."

Jocelyn knew a stab of remorse when she saw the delight leap into Aunt Clarissa's eyes, but next moment she was being dragged through her bedroom and across the patio, out of sight of the bus.

When they reached the shore, he pulled her along to the up-turned dinghy. She jerked back and got her hand free, but he lunged and caught her. She said, "All right, Magnus, that's enough of that silly nonsense. We're out of sight here. They'll go in a moment, and it doesn't take long to say no."

He gave her an incredulous look. "That's what you think. And you aren't saying 'no.' If you imagine I'm going back to the homestead to have the happiest day of my life all snarled up with tourists and Christmas puddings and toll calls from Auckland or cables from London, you're much mistaken. I've never known anything like it. We're going round to Thorkel's Voe. We're going to be completely alone. I can't think of a more ideal spot to take one's girl to."

It was too much for Jocelyn. She felt white-hot, and the words spilled out of her. "Yes, an ideal spot . . . and well used too. You take all your girls there, don't you, Magnus Isbister? Edna yesterday, Jocelyn Alexander today . . . only Jocelyn isn't going. She can tell you right here and now that she knows exactly who Edna is, what she meant in your life seven years ago, and what she means now!"

To her complete surprise he gave a great shout of laughter. "Oh, Jocelyn . . . *now* I know what's wrong. Splendid! You were jealous of me taking Edna to the Voe yesterday. That's all I need, some indication that you care enough to be jealous. Jocelyn, you're going to get into that dinghy. If I have to use force I will, and you know what happens in dinghies if you struggle! Think of James and Clarissa. Get in, or I'll carry you out to the launch and duck you on the way. If ever

182

I was determined on anything, I am on this. We're going to talk it out where it can't be interrupted. In with you, or take the consequences."

She got in. She said stiffly as he cast off, "It won't make any difference to the outcome, but all right. *I'd* like to get it said without interruption too *And stay dry.*"

IN SILENCE they transferred to the launch; Magnus started it up. In silence they headed out through the Gates of Lilliput and turned westward up the lake. He said, nonchalantly, "Now, just small talk, please, till we get to the Voe. I've a feeling that my actions will speak louder than words, and crush your opposition—but you can't embrace your loved one when you're at the wheel."

Jocelyn wouldn't deign to answer. She went to the stern seat, sat down, gazed stonily over the waters. He kept up a flow of small talk, did it cleverly, so the fact that she wasn't answering seemed of little consequence. It was intensely irritating.

As they tied up at the Voe she was jerked into speech. "Whatever's all that timber there for? And those stacks of tiles?"

"Good . . . it can speak after all," he said brazenly. This is what I brought Edna round to see yesterday. Come on up. It's a fine place for a proposal."

"For a discussion," she amended. "Up at Thorkel's Refuge?"

"Yes, come on. I've something to show you." He put out a hand and cupped her elbow.

She drew back. "I'm not exactly as feeble as Aunt Clarissa. I can manage."

"Then I'll lead the way." He sprang ahead of her. Jocelyn followed more slowly. He reached the top step, turned, smiled. She was staring past him. There were evidences of workmen everywhere. They must have come uplake by launch. Saw-horses, shavings, sawdust. There were shutters attached to each window, and newly-puttied glass replaced those panes

183

which had been broken. The chimney that had been almost a ruin was built up again with lake-boulders. Most of them looked like the ones Thorkel had used originally.

They had left the hollowed-out top step, but the rotting floorboards had been replaced. The entire roof was covered with decramastic tiles that would withstand generations of Fiordland weather. The whole place was clean. The inside walls were lined, but were yet to be sized and papered, she could see. A lean-to kitchen and bathroom had been added on.

Magnus said, "It's just a rock-gas stove, of course, because no power reaches here, but the lamps are good ones and work on pulleys. I like the way they've raftered the ceiling, don't you?"

Jocelyn swallowed, said, "But what's all this to do with me? How can I take an interest in the restoration when I want to get on with a bit of unfinished business. I might as well tell you, Magnus, I'm *seething* with all I want to tell you yet."

He stood looking at her and smiling. She was wearing the tussore-colored dacron dress of yesterday, and the coral ribbon tied her hair back in the endearingly small bunch at the nape of her neck. His smile made her heart, that traitor organ, turn over. But it made her angry too. He said, "I'm seething too, but not with anger. I refuse to be cheated out of the setting I'd planned. Look about you, Jocelyn. Know why I kept it secret from you? Because it's my Christmas present to your mother and father. Not just Thorkel's Refuge, but Thorkel's Voe. All the land including the Forgotten Headland. I've got it all drawn up. It was Thorkel's, and he left it to our family. Now it's being returned. Your mother told me they were saving for a beach house, that it would mean a lot to her in the somewhat nomadic life of a manse to know they owned a plot of land somewhere. So what place more fitting than this?"

A cry was wrung from her, one of sheer distress. "Oh, and how she would have loved it, but——"

"You're not to say they can't accept it. Nothing is more cruel than thrusting a gift back at the giver. I've had such fun planning it. Think of the fishing holidays your father will have here . . . and we'll be just over the hill. The utter peace for your mother . . . where no phone rings!"

She said stiffly, "How can they take a gift like this from a stranger?"

"That doesn't apply. It will be from their son-in-law-to-be. Jocelyn, we've fiddled about long enough. I told them when they were here that I hoped I'd be able to make you my wife some day. If you'd have me. I thought that old scandal might make you hesitate. Your mother said not to rush you, that once you said 'no,' you might stick to it. That you needed time to adjust yourself, after Leigh. Yet I've been pretty sure you *were* getting over him lately. I've been doing my best to blot his image out. I thought you were beginning to care for me. Two people as kindred as we are must surely marry. I told Edna yesterday I was hoping you'd marry me." The laughter warmed his voice, "When you were being jealous, you idiot! So. . . ."

What he'd hoped for in those hazel eyes wasn't there. They were as cold as agates. She said, "It won't wash, Magnus. It just won't wash. I just didn't believe Ina—about Edna. When Mike Forland rang yesterday I answered the ring in the study. I needed to get you as soon as possible. The binoculars were on the windowsill, so I looked out of that window to see if I could trace you. You were in the hawthorn glade. She held out her hands to you—and you kissed her. And . . . " her voice faltered, then firmed, "and I knew I was just a softy, a gullible softy. Ina had the right of it. She said you'd been together with Edna in Orkney, London, the Lake District, the Highlands. I knew you had, too. You'd both been quite open about that. But Ina also said she was the girl you'd weekended with seven years ago, here in New Zealand. So. . . . "

This time he didn't grip her. He moved back against Thorkel's table, and took a hold of it, each side of him. "I've wanted to tell you the whole truth, Jocelyn, but I must have been hoping for too much. I'm an idealistic sort of a bloke at heart. It goes with writing, I think. I suffered so much dis-

185

illusionment over Gillian I was testing you. I wanted to find out if it was possible that a girl who loved you could forgive a lapse as long ago as that. But——"

She interrupted him fiercely. "And I did. Oh, Magnus, I *did*. I hated the thought of it, but told myself I must be mature, that the folly of a man's youth oughtn't to be held against him. I knew there might have been other weekends, before that, but I really had reached the stage where I could put it into the limbo of all best-forgotten things . . . Magnus, what are you looking like that for? It doesn't signify now. I might have been willing to overlook the past. I'm certainly not going to share you with anyone now. Oh, and I loved Edna too . . . that's what I can't stand about it . . . Magnus, what *are* you doing?"

"Kissing you . . . like this . . . and this . . . stop talking, I can't do it properly. There, darling one, sweetheart . . ." When he lifted his mouth from hers he said, "Now, Jocelyn, you've had a fair go, so listen to me. That was the sort of love I hoped for." He gave her a little shake. "You look as if you're in a trance. Oh, Jos, try to take this in. I was kissing Edna because I was so happy for her. She'd just told me she's going to marry someone she met on the ship, a man from Tapanui. A fine chap. She's got Eric out of her system at last."

Jocelyn still felt as if she was in a trance. *"Eric* out of her system!"

She'd never seen those blue eyes look as tender as this. "Eric gave Edna a rough time, all told. They met too soon, perhaps. They were just kids. All her dreams of the future were woven round him, and Ronaldsay Downs. Then he met Jan and got swept off his feet. They were never engaged, you understand. I wasn't in New Zealand. Mother said Edna took it hard, but very bravely. Eric felt wretched over it, but she said she realized these things happened and she simply went out of his life. Are you with me?"

"No, not quite. Do you mean she turned to you for comfort when you came back? It would be so understandable, you and Eric were so alike."

"No, wait to hear it as I tell it. Ina played merry hell with

186

Jan's and Eric's marriage. I was fond of Jan, but she was weak. A married couple's first loyalty is to each other. Finally Jan took off, left Eric. I was back home then." Magnus fell silent, remembering. Jocelyn saw the lines etched on his face and knew that Eric's pain would be Magnus's pain.

"I hand it to Eric, he did all he could to patch up his marriage time and time again. Then, when it seemed it was irrevocably bust, we were afraid he was going to have a nervous breakdown. Dad thought he needed a change, and got him a job in Invercargill. We'd no idea Edna's people had moved there, Eric told me later she really saved his reason.

"For long enough, they managed to keep control of themselves, then finally they decided to give Jan cause for a divorce and make a new start. They went off to a motel together. They got there about eleven in the morning, and went in.

"Suddenly the enormity of what they were doing hit them. Eric looked at Edna and saw what it would do to her. She's a girl of high standards. And he was going to bring her low. At that very moment she turned to him and said, 'Eric, I don't know what this will do to you, but I can't go through with it.' He simply said, 'Me too,' and they came out. They were locking up preparatory to returning the key and telling the office, when Ina and a friend arrived for a few days. Ina thought they were leaving *after* a weekend together. It was a Monday morning, and Eric was just starting a round of calls on farmers in the Albertown area.

"Eric was appalled for Edna's sake. She was appalled for his. She had a pretty fair idea he'd never be happy without Jan and the children. So when Ina said: 'Eric . . . so this is what you get up to at weekends! All this talk of wanting Jan back is all eyewash!' Edna said, '*Eric?* I don't know who *you* are, or what business it could be of yours, but this is Magnus.' Edna said afterwards the words just seemed to say themselves in the horror of the moment.

"Eric got a terrific shock. He felt bludgeoned, but went along with it. Afterwards, they came straight to me. I thought we must play for time. Otherwise Ina would have rushed back and told Jan, and there'd have been no hope, ever, of that little family being reunited. I took Edna back to Invercargill from here. Eric went to Albertown, did his round, then went to his flat in Invercargill. And the whole thing suddenly became worth it. Just twenty-four hours after Eric got back, Jan walked in, most contrite, to ask if they could take up their lives together again. To the best of my knowledge they never again had a serious quarrel. Jan refused to ever let her sister set foot in her house again, but she used to go up and see her sometimes at their old home—very forgiving of her. But she said she'd never put her marriage at risk again. Then Ina married and things seemed to settle down. Till now."

He said, "But it played merry hell with *my* life. I left Edna in Invercargill and called to tell Gillian all about it. She was in Lumsden, with her sister. I'll never forget it. The worst week of my life. She was out when I called. I thought her sister seemed very ill at ease. She rang Gillian, where she was visiting, and Gillian came storming in. Now, this was natural. Ina had rung her . . . you know the way she'd do it. That it was on her conscience that Gillian ought to know what the man she was going to marry was really like. Any girl would have been flaming mad. But I never dreamed she wouldn't believe me. Very naïve of me. I finally lost my temper too, and we ended the engagement. Nevertheless, it wasn't very long before I felt it was for the best. I'd seen Gillian as she really was."

Magnus looked down on Jocelyn. "Understand why, when I met you, and found I loved you more than I'd ever imagined I loved Gillian, I wanted to find out if you could care enough to take me as I was, scandal and all."

"But I didn't need to. Why didn't you tell me the real truth?"

"Can't you see? Because you too might not have given it credence. Wouldn't it have sounded even more of a tall story? Wouldn't it have seemed pretty poor to try to blacken a dead brother's name to save my own? But if you could take me, reputation and all, it wouldn't matter. It would mean you

188

loved me in spite of it and then I'd be able to tell you and know I'd be believed."

"And I do love you, I do . . . oh, *how* I love you," said Jocelyn, putting up her hands to bring his face down to hers. He'd never seen those hazel eyes glow like this. "It's like a miracle. I'll never forget how it felt here—" she touched herself, "when I saw you dallying with Edna in the greenwood shade!"

"You idiot! *Dallying!* Couldn't you see it was a kiss of gratitude and that it lasted twenty seconds flat? Surely you saw it was just a peck? Even through binoculars!"

"I dropped them the moment it happened—I scratched the new windowsill. Fancy calling me an idiot at a moment like this. Still, at least you're not calling me a little devil in Norske as you did the first time we came here!"

The blue eyes were alight with fun, love, tenderness. "You should have asked your mother what I called you. *She* knew what it meant. Remember she got the giggles? Many Orcadians still have the odd endearment from their Scandinavian forebears, a legacy from the days before Orkney was deeded to Scotland. What else could *elsk-inne* mean but sweetheart? Or *kjele-degge* but darling? But tell me, love, maybe I hadn't needed to wait. How much time have I wasted?"

"Since the day before my parents came when I was in the garden talking madly to you about how you'd probably marry some day and give the children someone to care for them permanently. Oh, Magnus, what a lot of unnecessary heartache we've both suffered!"

"Well, let's catch up on wasted opportunity!"

Outside the bellbirds and *tuis* sang as sweetly as they had ever sung to Thórkel. A little sparrow hopped up the steps, and in, had a good look round for crumbs, cocked his head on one side and regarded the two people on the far windowseat with a hopeful eye, then, deciding it didn't look as if they were interested in food, flew away.

Finally Jocelyn lifted her head, said, "Magnus, you said a kiss of gratitude. But earlier you said delight because you were glad she was getting married. Remember? Edna, I mean." She laughed because he looked so bemused. As if what they'd been discussing had been completely forgotten.

"Oh, that. Delight *and* gratitude. Just before that she'd given me a piece of news that sets my mind at rest for ever. What's more, it could lay any doubt you might ever have—" he covered her lips with his fingers to still her protest. "Jocelyn, I thought, all these weeks, that I'd never have any evidence to offer you that it was Eric, not me. But now I have. Or Edna has.

"Shortly after she saw me off at Heathrow Airport, when I rushed home after they got me off that island, she got a letter, most unexpectedly, from Jan. It must be a very strange thing to see the handwriting of someone you know is now dead. That letter had chased Edna all round Europe; she'd been on the Continent, in Scandinavia, up to Scotland, back, and then she'd taken a job in the Channel Islands. It was a miracle it had ever reached her at all.

"The letter told her that Eric had told Jan about the incident. He'd realized that otherwise it might follow me all my life. That if I met someone else—as distinct from Gillian—it might interfere with my happiness. After those seven happy years with Jan he'd plucked up the courage. Jan had evidently reacted magnificently, because she'd said in this letter to Edna that if Eric had gone right off the rails, she'd only have had herself to blame. That she wanted to tell Edna how glad she was that *she* had been the one to play that part in his life; another woman might have taken him completely away from her. She hoped that someday Edna would find married happiness, that she deserved it much more than Jan herself."

He paused, drew in a deep breath, as if the more important news was still to come. ". . . And then Jan added that she'd not been able to rest till she'd gone to Ina and cleared my name and Edna's. Told her there never had been a weekend for anyone. And that if ever she tried to make out Eric *had* erred, Jan would never see her sister again as long as she lived. Ina had to accept it, or lose her completely. Jan said she'd be writing to me too, but they had to go to Christchurch first.

190

She was killed before she could." His face was sombre, remembering.

"If Edna had received that letter before I left Heathrow, I'd never have had any trouble with Ina at all. She must have hoped desperately that there'd not been time to let anyone know, and staked all on that, to get the children. She's got a warped mind. Perhaps we must pity her. She'll never touch our lives again, except that I'm going up there, to let Ina know, in front of Harold, that we now know she came into possession of the truth, but suppressed it. I don't want to sound unforgiving, Jocelyn, but it would be weak of me to ever allow her the opportunity of making mischief within our family circle again. Edna, by the way, is determined to show that letter to Gillian."

Suddenly his face changed, crumpled into laughter-lines. "I've just thought of something . . . if I'd known this before I left England, then I'd never have gone to such lengths to conceal from Ina, that morning, that an unknown and glamorous female had just spent a night under my roof, and you'd have gone out of my life! I'll change my mind . . . instead of bawling Ina out, I think I'll send her orchids with a note of profound thanks!"

"Magnus, you chump!" said Jocelyn fondly.

He got up. "Come on, *elsk-inne*, down to the shore. We must go home. On the way we can talk of lesser things . . . like my nearly saying when you talked of wanting to see Orkney, 'I'll take you there, some day,' and when your mother talked of Thorkel taking that blame for his brother, I thought because of it you might some day believe me. History repeating itself and all that."

"And me," said Jocelyn, smiling at the recollection, "blushing because I was hoping that your sleepless night might be due to thoughts of me . . . as mine had been because of thoughts of you!"

She was kissed for that. "Oh, Jocelyn, and I got mad with you because I thought you were advising me to go out on the town! Well, your father can marry us when they're up here in January. No point in wasting time. That's an ultimatum.

Home we go . . . a true home in every sense of the word now. Poor Aunt Clarissa, coping with those tourists! But she'll forgive us. I'll ring Scotty and tell him why I'd taken you on the lake, and offer to come to their hotel tonight to meet the tourists—sign books if they want that—and you'll go with me as my betrothed."

This was Magnus as he was meant to be . . . no inhibitions left, an extrovert, ebullient, sweeping everything before him. . . .

"Jocelyn, won't Ninian and Una be over the moon with delight? Una said to me last week that if I didn't ask you to marry me soon, she'd do it herself! Darling, you do realize it *is* a case of marrying *us*? That I can't give you what so many women have, in the first little while of marriage, a world of two? That we have a ready-made family . . . or the beginnings of one? Will you regret that?"

They had come to the bottom step. He stood on the lake-stones beneath it facing her. She was on the step itself. It brought her hazel eyes on a level with his blue ones.

All around was beauty . . . mountain and forest, birdsong and fragrance . . . the lap-lap of lake waters. It had been like this for eons of time. Across the lake of a thousand moods brooded the mountains of the mist, and in that vast hinterland of gorge and chasm, fiord and cascade beyond, waited countless delights for them through exploring years.

Jocelyn smiled into his eyes, leaned forward to kiss him on the mouth, then said, as he swung her down the last step, "But we *will* have our particular world of two, Magnus . . . that's what marriage is all about."

He caught her against him. "Like this?" he asked. "This . . . and much more?"

Above them, from a towering *rimu* that looked down on an old Orcadian's refuge where birds had never known fear or the sound of a firearm, the *riroriro* sang.